"No." Arms crossed, she tried, and failed, to stare him down.

He remained silent, waiting.

"You managed to get enchanted or some such nonsense after licking a measly clay fragment. If you think I'm going to let you anywhere *near* a room full of magical artifacts, books, and fragile instruments, you're insane."

"Why can't you humans keep your facts straight?" he finally said, his expression one of long-suffering. "I was gifted, not enchanted. It had nothing to do with me and everything to do with you. You're the one getting involved in dangerous plots. You're the one who needs help. Well, I'm it. Why won't you let me do my job?"

With those words, a soft glow began to emanate from him, barely discernible at first but growing brighter and brighter. As the glow increased, Lily's eyes widened till they were as big as saucers.

"Um, Kip, you're glowing," she said, clutching the door-frame for support, knuckles white.

"Am I?" He looked around at himself. "How fascinating. Apparently I had a point to make. The question is, have you gotten it?"

Also by Lydia Sherrer:

LOVE, LIES, AND HOCUS POCUS UNIVERSE

The Lily Singer Adventures:
Love, Lies, and Hocus Pocus Beginnings
Love, Lies, and Hocus Pocus Revelations
Love, Lies, and Hocus Pocus Allies
Love, Lies, and Hocus Pocus Legends
Love, Lies, and Hocus Pocus Betrayal
Love, Lies, and Hocus Pocus Identity
Love, Lies, and Hocus Pocus Kindred

The Lily Singer Adventures Novellas:
Love, Lies, and Hocus Pocus: A Study In Mischief
Love, Lies, and Hocus Pocus: Cat Magic

Dark Roads Trilogy (Sebastian's Origin)
Book 1: Accidental Witch

OTHER WORKS

TransDimensional Hunter (with John Ringo)
Book 1: Into the Real (releases April 2022)

We Shall Rise (A Black Tide Rising Anthology)

Ashes of Hope: A Dark Fantasy Post Apocalyptic Short Story

LOVE, LIES &
HOCUS POCUS
⊢⊤ REVELATIONS ⊤⊣

The Lily Singer Adventures
Book 2

LYDIA SHERRER

Chenoweth ❧ *Press*

LOVE, LIES, AND HOCUS POCUS REVELATIONS
The Lily Singer Adventures, Book 2

ISBN 13: 978-0-9973391-2-3 (paperback)
ISBN: 978-0-9973391-3-0 (ebook)

Published by Chenoweth Press 2016

Louisville, KY, USA

Cover design by Molly Phipps: wegotyoucoveredbookdesign.com

Interior illustrations by Serena Thomas

To Droopy, who keeps me sane (sort of)

Acknowledgments

Many overflowing thanks to the people who made this book happen. There were my faithful beta readers, who never complained about my ridiculous deadlines. Also to "blame" is my good friend Reggie Van Stockum, who first told me I should publish and lent me his copy of Writer's Market (he had no idea the maelstrom he was unleashing upon the world). Then there's my wonderful editor, Lori Brown Patrick, who took a chance with me. Much thanks to my exceptionally skilled and patient cover artist, Tony Warne, and my ever-helpful fellow authors, Robert Turk, Terry Maggert, Jessica Sherwood, and editor Alexandra Birr. I'm also indebted to Joseph Hagan; Maria Bowden and Richard Powell; and Brent, Karen, and Sylvia Hinton, whose generosity helped make this book happen. Most special thanks to my wonderful parents and sisters who have spent hours reading and editing my attempts at writing, never once discouraging me from doing what I love. And lastly, to my beloved husband, who, one cold winter night over a year ago, helped me conceive this story and has been my sounding board, biggest fan, and greatest supporter ever since.

Contents

Episode 3
Lost and Found

Chapter 1   3
Unexpected Conversations

Chapter 2   25
Two Sugars With a Pinch of Foreboding

Chapter 3   47
Major Magic

Chapter 4   67
Danger Walks Among Us

Epilogue   94

Interlude   99
Witchy Times

Episode 4
The Truth Shall Make You Free

Chapter 1   143
The Pitfalls of Well-Meant Interference

Chapter 2   167
The Stories We Tell

Chapter 3   192
Of Mothers and Men

Chapter 4   219
Sins of the Father

Epilogue   247

Glossary   261

About the Author   289

Episode 3

LOST AND FOUND

Chapter 1

UNEXPECTED CONVERSATIONS

BEAMS OF LATE-AFTERNOON SUNLIGHT POURED THROUGH LILY Singer's living room window, casting a bright patch of warmth on the rug. It was the only bit of July heat that made it into the air-conditioned refuge of her apartment. She sat cross-legged in the bright rectangle, surrounded by open books and scattered papers. Her cat, Sir Edgar Allan Kipling, lay artfully sprawled across the mess, paws in the air and fluffy tummy soaking up the warmth like a sponge. Being a cat, he always seemed to be lying on the exact paper she was looking for, no matter where she moved him.

Lily usually did her research and casting in the Basement, her magical archive beneath the McCain Library of Agnes Scott College, where she worked as archives manager. Yet, the Basement lacked natural light, so she'd relocated to her living room in an attempt to translate the cuneiform from a fragment of clay tablet the size of a matchbox. Its worn marks were exceptionally hard to see, so the sunshine helped.

Thus far, by cross-referencing her most reliable lexicon with archaeological accounts dating to the nineteenth century, she'd been able to confidently identify only a single grouping of marks. They made reference to Ninmah, the Sumerian goddess of the earth and animals. More fascinating than the cuneiform, however, were the *dimmu* runes hidden beneath, invisible to the mundane, non-wizard eye. They were easier to see but no less confusing, as they differed from the standardized runes in her *eduba*—her personal archive contained within a single, enchanted tome. She assumed the runes differed because they predated the centuries of study and research she benefited from. Whatever they meant, exactly, the runes appeared to be part of a controlling spell. Without the complete tablet for context, however, she couldn't know for sure.

Technically, she was supposed to be working on the engravings for her new ward bracelet. Madam Barrington, her teacher in the wizarding arts as well as the former Agnes Scott archives manager, had lent her a standard ward after her original bracelet broke under the strain of magical backlash. It was enough to tide her over, but it was no replacement for a true, personally crafted ward. While digging through the Basement's drawers looking for supplies, however, she'd come across this fragment. *Enkinim*, the language of magic and therefore her primary study, was related to Sumerian in the same way magical dimmu runes were related to cuneiform. Curiosity and the promise of a challenge had been too much to resist.

She was peering at the fragment when a ringing interrupted her. Laying the piece of clay down on a pile of reference papers, she headed for her purse in the bedroom. As an introvert, she had few friends, and an observant, rather than interactive, presence online, and so rarely kept her phone nearby. Glancing at the caller ID, she was surprised but delighted to see who it was. Madam Barrington didn't often use the phone.

"Good evening, Ms. B."

"Good evening, Miss Singer," she replied. Despite having been Lily's mentor for the past seven years, Madam Barrington was old-fashioned to the core and rarely addressed anyone by their first name. "I trust I'm not interrupting anything important?"

"Nothing that can't wait. To what do I owe the pleasure?"

"If you are able to excuse yourself from holding office hours tomorrow, an opportunity to further your professional and magical knowledge has arisen. The Tablet of Eridu exhibit at the Clay Museum will be closing at the end of the month. The artifact is on loan from the Hermann Hilprecht Museum of the University of Pennsylvania and has great historical as well as magical significance. I worked in partnership with the Clay Museum's curator two years ago when the exhibit opened; they have requested my help again to ensure the artifact's safe return. I agreed on the condition that you be allowed to assist. I am, after all, retired." Lily heard the faintest hint of dry humor in her mentor's voice and smiled. Like all wizards, Madam Barrington was long-lived and well preserved. She'd retired to let Lily take over management of the archives, not because of age or infirmity.

"I'd be delighted to join you. Fall term is a good month away and the summer students rarely darken my door. When and where shall I meet you?"

"Nine o'clock tomorrow morning at the Clay Museum. It is located on Emory University grounds."

"I'll be there," Lily said, making a note in her datebook.

"Very good, Miss Singer. I shall see you then."

They exchanged farewells and Lily hung up, thoughtful. She was familiar with Emory. It was a private research university north of Agnes Scott in the Druid Hills area of Atlanta. She'd been to their archives once or twice, as well as taken a few of their library science classes to augment her work experience at McCain Library, but she had never visited the Clay Museum.

Returning to her patch of sunlight and pile of papers, she was horrified to find Sir Kipling licking the clay fragment.

"Stop that! Shoo, shoo!" Lily hurried over and Sir Kipling, knowing he was in trouble, fled to relative safety underneath her desk.

"You ridiculous cat. Why must you bother everything?" she lamented to herself, picking up the fragment. Examining it, she was relieved to see it was barely damp at all, with no damage to its markings. A glance under the desk revealed her errant pet, who was now cleaning his paw with supreme unconcern, pausing occasionally to blink at her.

"Cats," she grumbled, settling back down in the patch of sunlight. She needed to get more deciphering done before the daylight weakened and she had to start thinking about bed. Nine a.m. came early and she wanted to look, and feel, her best for an appointment at a prestigious university museum.

Lily woke Wednesday morning, not to the sound of her alarm clock, but to the soothing vibrations of a purring cat. She had an uncomfortable feeling she'd overslept, but she was distracted from it by the warm, heavy ball of fur settled comfortably on her chest.

Groaning, she tried to push him off. "Kip, you better not have turned off my alarm again."

Sir Kipling, however, didn't want to move. He dug his claws into the sheets and resisted her groggy attempt to dislodge him. "Well, if it weren't so loud and annoying, I wouldn't have to take matters into my own paws," he protested.

"It's *supposed* to be loud and annoying to wake me—"

She froze, going cross-eyed in an attempt to see the feline perched atop her. Her muddled, half-asleep brain tried, and failed, to make sense of what she'd just heard. It'd sounded like meowing, but also like words. She stared at her cat and he stared back, eyes half-lidded.

"Did you...?" She paused, giving her head a shake to dislodge the cobwebs in her brain. "I thought I heard... good grief, I'm imagining a conversation with my cat. I need a hot shower." She sat up for real this time, her movement threatening to spill Sir Kipling onto the bedcovers.

Twisting with cat-like agility, he launched off her chest and landed on the edge of the bed in a dignity-preserving move, then turned to lick his mussed fur into submission. "A hot shower won't fix your problems," he commented between licks.

Lily stared, speechless, no longer sure of her own sanity.

Sir Kipling paused his ministrations to look at her. "If you insist on sitting there being shocked, you might as well make yourself useful and pet me."

"I—" She stopped, then tried again. "You...talk?"

A smug look was all the reply she got.

"Wait, that's not—since when?" Lily was still shocked, but her brain at least had started working again. She'd adopted Sir Kipling as a stray kitten during her last year of college and had never gotten the slightest inkling he was anything but a normal cat.

"Since now," he stated matter-of-factly.

"Don't be silly. Cats don't randomly start—" she paused, suddenly suspicious. "Was it that fragment of tablet? Wonderful. Just splendid. What did you do?"

He sniffed archly. "You'd think you weren't happy to talk to me. Well, good morning to you, too. I'm just fine, thanks for asking."

Lily rolled her eyes. He was perfectly healthy but probably wouldn't cooperate unless she mollified him. Typical cat.

"I trust you're well this morning? Did whatever you got up to last night damage anything vital?" She couldn't resist a bit of sarcasm, but he ignored it.

"Now that you mention it, there *is* this place on my back that's been itching all night—"

"Sir Edgar Allan Kipling," she interrupted in a voice that brooked no nonsense. "To the point, please."

"Well, if you insist," he said, taking his time to stretch and yawn before continuing. "I did nothing at all. I was just minding my own business when that piece of dirt you've been staring at—"

"You mean the clay fragment?"

Sir Kipling stopped, ears tilted back in annoyance. Lily closed her mouth. After a deliberate pause, he continued. "Yes, the piece of dirt. It started glowing and then…well, let's just say interesting times are coming, and someone thought you could use a little help."

"What? What's that supposed to mean? What's coming? Who are you talking about?"

"Well, I *could* answer your questions, but then you'd be late for your meeting."

Glancing at her alarm clock she yelped and jumped out of bed, heading for the shower. She had barely thirty minutes to do what normally took an hour, and she would have to skip breakfast.

Hand on the bathroom door, she turned and glared at her cat, who had settled comfortably onto the warm spot she'd just vacated. His eyes had closed, as if in sleep, and all four paws were tucked under him, making him look like a fluffy loaf of bread—a catloaf.

"This isn't over, Sir. You and I will be having a very long conversation when I get home."

She didn't wait for his reply as she rushed into the bathroom to get ready.

The A.T. Clay Museum, named after American Semitic archaeologist Albert Tobias Clay, was a modestly sized but nonetheless impressive building. Its columned marble facade was draped on either side with banners declaring its latest exhibits, and wide steps led up to a set of beautifully carved wooden doors.

Picking up her pace as she hurried toward it, Lily tried to push thoughts of Sir Kipling's shocking new skill to the back of her mind, needing to focus. She glanced at her watch. One minute to nine; at least she wouldn't be late. She'd had the sense to prepare her outfit the evening before, thus avoiding any rushed fashion decisions. Her leather and mesh pump oxfords were vintage 1950s, their soft gray hue matching her linen suit worn over a cream chiffon blouse.

As she neared the marble steps, she got a faint impression of magic in the air. Before she could examine the feeling further, however, she was distracted by the sight of Madam Barrington on the top step speaking to a man in the process of unlocking the large wooden doors. They both turned at the sound of her heels on the marble.

"Ah, here she is," said Madam Barrington. "Mr. Baker, may I present Miss Lily Singer, my replacement as archives manager at the McCain Library. She has graciously agreed to assist in preparing the tablet for return and is an accomplished curator and wizard in her own right."

Lily barely managed to hide her start of surprise at Madam Barrington's word choice. Mounting the steps and grasping Mr. Baker's hand in an uncertain shake, she probed gently, looking for signs of his magical gift. There were none. He was quite clearly a mundane.

Seeing her look of confusion, Mr. Baker chuckled, his voice rich and jolly with the faintest trace of an Irish accent. "No, Miss Singer, I'm no wizard myself. But I've got a few in my family tree, and the smart ones know to stick together." His short stature, rotund belly, and twinkling eyes put her in mind of a halfling. She wanted to ask what he meant by "the smart ones" and "stick together," but she knew now was not the time. So she tucked the question away and moved to follow her mentor into the dark, echoing hall.

She didn't get far. As she attempted to step over the threshold, something stopped her and there was an unpleasant prickling on the back of her neck. A second attempt got her no further, and the unpleasant feeling of being repelled grew. Herself several steps into the hallway, Madam Barrington finally realized Lily was not following her and turned.

"Oh, good heavens, I do apologize, Miss Singer," she said, and came back. "This is partly why you are here, to study and help renew the magical wards on this building, one of which is a ward against magical blood, both man and beast. Here, take my hands."

Lily took them and found she could now pass through the doorway.

"Once you add your magic to the ward, you will be able to pass unhindered," Madam Barrington explained as they followed Mr. Baker to his office and he went through the process of waking the building's systems from their nightly slumber.

"What about all the other wizards?" Lily asked.

Madam Barrington smiled dryly. "What other wizards? As you know, we are not precisely a thriving community. We do get a visitor now and then, but anyone who knows of the tablet also knows it is well protected, and therefore only accessed with approval from the local caretaker."

"I'm sorry, the local what?"

"The wizard tasked with maintaining the tablet's protection wherever it is on display. I have been its caretaker these two years it has resided in Atlanta."

"I see," Lily said, mind dancing with even more questions than before. Madam Barrington had given her a thorough education in magical theory and spell-casting, including all the major highlights of magical history. But the older woman had always been decidedly vague about current wizard society and customs, and there was a dearth of modern works in the Basement. She suspected Madam Barrington's vagueness was connected to whatever had caused Lily's own mother to divorce and move to the backwaters of Alabama when Lily was barely a toddler. Since then her mother had remarried, raised a family, and built a quiet country life, all while flatly refusing to talk about her past. She'd never breathed a word about magic to Lily. Lily grew up knowing she was different, but not why, and by the age of eighteen she'd had enough. After a huge fight with her mother, she'd left for Atlanta to attend Agnes Scott College and discover her past on her own.

To her knowledge, her mother and Madam Barrington were not acquainted. Then again, you never knew. Her mentor had always been guarded when it came to personal questions. Lily respected the older woman's privacy, but it was times like these that sorely tried her patience. It felt like she was part of a game where she knew all the moves, but none of the rules. Perhaps today's work would shed more light on the rules, and players, she sought to understand.

Mr. Baker returned from his office, his smile now lit by the soft glow of museum lights all around them. "The doors don't officially open 'til ten, so you have a good hour to work before any visitors arrive. I'll be in my office. If you need anything, just pop right in."

"Thank you Mr. Baker, I am greatly obliged," Madam Barrington said, inclining her head, then turning to Lily. "Come, Miss Singer. We shall begin by examining the tablet."

Madam Barrington led her down the marble-floored lobby, their steps echoing loudly in the silent museum. At the end of the hall, a security grill blocked access to a café and gift shop area. To the left were closed doors with a plaque that read "Reception Hall." They turned right through large doors that opened onto a room filled with lit displays of ancient Roman and Greek pottery, jewelry, and artwork. They passed through this to a hall hung with drawings from Renaissance-era Europe. She caught a glimpse of Oriental art to her right, but Madam Barrington turned left and she followed.

Lily's skin tingled with anticipation and the ghost touch of more spells as they entered a large room filled with ancient Egyptian and Near East artifacts. At the end of the room stood two giant pillars, their tops touching the ceiling. Crooked joints were faintly visible where they had been pieced back together from whatever ruins they'd been pulled from. Between them was a single pedestal brightly lit by recessed lights in the ceiling above. Suspended within its display case was a tablet intricately stamped with tightly packed lines of cuneiform. Twice the size of her palm, it was missing most of the right edge so that each line of script disappeared into speculation. The three-quarters that remained had been painstakingly reconstructed from several large fragments and many smaller ones.

Her mentor remained silent as Lily walked around the pedestal several times, inspecting the exquisite example of ancient Sumerian literature from every angle.

"This," Madam Barrington began, "is the Tablet of Eridu. As you know, Eridu was considered the first city in the world by the ancient Sumerians. According to myth, it was founded by the gods, specifically Enki, and from it was spread civilization as a gift from god to man. Undoubtedly an important center for trade, religion, and the arts, some sources even equate it to the Biblical city of Babel. Pulled from that great city's ruins, this tablet contains incomplete accounts of the origins of the world, the gods, and mankind. It is not the only such work. The Nippur Tablet, for example, holds similar accounts. But this is the only tablet we have that was added to by the hands of our wizard ancestors after being stamped into being by the historians of that time.

"We know little about the first great wizards, purportedly descendants of the mythological Gilgamesh, the original recipient of magic from the gods. What we do know is that they took it upon themselves to preserve the first spells, hidden in plain sight, upon historical documents of their time. Dimmu runes beneath the cuneiform on this tablet

outline some of the most primitive yet potent and dangerous spells known to wizardkind. Unfortunately, or perhaps
fortunately, depending on your point of view, the tablet was
broken many centuries ago. The pieces you see here—rediscovered during the 19th century by wizard archaeologists
in search of links to our past—contain only parts of those
spells. Despite the tablet's relative uselessness, however, its
potential was obvious. Thus, the wards."

Lily stared at the innocuous-looking piece of clay, the
sharpness of its script speaking to the preserving power of
the sand in which it had been buried. Both her imagination
and scholarly instincts were excited by Madam Barrington's
words. "But what's so dangerous about the spells? Wouldn't
the benefit outweigh the danger?" she asked.

A humorless smile graced Madam Barrington's lips.
"When one can animate the dead, take dominion over creatures both man and beast, and control the elements themselves, then even the best of morals are susceptible to the
realities of human nature. The saying that absolute power
corrupts absolutely is no empty aphorism. Where magic is
concerned, it is a deadly reality."

Lily's eyes widened. "The tablet has such spells?"

"So says ancient myth," Madam Barrington replied,
her expression dubious. "Without the complete tablet, we
can only speculate. Regardless of the danger it poses to one's
morals, it has been many centuries since wizards possessed
the power and force of will to cast such spells. Those who
have tried have inevitably lost control and suffered the lethal
consequences."

"Indeed," Lily murmured, bending to examine the tablet again. During Madam Barrington's speech her mind had
instantly turned to the clay fragment carefully shut away in
her desk. With such worn script, it must have been unburied

long before the tablet, but she could see where it might fit on one of the corners. Her boundless curiosity was tempered by common sense, however. Despite the enticing prospect of reuniting the pieces to learn their legendary spells, she wasn't fool enough to think her abilities were up to the task. She wondered if her mentor knew of the fragment and considered mentioning it, but some impulse held her back. Surely Madam Barrington knew; she'd been the Basement's caretaker for decades. There was no need to bring it up. Yet.

"Well," Madam Barrington said into the silence, clapping her hands together. "Enough history. Our duty at present is to protect and preserve, not study. I am sure you have noticed the many wards around the case and room. We will be renewing them and adding a few improvements I have developed since my last visit."

They spent the next fifty minutes casting spell after spell. In each room they joined hands to make a circle of power—helpful when doing joint spell work—and together spoke words of power that shaped the magic laid over door mantels, sunk into floors, and woven through the walls. As they renewed each ward, Lily could see the myriad of dimmu rune anchors glowing in her mind's eye. Wards could be cast without such anchors, but they were never as potent or lasting. Madam Barrington had already done the hard work two years ago when she'd meticulously engraved each rune, inlaying them with aluminum, whose high-energy density acted as a storehouse for magic. Lithium worked even better but was too reactive to use safely.

Though she knew all the standard ward spells, there were a few specialized ones her mentor taught her for the first time. She made careful note of each and committed them to memory, so as to record them in her eduba later. When Madam Barrington got to one of her customized "improvements," Lily simply fell silent and fed her power into their combined link, letting her mentor shape the magic. Though not particularly complicated, the wards took time to shape and settle, and, like all spells, required concentration and force of will. When they stopped for a break halfway through, Lily went in search of water and brought back two folding chairs graciously provided by Mr. Baker. Madam Barrington nodded appreciatively when Lily reappeared: sitting on the floor was no longer as easy for her as it once was. Though neither of them were so fatigued they couldn't stand, there was no point in wasting energy when so much was already being poured into their magic.

About to resume their work, however, they were interrupted by *Bewitched's* lively 1960s theme song. It echoed through the empty hall, the notes emanating from Lily's suit pocket. Madam Barrington's eyebrows raised almost into her hairline, but she made no comment as Lily hastily withdrew the phone and put it to her ear.

"What is it? I'm rather busy."

"Well, hello to you, too, grumpy-face," Sebastian chortled, unfazed by her repressive tone. His status as Madam Barrington's great-grandnephew was made complicated by the fact that he was also a witch—a disgrace to wizardkind in the Madam's opinion, which was why she had disowned him. That made talking to him in front of her a bit awkward.

"To the point, Sebastian. I'm in the middle of spell-casting."

"Okay, okay. We need to talk. There's been some… well, I've recently heard something you ought to know. It's important."

Resisting the temptation to demand more detail, Lily simply replied, "Why don't you call back in an hour, I can talk then."

There was a pregnant pause. "I'd rather not discuss it over the phone."

"At my apartment, then, this evening?"

"Nope. I have to move on this now, or not at all. What I do depends on what you think of my information."

Lily sighed, amazed, as usual, at Sebastian's talent for finding trouble, as this no doubt was. "Fine. I'm at the Clay Museum, on Emory campus. I'll be done with my work by ten. You can meet me here."

"Got it. See you then," he said, and abruptly hung up.

Confused, Lily stared at her phone, then looked up to see Madam Barrington's eyes on her. If her mentor was curious, it didn't show. She simply looked politely impatient to return to their task. Taking a deep breath to clear her mind and refocus, Lily joined hands with her once again and they got back to work.

Five minutes before ten they finished their last spell. Letting the power sink into its dimmu anchor, they took several long moments to slowly withdraw from their combined link to the Source and settle themselves. Afterwards, Lily gathered the chairs and they returned to Mr. Baker's office. He was expecting a large group of middle schoolers on field trip just then, so they simply thanked him and departed for the parking lot.

"I would be delighted to have you over for a bracing cup of Irish Breakfast and a sit down," Madam Barrington commented as they walked. "But I seem to recall you have a pending appointment."

"Um, yes. Sebastian needs to discuss something, and…" she paused, thinking of the long, long conversation she needed to have with her cat. "I'm afraid I'm rather busy the rest of today," she finished regretfully.

"Well," her mentor said, "it has been too long since we shared a cup. You must join me for tea Saturday afternoon."

"That would be wonderful," Lily said, hoping against hope whatever Sir Kipling had gotten himself into would be resolved by then. Speaking of Sir Kipling... "I don't suppose you've ever heard of a cat who could talk?" she asked. "In wizard histories, that is," she added hurriedly at the look on her mentor's face.

Madam Barrington thought about it as they approached her car. "Beyond myth and ancient folklore, I know of no historical documentation of any such thing. Spells to impart human speech and intelligence on creatures have been attempted, of course, but with no success."

"I see," Lily said, shoulders slumping. "Well, I'll see you Saturday. Four o'clock?"

"As always," Madam Barrington said with a smile, and got into her ancient Buick.

Once her mentor had left, Lily returned to the museum and entered the now-open café in search of something hot to drink. Much to her disappointment, though not surprise, they had only coffee. Resigned, she settled at a café table with an overpriced bottle of water, a banana, and a plain bagel. Meager fare, to be sure, but it would have to do.

After breakfast, she got started satisfying her curiosity with a thorough tour of the museum's exhibits. She was leaning over, engrossed in her examination of a terra-cotta kylix—a type of Ancient Greek drinking cup—when she felt a light prickle on the back of her neck. It was so similar to the tickle of creepy-crawly spider legs that she let out an involuntary scream, shooting upright to writhe frantically, brushing the back of her neck. She loathed spiders.

A loud guffaw sounded behind her and she spun to see Sebastian bent over, slapping his leg in glee. Several people looked their way in disapproval, obviously disturbed by the noise.

Blushing beet red, Lily grabbed Sebastian's elbow and towed him to an out-of-the-way alcove in the lobby. His guffaws had subsided by the time she spun him toward her, glaring daggers up into his amused face.

"That was absolutely—"

"Hey, I'm sorry, okay? I'm sorry!" Sebastian cut her off, holding up his hands. "I couldn't help it. You were so enthralled by whatever ancient kitchenware you were looking at, you didn't even hear me calling your name. How could I resist?"

Lily's mouth snapped shut as a fresh wave of heat flared in her cheeks, though her expression didn't soften. "You could have tapped me on the shoulder like any other decent, well-bred, sane person."

"Weeell, since I'm none of those things…" he said slowly, unable to suppress his grin.

She stood, arms crossed, wanting to stay angry, but knowing it was a waste of effort.

"You," she finally said, "are an incorrigible…obstreperous…indecent…heathen!" Her words were punctuated by fulminating pauses as she searched for words worthy of her ire. It was one thing to play pranks on her in private. But to do it in public…at least neither Madam Barrington nor Mr. Baker had been present.

Sebastian cast his eyes downward, undertaking an honest show of remorse. Unfortunately for him, it was ruined by the echoes of laughter still shining from his eyes and tucked into the corners of his mouth when he looked back up at her.

"I'm terrible, I know. But now that we're all agreed, can we get to business?" he asked.

"Well, *I* wasn't the one keeping us from it in the first place, you—oh, never mind." Lily took a deep, calming breath. "What did you need to tell me?"

At that, Sebastian's expression lost its mirth. His eyes darted from side to side, checking the lobby for occupants. Apparently satisfied, he drew Lily close as he stepped further back into the alcove.

"Word on the street is someone's looking for a grifter. Specifically, a grifter of the, uh, witch persuasion, so to speak."

"Wait, so…someone's looking for you?" Lily asked, misunderstanding with studied deliberateness.

Sebastian adopted an affronted look. "How dare you suggest such a thing! I don't swindle people, I'll have you know. All my tricks are completely honest and legitimate."

That got him an eye roll.

"No, it's for a job," he said, forging onward. "Someone, somewhere, is looking to hire a witch with…less-than-legal skills. I, of course, don't fit their bill. But I keep my ear to the ground, and I know people. I usually hear about it when this sort of request gets circulated. My question for you is: what should we do about it?"

"Why are you asking me?" Lily said, now genuinely confused.

"Isn't it obvious? If they want a witch grifter, they're after something magical. And stealing something magical is never a good thing. You're the most magical person I know—well, the most magical person I trust, anyway—so I'm telling you."

"But why?" Lily asked again. "It could literally be anything under the sun, and it's usually a bad idea to get involved with unknown magic or magic users. We have no idea what we might be getting into, and I'm tired of you dragging me into situations like that."

"Okay," he said, "so, what if I get more information? More detail. If we know what it is, we can stop it."

"Or, you could just apply for the job, and when they pick you, turn them over to the police. Quick and easy."

Now it was Sebastian's turn to roll his eyes. "Don't be naive on purpose, Lil. It's unbecoming. No one with the balls to get involved with witches would be idiotic enough to give their hired criminals a loaded gun. They'll make sure there's no way to connect them to the crime; they'll use middlemen. But even if we can't catch the mastermind, we can stop them from getting their hands on what they want."

"I suppose," Lily said, grudgingly. She'd given up trying to stop Sebastian from calling her "Lil." He enjoyed it more when she complained.

Contemplating Sebastian's news, her mind went to the mysterious wizard they'd met in Pitts. The problem was that she knew too little about him to even guess if he was behind this shadowy plot. They'd already foiled one of his attempts to get a magical artifact, but he'd claimed it was a family heirloom and so rightly his, anyway.

Speaking of magical artifacts...

"Follow me," she said, and stalked away. Though still annoyed, she knew she should do something. Madam Barrington had always taught her magic was a gift, not a privilege, and all wizards were duty-bound to be responsible stewards of it. Having the knowledge and skill to help, how could she justify hiding in her library and hoping the problem would go away? She just hoped *this* problem didn't attract FBI attention. Having claimed ignorance during their interview about the Pitts incident, she didn't know how long that song and dance would remain convincing if she kept popping up on their radar.

Sebastian ran to catch up as she wove around small groups of museum visitors, headed for the Near East exhibit hall. They stopped in front of the Tablet of Eridu's pedestal.

"What is it?" he asked, bending down to take a closer look.

"It's a very ancient tablet inscribed with Sumerian myths," Lily said, then glanced around. Several people stood nearby looking at other artifacts, so she lowered her voice before continuing. "Underneath the writing are some incomplete but powerful spells that could wreak havoc in the wrong hands."

"Hmm. You think this could be it, then?" he asked, matching her low tone.

She shrugged. "I don't know. I doubt anyone could get to it. Madam Barrington and I just renewed the wards this morning. But take a good look, anyway, so you'll remember it."

He did so, examining it from several angles. Stepping back to get a wider view, he accidentally bumped into an older woman with large glasses and various drawing implements behind both ears. Probably an amateur artist, she'd been sketching the ancient Egyptian statue of Ra that sat across from the tablet's pedestal. They apologized profusely to each other, then returned to their respective tasks.

"It's not much to look at, is it?" he finally commented.

Lily rolled her eyes. "It's not supposed to be, silly. It's impressive because it's one of the oldest surviving written records of any kind. This is basically the oldest book in the world."

"Kinda makes ya drool, doesn't it?" said a perky voice beside her, and she jumped for the second time that day.

A young woman, cute as a button with brown hair in a pixie cut, had moved up silently beside her and was examining the tablet with a thoughtful expression. Though probably in her mid-twenties, she was so slender and petite she looked barely legal. Her garish metal-band t-shirt—complete with unreadable words and an overabundance of skulls—along with ripped jeans and grunge boots almost gave Lily a fit.

"Um…excuse me?" Lily said, trying for an arch tone but sounding distracted instead as she tried to recover from the assault on her fashion sensibility.

"I said, doesn't it make you drool? I mean, come on, the oldest book in the world? Who wouldn't want that?"

Before Lily could reply, Sebastian inserted himself into the conversation. "Well, I'm drooling, but I don't think it's because of some lump of clay, no matter how old it is." He winked and gave the girl his most charming smile. "I'm Sebastian. Wanna get a drink?"

The girl laughed, a tinkling sound that made Lily cringe more than the outfit had.

"Nice try, sweetie. But you couldn't keep up with me."

"Try me. You haven't seen the things I normally have to keep up with."

His bold words made the girl laugh again, and Lily gritted her teeth. She cleared her throat, trying to get Sebastian's attention, but he ignored her.

"That's cute," the girl was saying, "but I'll pass. I wouldn't want to bruise that ego of yours, since it's probably the only big thing you have." With a wink she walked away, leaving Sebastian with his jaw hanging open.

Lily snorted and covered her mouth, trying only half-heartedly to hide her smirk. She was secretly pleased at the rebuff but avoided thinking about the hot flush she'd felt during the exchange. It was different from the prickly annoyance Sebastian often evoked, more intense, almost primal. She told herself it wasn't jealousy—that would be ridiculous—and put the matter from her mind.

"Serves you right for flirting with strangers," she said loftily, partly to poke at him but mostly to distract herself from where her thoughts had been headed.

Sebastian closed his mouth and turned back to the pedestal, flashing her a confident but wholly unconvincing grin. "She totally digs me," he declared.

"You're an idiot," Lily said. "Now will you please focus? We have work to do. Go ahead and move on the job. Find out as much as you can and come by my apartment tomorrow evening. I guess we'll decide what to do once we know more."

Sebastian nodded and hurried off, leaving Lily staring at the tablet, lost in thought. She had a talking cat and a heist on her hands and had no idea what to do about either. Her week was becoming very interesting in a Chinese curse sort of way.

Chapter 2

Two Sugars With a Pinch of Foreboding

I T WASN'T QUITE NOON WHEN LILY PULLED UP TO HER APARTMENT. She'd run errands after leaving the museum, so she had a lot on her mind and in her hands as she got out of the car. It wasn't until she was almost upon him that she noticed Sir Kipling sitting primly on the low wall in front of her building.

She started in shock, causing one of her bags to tilt to the side and spill canned goods onto the sidewalk where they scattered in all directions. "What are you doing outside?" she demanded, torn between concern and annoyance as she bent to gather her things.

"Enjoying the sunshine."

"What?" She was distracted by a particularly enterprising can of soup that had rolled off the sidewalk and under her car.

"You asked what I was doing outside."

Lily groaned and straightened. "What I meant was how did you *get* outside?"

"By walking."

"But how did you walk out of a locked apartment?"

"Cats go whither they please," he said cryptically. "Locks are meaningless."

Eyebrows raised, Lily snorted. "Oh really? Well, then I suppose solid walls are meaningless, too?"

"Obviously," he replied, the word oozing feline smugness.

Lily didn't reply, simply tried to figure out how to rearrange her bags without spilling everything so she could carry him inside. She hoped he wouldn't run away. Normal cats were difficult enough to control; she had no idea what to do with a magical one.

Sir Kipling must have caught on to her dilemma because he got up, fluffy tail twitching back and forth. "Don't bother. I'll let myself back in." With that, he jumped down behind the wall and disappeared from view.

Hurrying over she looked behind the wall, but there was no sign of him.

"Great, now he can talk *and* vanish into thin air," Lily sighed, resisting the urge to bite her lip in worry. He would come back. Probably. It was an obvious waste of effort to go looking for him if he didn't want to be found. She climbed the steps, juggling bags to extract her keys and unlock the door.

Depositing the groceries on the kitchen counter, she went into her bedroom to change but stopped in her tracks at the sight of Sir Kipling lazing on the bed.

He gave her a blithe look. "Vanish, yes. Into thin air, hardly."

"I...you...did I leave a window open or something?" she asked.

"No, you didn't. I told you, cats go where they please."

"No, they don't. They're governed by the laws of nature and physics. But you seem to be flaunting those with aplomb. Did the fragment do that to you, too?"

"Don't be silly," Sir Kipling said. "Cats don't defy physics. We simply have a better understanding than humans of how the world works."

Lily stared, then shook her head. "Just do me a favor, all right? Don't run off."

Sir Kipling huffed, looking hurt. "What do you think I am, an alley cat? You're my human. *Somebody* has to look after you. And you feed me," he added as an afterthought.

That startled a laugh out of her, and she felt her worry fade. Giving up the effort to fathom feline logic, she proceeded to change clothes, make a large pot of tea, and eat lunch.

Once fed and more relaxed, she returned to the bedroom. Sir Kipling appeared to be fast asleep, though an ear twitched when she climbed onto the bed and sat cross-legged with her back to the headboard.

"All right, Kip. Out with it. What's going on?"

He ignored her, so she nudged him with a foot. She was rewarded with a yawn, a stretch, and a reproachful look.

"Must we do this now? I was in the middle of my hourly nap."

"You'll survive. Now talk. That's what you do these days, right?"

"No, not really."

"What?" She was getting annoyed by his ambiguous answers and wondered if all cats were so vague.

"I've always talked to you this way, but now you under-stand me."

"Wait, you mean…" she paused and considered. If she actually *listened* to the sounds he made instead of focus-ing on the words interpreted by her brain, they did indeed sound like meows.

"That's fascinating…so, what do I sound like? Under-neath the words, I mean," she asked, curious.

He flicked his ears at her, considering. "Like a human."

Lily rolled her eyes. "You're not very helpful."

"Humph. If someone asked you what a cat sounded like, what would you say?"

She paused, flummoxed, and shrugged. "Like a cat, I guess."

"Now who's being unhelpful?"

"Still *you* as far as I'm concerned, Mr. Evasive." She pointed at him accusingly. "You haven't explained what you did last night."

"As I said, nothing. I was minding my own business when the drawer containing your piece of dirt started glow-ing. So I went to investigate."

"I knew it! You licked it again, didn't you?"

"Hardly," Sir Kipling said, scrunching up his nose. "Dirt tastes bad. I simply sat on your chair and observed. Pieces of light were leaking out and getting all over the place. Some must have touched me, and then…" He stopped.

"Yes?" Lily leaned forward eagerly.

"I…can't really say."

"Kip, don't be stubborn, even if you *are* a cat."

He shot her a perturbed look and shifted, reposition-ing into a catloaf so that all four paws were tucked beneath him. For a while he just gazed at her, eyes two unfathomable pools of yellow. Finally, he spoke. "I can't say because I don't know. Something was there, then it was in me, then it was gone. It was big like the sky, and strong like the earth, and good like a friend. It told me danger was coming, and you would need me. That's all."

Lily stared, shocked into silence. She believed him—for a cat, his little speech was surprisingly straightforward—but had no idea what to make of it. Ever since she'd learned she was a wizard, her preconceptions about the world had been routinely turned upside down. Fae were real. Demons and spirits were far more common than was comfortable, and who knew what else lurked about, hidden in the forgetfulness of mankind? Maybe it was an elemental or a god... if they even existed. And what about the warning? What danger was coming? Should she even believe it? Experience told her it was dangerous to dismiss a thing simply because you didn't understand it. She would have to do research. A lot of it.

"Are you sure you're all right?" was all she could think to say.

"I'm a cat," he replied. "We're always all right. But if you insist on being concerned, there *is* this spot on my back..."

With a roll of her eyes and a fond smile, Lily leaned forward to give her cat a very thorough petting.

The next evening, Lily got home late from work and was surprised not to see Sebastian waiting on her doorstep. She'd expected him to come by as early as possible to share whatever information he'd found. With an internal shrug, she carted in her pile of books retrieved from the Basement—extra research material in light of recent events—and got started on a double batch of cranberry almond scones. Her current stash would disappear soon after Sebastian arrived, and she hated running out of scones. Sir Kipling wanted to sit on the counter to observe her labors, but she flatly refused. Just because they could communicate didn't make him shed any less fur. The counters were still a no-cat zone.

Seven o'clock came and went, and so did eight. By nine, she was thoroughly annoyed. By ten, it was raining and she'd started to worry. Sebastian wasn't answering his phone. She wondered if he'd simply forgotten their appointment. That didn't seem likely, though, given how up in arms he'd been about the whole affair yesterday.

As she tried to decide whether to go to bed or drive to his apartment to find him, her doorbell finally rang. She opened it in a rush and got a face full of rain as Sebastian hurried inside, dripping wet and muttering curses at the foul weather.

Relieved, she ushered him into the bathroom to dry off. Not having a single stitch of clothing that would fit his tall, lanky frame, she instructed him to lay his wet clothes outside the door. Once they were no longer on him, it was easy to dry each piece with a simple evaporation spell, though she blushed a little when she picked up his boxers. She left the now-dry pile of clothes by the bathroom door and went to the kitchen to make tea.

Sebastian emerged, back to normal except for his damp, tousled hair, and sat down at her kitchen table. He sagged in his chair, looking exhausted. Sir Kipling immediately appropriated his lap, eager for pettings now that the man wasn't soaking wet. Sebastian rubbed him behind the ears, his tired expression brightening as he spotted the neat rows of scones lining Lily's counters. She smacked his hand when he reached for one.

"Finish the old ones first," she scolded, pointing to the glass cake dome on her table.

A hot cup of Assam tea and five scones later, he finally slowed down enough to talk.

"Sorry for being late and wet and all. It was a chore trying to find out what we needed to know, then I got a flat tire, then it started raining and I don't think I even own an umbrella."

Lily's annoyance was tempered and she decided not to mention how worried she'd been. "Why didn't you call me? I could have picked you up."

"My phone died," he said.

"And you don't have a car charger?"

"Er, it broke a while ago and I haven't replaced it," he admitted sheepishly. "Electronics don't really like me."

She rolled her eyes.

"Hey, at least I got what matters, right? I got the scoop on what's happening."

"Yes, that's definitely good. It means you haven't soaked my living room floor and consumed my scones for nothing. Do tell." She smiled, knowing he enjoyed her sarcasm.

He leaned forward, expression turning serious. "I hope it's not for nothing, anyway. Apparently the job got offered to a couple known players first, and there was argument about who would get it. So they put out feelers for alternate options. That's the part I heard about. After more digging, all I came up with is that the candidate has to know about museum security systems. That's besides being a witch of course. So we know they're robbing a museum, and there's magic involved. They wouldn't need a witch otherwise, since witches are the only people besides wizards who know magic exists."

"So why aren't they looking for a wizard?" Lily asked, confused.

"No idea, but I think we can be pretty sure what they're after."

"Not necessarily," she cautioned. "Did they mention the item or location?"

"Nope. You don't get that stuff unless you're picked for the job."

"Which you weren't?" She raised an eyebrow.

He shook his head. "Not even close."

"What a relief," she said sarcastically. "But we still don't *know* they're after the tablet."

"Oh, come on, Lil. What else could it be? Do you know of any other highly protected magical artifacts in Atlanta? Why else would they ask for a witch and not a wizard unless they were stealing something that was guarded specifically against wizards?"

That brought Lily up short. She remembered her difficulty getting into the museum with its ward against magical blood. "You could be right..." she said slowly.

"More like I'm probably right."

"Only probably? Such modesty, Sebastian."

"Well, I *am* a paragon of humility," he said with a straight face.

Lily managed to hold in her snort—it was such an unladylike thing to do, after all—but Sir Kipling had no such qualms. He let out a chuffing cough that, to Lily's ears, sounded like amused disbelief. Apparently he could understand human speech across the board, not just hers.

"If he's a paragon of humility, then I'm a saber-toothed tiger," the feline said.

This time she did not manage to suppress her snort.

"What's so funny?" Sebastian asked, cocking his head.

"Oh, um, well..." Lily hesitated. It occurred to her that no one else would be able to understand Sir Kipling but her.

It was a delightful secret she wasn't quite ready to share. "It's nothing," she finished lamely.

He looked at her, a knowing expression on his face as he produced his silver coin from nowhere and started rolling it over his knuckles. But whatever he thought of her response, he kept it to himself. "So, what are we gonna do?"

"Do?" Lily asked, tearing her gaze from the annoyingly mesmerizing display. "What *can* we do? We don't know who the thief is or when they'll strike, and we only *think* we know what they're—" She broke off, eyes snapping back to his coin as she suddenly realized something she'd seen. "Where did you get that, Sebastian?" she asked, reaching for it.

He snatched it away defensively, putting it back in his pocket and out of sight. "It's nothing. Just an old coin my dad gave me."

"I don't think so," Lily said. "I never got a good look at it before; I just assumed it was a silver dollar. But I suddenly realized those markings on it were dimmu runes. It could be enchanted with all sorts of magic. Let me see it, please." She held out her hand.

But Sebastian shook his head, not meeting her eyes. "It's just an old coin. Dad had all sorts of weird stuff lying around. Forget about it."

Taken aback, Lily wondered why Sebastian was acting uncomfortable all of a sudden. Those were most definitely dimmu runes she'd seen.

"What about the ol' Bat?" he said, bringing them back to their original conversation with studied effort. "I bet she knows all the big names in magic. She would know who's after the tablet. Plus, you said the other day you two were working on the ward spells together. She could help us plan our defensive strategy."

Lily let the subject of the coin drop for the moment, her mind switching gears to keep up with her errant friend. "Don't let her catch you using that name, not unless you want to be a bat yourself."

Sebastian's lips twitched in a suppressed smile. "Fine, Aunt B. then. Why don't you ask her?"

"Because," she said, "I try not to bother her with your harebrained antics on too regular a basis. She may not be inclined to believe this, coming from you."

"Then don't tell her I told you," he insisted.

Lily sighed. She'd more or less known things would go this way. There'd been a tiny glimmer of hope Sebastian's information was incorrect, but now it seemed much less likely. The threat was real enough that she couldn't ignore it, even if all she wanted was to hide her face in a book.

"All right, fine," she relented, slumping back in her chair. "We're having tea this Saturday. I'll ask her then." And hopefully Madam Barrington would take her seriously, she added to herself.

"Excellent! I'll see what else I can dig up. Maybe I should read up on museum security systems. You never know when it might come in handy," he said with a wink.

"Read?" Lily scoffed. "That would be impressive. I've never seen you even pick up a book of your own volition, much less read one."

"Who said anything about books? That's what the Internet's for." Sebastian got up, forcing Sir Kipling to leap to safety before he was dumped unceremoniously onto the floor. The feline retreated to the living room, disgruntled.

"I'll be off then. Mind if I, er, take some for the road?" her friend asked, eyeing the freshly baked scones hopefully.

Lily hid a smile and bagged half a dozen for him. She knew they would all be gone by the time he got home.

The rain had more or less stopped, so she stood in the doorway and watched as he disappeared into the darkness.

"Do you suppose he'll make it?" Sir Kipling asked from where he sat on the couch. The floor by the doorway was still damp and therefore thoroughly uninviting.

Lily closed and locked the door. "As long as he doesn't eat all the scones at once and go into a food coma, he'll be fine."

"I wouldn't put it past him," her cat commented, jumping down to join her as she headed to the bedroom.

"Neither would I, Kip."

Friday was a full day so work went by quickly. When she came home, she once again found Sir Kipling waiting for her on the garden wall. This time, however, he deigned to accompany her inside using the normal method: the front door.

She spent the whole evening reading—not only her eduba but also books she'd brought from the Basement—searching for any reference to animals gaining human understanding. Sir Kipling convinced her to read on the couch so he could discharge his duty as a lap warmer. Flipping through book after book, she found occasional speculation about mythological beasts having intelligence and speech, but very little about ordinary animals. The most on that topic concerned familiars, used differently by wizards and witches.

According to *The Wicce and Their Ways,* since witches had no innate connection to the Source's power, they often made bargains with various spirits and creatures to form partnerships. Some such beings could take the appearance or form of animals to avoid detection, thus the stereotype of witches having black cats. These dealings could be dangerous, however, and often led to the practitioner changing, knowingly or not, by simple association. "Something given, something gained" was the witch's way and, according to the book, the main reason why most wizards scorned witchcraft.

Reading between the lines, Lily got the impression wizards stuck to their own spells and rarely dealt with other magical beings out of a historical perception of their own superiority. She thought this was quite silly, but then she'd witnessed enough racism growing up in Alabama to understand what historical perception could do to a group of people.

Mulling over the cultural repercussions of elitism, she finally hit pay dirt when she found a reference to a title she'd seen in her eduba before but had never read. It dealt with crafting, the field of spell-casting that involved making enchanted objects. Calling forth the book to her eduba's pages, she started skimming *Ergonomics of Advanced Thaumaturgy*. According to the chapter on constructs, most familiars were nothing more than loyal pets wearing enchanted collars. In rare cases, however, a skilled wizard could create their own familiar by crafting a mechanical body and enchanting it with abilities. These construct familiars were used for everything from manual labor to acting as mobile wards, messengers, protectors, spies, and more.

Lily closed the tome and laid it aside, scratching Sir Kipling thoughtfully behind the ears as she processed the information. She came to the conclusion that, though fascinating, it didn't help much. Her cat was neither a mechanical creation nor did he wear a fancy collar. She'd not called forth any spirit to bargain with, nor was her cat the physical manifestation of some mysterious being. It might have been a spell she'd inadvertently activated, but that didn't fit

Sir Kipling's description of events. He'd said something was there, a force or entity, that had communicated with him. She only wished he could tell her more.

"Kip," she said, breaking the silence, "why didn't you ask its name? I mean, if something had given me strange powers and told me danger was coming, I'd have asked for a bit more detail before accepting what it said."

Sir Kipling yawned and turned slightly, curling in her lap so that his tummy was available for pettings and he could examine her with half-lidded eyes.

"I accepted it because that was all there was to be done," he said. "Humans like to ask all sorts of questions that get them nowhere and accomplish nothing. Cats simply accept things for the way they are. Now stop talking and pet me."

She rolled her eyes but complied, burying her hand in his soft fur. She considered the possibility he was possessed or gifted. But what sort of entity had the power to grant understanding not just to Sir Kipling, but also to her? Such a thing was beyond any creature, being, or force she'd ever read about. Of course, there were the ancient Sumerian gods from myth. But those were just creative explanations of the Source and its workings that were beyond human understanding. At least that's the line more modern wizard texts took. More modern texts explained the Source in scientific terms as a well of boundless energy in some other plane or dimension. People with certain genes had the ability to sense and utilize that energy to do things mundane science hadn't yet discovered.

While plausible, that explanation didn't sit right in her mind. When connected to the Source, she felt part of something bigger than herself, bigger than the whole world. And what about Enkinim? If the Source were simply energy, why couldn't it be controlled by any word or language you felt like using? It didn't make sense apart from the idea that magic was created to be used in a certain way and was given to humankind by someone or something greater than themselves.

This idea made Lily more inclined to consider the existence of a god or greater entity. It made the most sense in Sir Kipling's case. Yet, if it were true, she wondered what the entity's motivations were. It seemed benevolent, but she and her cat could just be pawns in some cosmic game, for all she knew.

All that reading and thinking made her eyes sting and her head hurt, but it wasn't until after midnight that she finally cleaned up the piles of books and crawled into bed. The last thing she remembered before passing out was the sight of Sir Kipling, sitting erect and watchful at the end of her bed, eyes glinting in the reflected light of the street lamps outside.

She let herself sleep in Saturday morning. Once up, she spent a few hours cleaning her apartment before getting ready to join Madam Barrington for tea. Leaving the house was not an easy task, however, because Sir Kipling wanted to come with her.

"No. Absolutely not." Lily stood firm before the front door, hands on hips.

Sir Kipling's tail twitched back and forth, the only sign of his agitation. "Why not? I can take care of myself."

"So you think. But that's not what I'm worried about. I need time to…explain to Madam Barrington what's going on. It's going to be enough of a shock without you there prancing around and showing off."

"I can be discreet," he pouted.

"*Can* and *will* are two different things. Now please, *please* stay in the house."

He glowered but then sniffed a grudging acknowledgment before stalking off, tail held high.

"Drama queen," Lily muttered, and left the house. She'd carefully packed the fragment of tablet in a warded, metal carrying case the size of a shoebox. The time had come to show it to Madam Barrington.

With so much on her mind as she pulled up to Madam Barrington's house, she barely spared a glance at its grand three-story facade. Heat waves shimmered off the front as it bore the full brunt of the July sun. The rest was shaded by a few large maples and oaks crowded into her small yard. Lily hurried up the front steps to escape into the house's dim, cool interior. She hesitated at the door, apprehensive about her teacher's reaction to the news she brought. Yet, there was nothing to do but push onward, so she rang the doorbell.

Madam Barrington let her in and they proceeded to the kitchen where Lily helped finish the tea preparation. The sight of the familiar room and the fragrance of baking calmed her. Her mentor had made savory rosemary and ham scones, delicate benedictine sandwiches, and a variety of sweet treats. She'd picked out two different teas: the obligatory Earl Grey along with a Peach Melba black tea.

Armed with trays of steaming tea pots and culinary delights, they settled into the Madam's afternoon parlor—the sun room was a bit too warm—and enjoyed the simple delight of each other's company. They spent a while catching up; Lily found plenty to say about her progress on the ward bracelet and her work in the archives, putting off the inevitable conversation she'd actually come for.

Finally, it could be avoided no longer. Lily set down her cup and picked up the warded case she'd left by her chair's foot. Madam Barrington gave no hint of surprise, as if she'd known something was going on.

"I found this tucked away in one of the Basement's artifact drawers," Lily began, opening the case and presenting it to her mentor. Madam Barrington took it and examined the fragment closely, expression suddenly closed and unreadable.

"I wanted to translate the script and the Basement didn't have any natural light, so I took it home…" she faltered, reluctant to mention Sir Kipling, then decided to skip that part for now. "I've made some progress, but as you can see there's little to go on, and I don't know where the rest of the tablet is…might you know what it is or where it came from?" she finished hesitantly.

The older woman stared at the fragment for several long moments, eyes distant and thoughtful. After a while, Lily made a polite noise that seemed to pull her from her reverie. "I am surprised you stumbled upon it," her mentor said. "It was given to me many years ago to keep safe until it was needed, and that is all which ought to be said about it." She closed the case decisively and handed it back to Lily. "Put this back where you found it and never touch it again."

Lily's insides clenched with guilt even as her curious side rankled at being so casually dismissed. She was *very* glad she hadn't let Sir Kipling accompany her. She could easily keep silent on the matter, yet should she?

"But what would it be needed for?" she ventured, probing for more information. "How will we know when 'the time' comes?"

"That," Madam Barrington said with a tone of finality, "is a burden given to me that I alone must bear. Do not concern yourself with it."

Well, Lily thought, so much for discussing Sir Kipling. Without the truth, she couldn't make an informed decision on what to do. Instinct told her this fragment had a part to play in whatever was coming and that it was meant to be used. For good or ill, she had no idea. A visceral reluctance to hide the fragment away again gripped her, but it seemed Madam Barrington was not to be reasoned with. She felt a moment of frustration at her mentor and resisted the urge to purse her lips. Remembering the phrase carved into the rafters of McCain Library, *the truth shall make you free*, she longed for the day when she knew everything and would be free of this carefully constructed web of truth and lies.

Madam Barrington must have sensed her reluctance, because her teacher's expression softened and she sighed. "Miss Singer, you must understand. Though you are a mature and highly skilled woman, you are still in the early stages of your journey as a wizard. You easily mastered the basics and have quite impressed me with your grasp of more advanced skills. Yet seven years is only a fragment of the lifetime one needs to truly come to terms with all the Source reveals to us. You have the disadvantage of starting late in life. I myself was tutored from the age of six until my eighteenth year when…well, in any case I continued my studies on my own and it has taken me decades to become who I am today.

"Skill and wisdom come with time. Attempting too much too soon is often disastrous to a young wizard. You have many years in which to flourish, and what I decline to share I do only for your benefit. For everything there is a time, and all things come about in their proper season. Think no more of this fragment. Put it away, and when the time comes, all will be clear."

So many things raced through Lily's mind that all she could manage was a nod as she set the case back on the floor. Though she respected Madam Barrington and would be the first to admit to her wisdom and power, in this matter she disagreed. Her whole life, people had been hiding things from her, and she was fed up with it. She was fully aware of her sometimes reckless curiosity, but this had become much more than just curiosity. She had a strong premonition that something big had begun and it would not wait for her to "flourish." Putting aside the matter of the fragment, she gathered herself to discuss the other reason she'd come.

"You may recall I met with Sebastian recently," she began, heart sinking as Madam Barrington's lips pursed at the mere mention of her nephew's name. Lily forged onward. "He had some interesting information. Someone in the area has been looking to hire a witch to steal a particular item—we don't know what—from a museum. Now, I know you said the Tablet of Eridu exhibit closes at the end of the month." She paused in thought. "That would be next Saturday, correct?"

Madam Barrington nodded.

"Being in transition makes the artifact vulnerable. That's one reason we think the tablet is the most likely target. But it's also because they specifically need a witch, not a wizard or mundane. That implies the thief will need an awareness of magic while not being magical themselves, perhaps to foil specific wards..." Lily let the sentence dangle, knowing by the sharp look in the other woman's eyes that she followed.

"Obviously, we can't know for sure," she continued. "But I believe the threat is great enough to warrant extra precautions, possibly even closing the exhibit early to transport the tablet before the thief is ready to strike." She stopped, eyeing her mentor's skeptical expression.

"And you believe my nephew's information is...accurate?" Madam Barrington asked stiffly.

"I do. He may be flippant and reckless sometimes... well, most of the time. But what he does, he does well, and he's good at finding things." She had a brief vision of Grimmold, the tracker fae he'd befriended. "If he says there's a plot afoot, I believe him."

Madam Barrington looked away, gazing out the parlor window at the greenery outside. Finally, she turned back. "Have I ever told you why I disowned my great-grand-nephew, Miss Singer?"

Lily recoiled at the look of pain and disapproval on her mentor's face, relaxing only when she realized it wasn't aimed at her, but rather at whatever memory her mentor had been considering. "Well, I always assumed it was because he's a witch. At least, that's what he says."

"He is right, on the whole, but the root of the matter goes deeper. I tell you this not because I want to, but because you deserve to understand the person in whom you put your trust."

Wary, Lily nodded understanding.

"After—" Madam Barrington visibly struggled to say his name, "—Sebastian's parents died, I took him in. I was his only family, at least his only suitable family, and it had been decided long ago that I would look after the boys should anything happen to their parents. Thomas, their father, was of course a wizard. But he refused to use his gift, just as his father had before him. I sometimes wonder if they might still be alive today, had only Thomas accepted his birthright..." her voice grew distant and terribly sad, but she shook herself and returned to her story. "Frederick, the older brother, was already twenty and halfway through college at the time. He coped by burying himself in his studies. But Sebastian..."

she sighed. "He was troubled. So traumatized by his parents' death, so full of anger and loss. He refused to attend school and often ran away, involving himself in who knew what mischief. I regret I did not try harder to comfort him. I have never been a tender woman, raised as I was in the 'stiff upper lip' fashion common among my fellow Englishmen.

"I finally decided to take a firmer stand and discover what my nephew was up to during his long truancies. Finding him proved difficult, and when I did I almost wished I had not. I caught him…" she stopped, as if she dreaded saying what came next. She finally spat out the words, disgust tinged with regret and shame. "I caught him in the throes of a ritual summoning, attempting to bargain with a demon to resurrect his parents."

Lily gasped, horrified.

"I knew he had been dabbling in witchcraft for several years, being a mundane like his mother and not liking it one bit. But I had no idea it had progressed past a boyish fancy. I understood enough of the craft to know his symbols were accurate and potent. I arrived just in time to stop him trading half his soul for the lives of his parents. The fool knew enough to cause immense damage but had not the sense to realize one cannot live on half a soul. It would not have worked in any event. The supernatural operates within and through the realities of the universe, not contrary to them. Those who have passed beyond the veil do not return and are only mocked by any attempt to recreate their semblance in our mortal world."

Realizing that her grip on her teacup threatened to break the delicate china, Lily laid it down as she tried to reconcile the man she knew with the boy her mentor described. "What happened next?" she asked timidly.

"I taught him a lesson he would never forget and forbade him under any circumstances to so much as think about witchcraft again. I took an active role in his upbringing his last years of secondary school, and he seemed to settle down. Realizing he had almost sold his soul to an embodiment of evil bent on his eternal torment had a sobering effect. But as soon as he turned eighteen, he informed me he was leaving to becoming a witch—a good one this time—and that there was nothing I could do to prevent it. Apparently my firm hand had simply taught him to conceal rather than give up his foolish ways. I was…frightened for him, and naturally could not approve of such a thing. Perhaps I acted too harshly in my threat to disown him. Yet, he had always been his own man, and so he walked away without another word."

Now that sounded just like Sebastian, Lily thought. He always did his own thing, consequences be damned. Still, he'd never seemed truly foolish. She gave him unending grief about his behavior, but most of it was for show. She sensed his wisdom—well, street smarts, in any case—and he *was* a good witch. Most important, he seemed to know his limits. Obviously he had learned much on his own in the intervening decade since he'd walked away from Madam Barrington's blessing.

"As I said," her mentor finished, "I do not tell you this to harm your friendship with my nephew. He needs sensible friends. I only wish to offer fair warning of what he is capable of. Admittedly, I might have told you this when you first made his acquaintance. But I did not wish to…color your perception of him. There has been very little contact between us since he came of age, and I hope he has grown into a man worthy of trust. Yet, you can understand my reluctance to rely on his judgment."

After a long, thoughtful moment, Lily nodded. "I understand. But in this instance, I think it's too risky to ignore his information. He may be reckless, but what he knows, he knows. Would you please speak to Mr. Baker about returning the tablet early? At the very least we should pay the museum another visit and add additional wards."

With a sigh, Madam Barrington nodded and rose, gathering up their empty teacups and plates. "I suppose it would not hurt. I will speak to him on the morrow."

"Thank you," Lily said, relieved.

They cleaned up in silence, neither having the need or desire to converse further. Lily left the house even more preoccupied than when she'd arrived. She spent the drive home lost in thought about a sixteen-year-old boy bargaining with the devil for his parents' souls.

Chapter 3

MAJOR MAGIC

LILY WAS WRAPPING UP HER WEEKLY YOGA ROUTINE WHEN SHE got the call from Madam Barrington Sunday afternoon. She liked exercise, or being sweaty in general, about as much as she liked bad grammar or public speaking: that is to say, not at all. Yet, it was important for good health, so she'd picked yoga as the least uncomfortable exercise option. Sir Kipling, having always watched her yoga sessions in rapt fascination, now reveled in his newfound ability to make sarcastic remarks about her ridiculous contortions. He especially enjoyed mimicking her positions as he cleaned himself, pointing out that cats invented yoga and giving her pointers on how to get her foot behind her head. Thus, she eagerly abandoned her cow face pose—where in the world they got such names, she had no idea—to answer the phone.

"Good afternoon, Miss Singer. I am afraid I have rather unfortunate news," Madam Barrington said, voice clipped and to the point. "It is quite impossible for the museum to close the exhibit early. A fundraiser gala is planned for this coming Saturday, and the Tablet of Eridu is one of their star exhibits. Mr. Baker, of course, welcomes us to add further magical protection as we deem necessary. He has already alerted the appropriate authorities of the possible threat, but that is all that can be done."

With a sigh, Lily thanked her mentor and they agreed to meet the following morning to put additional wards in place. She then texted her assistant, Penny, that she would be late for their Monday meeting.

Sitting down at the kitchen table, Lily massaged her temples. She had a sinking feeling the gala would be the thief's entry point. It would be noisy, flashy, and crowded, thus straining the wards that normally only dealt with a few odd museumgoers. The question was, why hadn't the thief struck before now? Though the museum had a few security guards, it wasn't exactly Fort Knox. Was it simply because the job hadn't been open before? But what had changed recently to make the mastermind behind it move now? These questions bothered her, but there was no way to answer them.

"You know they're going to do it during the party," Sir Kipling commented.

Her head came up to see him perched on the back of the sofa, examining her through the archway to the kitchen. "How did you..." she started, shifting uncomfortably.

"I'm a cat."

"Kip," she said in a warning tone.

"If you would just use your head..." he said, then changed tack at her dangerous expression. "Fine. I have good hearing. And as I'm sure you've already logically concluded, the party provides the perfect diversion as well as access point."

"But you're a cat. How would you know anything about robberies?" Lily asked, arching an eyebrow.

"Well, you're a human. How would you know anything about cats?" he shot back.

"Because I have one."

"And yet you clearly don't understand them. Why do you think some robbers are called cat burglars?"

Lily paused. He had a point. "Well, never mind," she said, waving a hand in dismissal. "I still have reading to get through if I'm ever going to finish my ward bracelet. I should get busy. Though, speaking of wards..." She eyed Sir Kipling, remembering what she'd read about animal familiars and their enchanted collars.

"How do you feel about wearing a collar?" she asked, and explained her idea.

Sir Kipling was not pleased.

Monday, being Monday, did not start out well. Lily hadn't slept much the night before, plagued by vague dreams that left her apprehensive without knowing why. Everything about her morning felt off, and she was relieved when she finally made it to her car, rushing to get to the museum by nine. Halfway there, she glanced in her rear view mirror and saw—

"Sir Edgar Allan Kipling! What in the world are you doing in the back seat? How did you get in the car?" She twisted to stare at him, barely believing her eyes. At his meow of alarm, she turned back just in time to slam on the brakes and avoid a rear-end collision. When she glanced at her rear view mirror again, Sir Kipling's claws were dug into the seat and his hair was standing on end.

"Might I suggest you do more driving and less shouting?" he offered, his meow sounding high-pitched.

"Well, what did you expect?" she bit out, heart thumping from their near miss. "You are seriously trying my patience."

"Well, what did *you* expect?" he said. "I *am* a—"

"—cat, I know," she finished for him. She considered turning around and taking him back, but she was already late. "What am I supposed to do with you? You'll get hot staying in the car and I can't take you into the museum. No pets allowed."

"Well, isn't it convenient that I'm not a pet? I can look after myself. No one will notice."

"People will most certainly notice a cat in a museum. Why would you want to go in there, anyway?" she asked, eyes narrowing as she glared at her rearview mirror.

"I have my reasons," he said evasively. Lily gave him The Look, the one parents use on misbehaving children. He twitched his tail and elaborated slightly. "I'm curious to see what all the fuss is about."

"Madam Barrington will spot you if you so much as set a paw near that tablet."

"No, she won't," he assured her with a smug expression.

"We'll see," Lily grumbled, and fell silent. Obviously, intelligence hadn't made Sir Kipling any less cat-like; there would be no controlling him. She could only hope he stayed out of trouble. One thing was for sure: he was no pet anymore.

True to his word, Lily saw neither hide nor hair of her fluffy feline in the museum. She and Madam Barrington worked together casting extra protections around the exhibit hall and on the tablet's pedestal, including an anti-breaking spell for the glass. Her mentor even put a conveyance spell on the tablet itself. Such spells could transmit sensory input, whether audio, visual, or tactile, from one item to another, even over great distances. She would know if the tablet was touched. Variations of this spell class could be used for many things, even a wizard version of the mundane cell phone.

Lily wondered what good a conveyance spell would do if her mentor were all the way at home, but Madam Barrington gave her a knowing look. "In addition to warning Mr. Baker, I took the liberty of acquiring two tickets to the fundraiser. I am not fond of parties, especially late ones, but as this is for a good cause…"

Lily frowned. "Only two? What about Sebastian?"

"I see no reason for him to accompany us," Madam Barrington said, her posture stiffening.

"With all due respect, Ms. B., he has every reason to come. He's a witch."

"Yes. That is what concerns me," the older woman said, tone dry as paper.

"I know he's done foolish things in the past…well, he still does foolish things. But the point is, if we're dealing with a witch, he'll know how to counter them better than either of us would."

Madam Barrington looked away, busying herself with a minor adjustment of the spell she'd just cast.

Lily held her breath.

Finally, her mentor looked back, expression resigned. "Very well. I shall request a third ticket. I only pray he has learned a modicum of sense since he was under my roof."

"He has," Lily assured her. She only hoped she was right.

Unlike their previous visit, Mr. Baker had no pressing engagements and welcomed them into his office for a cup of tea once they finished their work. To Lily's delight, he even served digestives, that British biscuit which didn't actually help digestion but allowed you to eat cookies under the guise of being healthy. As they sat, sipped, and ate, Mr. Baker explained the extra precautions the museum would be taking for the gala.

"We'd originally planned for one of our regular security guards to cover the fundraiser. But in light of your news, which Madam Barrington assures me is reliable"—Lily glanced at her mentor, eyebrows raised. Madam Barrington had gone out on a limb, saying that—"we have contracted with private security for the event and notified the university police to report anything suspicious. Besides that, and your extra wards of course, there isn't much to be done. It *is* an open fundraiser. Anyone who buys a ticket will be admitted."

They both thanked Mr. Baker and took their leave. On the way out, Lily happened to glance toward the exhibit hall entrance and caught sight of slight girl wearing a neon shirt, ripped jeans, and Doc Martens disappearing into it. With a start, she recognized the girl's pixie haircut. Hurrying forward, she tried to catch another glimpse, but when she rounded the corner, the girl had vanished. Several pairs of people and a family with small children were quietly browsing the exhibits, but the girl was nowhere to be seen.

"Great, more people who can vanish into thin air," she muttered, turning to leave the museum.

"Looking for someone?" came a voice by her feet.

Lily jumped so high she nearly lost her balance.

"Sir Kipling!" she hissed at the cat, who had materialized out of some dark corner. "People can see you."

"Nobody's looking at the moment. That girl you were following didn't disappear, by the way, she just ducked into one of the other rooms. Is she important?"

Ignoring the question, Lily hesitated, wanting to pursue the girl but not knowing what she would say should she find her. Wheedling information out of someone was more Sebastian's specialty. Besides, she was already late for her meeting with Penny. "I'll explain later," she finally answered him. "Now, go do whatever you did to get in here unnoticed. We're going home."

On the way back to McCain Library and a full day of work, Lily called Sebastian and told him about the gala. When she mentioned the pixie-haired girl, he agreed it was odd to see the same person there two weeks in a row. So, Lily suggested he visit the museum for the day to keep an eye out in case she reappeared. It seemed unlikely she was the thief, but better safe than sorry. Perhaps Sebastian could dig something up.

For an activity as boring as a stakeout, Sebastian was suspiciously enthusiastic. Given his reaction, Lily liked the idea of him being around this mysterious girl less and less. Yet, there was no way for her to join him. She had several important meetings that day and couldn't skip work just because she was...what? Jealous? She pushed the thought away. It was a ridiculous notion. Sebastian was smart—usually—and capable. He would be fine by himself.

Later that night, after a relaxing bubble bath, Lily was getting some reading done when Sebastian called back to report.

"No sign of her," he said.

"Hmm. It was worth a try. For all we know, she's a student doing a project and had to go back for more research."

"Maybe," Sebastian said, but he sounded skeptical.

"Well, if you're worried about it, you can always conduct more stakeouts," Lily suggested, ignoring her rebellious emotions.

"I'll see what I can do," he promised.

She spent the rest of the evening buried in ward research. It was time to buckle down and finish that bracelet. Something told her she would need it on Saturday.

Tuesday evening after work, Lily spent hours in the Basement perfecting the dimmu runes meticulously carved into the aluminum beads that would make up her bracelet. It was draining work, and by the time she'd dragged herself home it was after midnight. Her back, eyes, and head ached. To her surprise, Sir Kipling was waiting for her on the garden wall, tail twitching furiously in feline annoyance.

"Out a bit late, aren't you?" he asked, jumping down to sniff at her shoes and rub on her leg. "Humans aren't supposed to be up at all hours, even I know that. I was about to come looking for you."

Despite her weariness, she couldn't help smiling. "What are you, my mother?"

Apparently satisfied she was in one piece, his worry gave way to the usual sarcasm. "No, you're my human. Besides, I can see the bottom of my food bowl. I might have starved if you'd stayed out much longer."

"Perish the thought," she muttered, mounting the steps to her apartment, Sir Kipling following behind.

On a hunch, Lily peeked in her car's back window before she left for work Wednesday morning. Sure enough, there was Sir Kipling, crouched on the floorboards behind the driver's seat.

Jerking open the back door, she gave him her sternest glare. "Out!"

Caught red-handed, he sat up and started casually cleaning a paw as if he'd meant to be found all along.

Lily sighed. "You can't come to work with me, Kip. Now, shoo, or I'll be late."

He jumped up on the back seat but made no move to exit the vehicle. "I see no reason why I can't go. You're going, after all."

She bent slightly so she could fix him with a glare. "You're a cat. I'm a human. Pets aren't allowed on campus."

"Neither are men."

"I—what?"

"You complain all the time about Sebastian visiting when men aren't supposed to be wandering around campus. If I let him ignore rules more than I do, I wouldn't be much of a cat, now, would I?"

"It's not a competition, and I'd get in trouble if you got caught." She stood up, hands on hips.

"O, ye of little faith," he quipped.

Lily rolled her eyes. "You can't follow me around everywhere. You might as well get used to that now."

"I don't follow anyone. That's a dog's job." He sniffed, his disdain evident. "I'm simply keeping an eye on you."

"Thanks, but I've taken care of myself perfectly fine up until now."

"Things are changing. Who says it's you I'm worried about?" he said cryptically.

About to protest, Lily stopped, thought about what he'd said, and closed her mouth. She wanted to ask what he meant, but she knew it would be a waste of breath; she'd have to take his word for it.

"Fine," she said, throwing up her hands and closing the car door. She climbed into the driver's seat and turned around to fix him with a stern look. "But no wandering around the library. You stay outside. I can't risk someone seeing an animal loose inside a school building."

Sir Kipling made no reply, simply settled down on the back seat with a smug look.

Despite her fears, no one burst into her office demanding to know why she'd brought a cat to school. In truth, Penny was the only one who would recognize him as Lily's cat, anyway. She needed to make that ward collar soon, though, and get tags for it if he was going to be wandering around on a regular basis. It wouldn't do for someone to mistake him for a feral cat and call animal control.

After work, she again descended the steps into the lower-level archives and headed for the closet that doubled as the magical entrance to the Basement. Only because she was half expecting it did she catch sight of Sir Kipling's gray form slipping into the closet with her.

"Oh no you don't!" She snatched him up, intending to deposit him outside the door. "The Basement is no place for a cat, especially one that's already gotten himself into trouble messing with a magical artifact."

He squirmed vigorously, so she dropped him rather than let him claw her blouse in an attempt to escape. Turning to sit just out of reach, he glared up at her, unblinking.

"No." Arms crossed, she tried, and failed, to stare him down.

He remained silent, waiting.

"You managed to get enchanted or some such nonsense after licking a measly clay fragment. If you think I'm going to let you anywhere *near* a room full of magical artifacts, books, and fragile instruments, you're insane."

"Why can't you humans keep your facts straight?" he finally said, his expression one of long-suffering. "I was gifted, not enchanted. It had nothing to do with me and everything to do with you. You're the one getting involved in dangerous plots. You're the one who needs help. Well, I'm it. Why won't you let me do my job?"

With those words, a soft glow began to emanate from him, barely discernible at first but growing brighter and brighter. As the glow increased, Lily's eyes widened till they were as big as saucers.

"Um, Kip, you're glowing," she said, clutching the door-frame for support, knuckles white.

"Am I?" He looked around at himself. "How fascinating. Apparently I had a point to make. The question is, have you gotten it?"

Lily nodded. Anything to stop whatever strangeness was going on. As soon as she did, the glow vanished, leaving Sir Kipling looking as surprised as she felt. Weary, confused, and worried, she closed her eyes and tried to think. Whoever or whatever had given Sir Kipling intelligence had an agenda. It seemed the agenda was to protect her, like some sort of guardian spirit. But what did she know? Maybe it was using Sir Kipling for some other end. Yet he'd said it was "good" and here to help.

It came down to whether or not she trusted her cat, as ridiculous as that sounded. How many people had to ask themselves such a question? Looking into those yellow orbs, she saw confidence, certainty, and mystery. She thought about how warm and safe she felt when he curled up beside her as she fell asleep. Then there were his constant attempts to groom her, despite loud and vociferous protest on her part. He kept her company, listened patiently when she complained, and always made sure her clothes were thoroughly covered in cat hair. They were family. He was her cat; she was his human. It seemed crazy, but that was enough.

"Fine," she said, reflecting on how frequently she used that word these days. "But no scratching any of the furniture, no licking, no jumping up on things, no opening drawers or cabinets"—she'd never seen him do it, but it was safer to assume he could—"and do not touch *anything*. Got it?"

He blinked at her. "I promise to be perfectly civilized."

Throwing up her hands, she turned, knowing that was the best she could expect. He darted in to join her in the dark closet, and she opened the magical door to the Basement. Before she could wonder if she'd have to carry him through, he'd already disappeared into it.

"Well, aren't we just special today," she grumbled, following him.

An hour later she'd finally finished the setup for creating her ward bracelet. Realizing it was an exercise in futility, she'd given up trying to keep an eye on Sir Kipling. Either he would behave or he wouldn't. So far, the worst she'd seen him do was sniff daintily at the leg of one of her chintz chairs. Though he *had* spent an inordinately long time staring up at the stone gargoyle atop the antique card catalog cabinet, as if he expected it to come to life and attack him. After ensuring the gargoyle was not an imminent threat, he'd disappeared for a time to explore, eventually reappearing underneath the oak worktable to watch her intently, eyes following her every move. He seemed fascinated by her preparations, though he neither commented on them nor asked questions. Eventually she forgot he was there and went on with her work.

Now, everything was ready. Her workspace was a large portion of bare floor, already marked by a spell circle carved deep into the wood, surrounded by powerful warding runes. This circle was why she did most of her casting in the Basement. It had been carved long ago, even before Madam Barrington's time. Each successive caretaker had added to it, Lily included. It could make the weakest, most inexpertly cast containment spell strong enough to restrain any magical mishap. Along its edge were runes for increased concentration and calm so strong that Lily didn't bother burning sage to help her focus. It was one of the components that made the Basement so useful, a true wizard's paradise.

Laying each silver bead of her bracelet down carefully, she arranged them in a perfect octagon around the edges of a dimmu rune drawn on the floor. Next, she took out the bundle of eight hemp strands that held her amulet and laid the whole thing within the octagon. In conjunction with her amulet, this rune would focus and amplify the magic she channeled into each bead. Because the beads were aluminum, they could be imbued with significant warding power, despite their small size. Plus, each bore runes that would let her bolster the ward's strength for a short period by pouring magic straight into it from the Source. It was, she reflected, almost like the force field shields described in science fiction novels. The beads were the projectors with built-in "batteries" that could be recharged or boosted by the Source as the "backup generator." It was all very scientific, thus the common saying: magic was simply science the mundanes hadn't figured out yet.

With the easy part over—runes carved, workspace prepped—she got down to business: using willpower and her mastery of an ancient language to shape pure energy into a form that would protect her from a multitude of harm.

Settling cross-legged on her favorite cushion, she noticed Sir Kipling sitting just outside the spell circle. His paws were tucked comfortably underneath him in a catloaf position and he seemed content to simply watch the show with unblinking yellow eyes. Lily smiled and closed her own, letting the knowledge of his presence slip away along with every other worry, thought, and care. It had taken years to master the deep calm necessary to control complex spells, a skill that required constant practice and firm discipline.

Slowly, carefully, she tapped the Source, reaching deep inside until she felt its intense glow. It was like a bottom-less well of light inside her, and she split off a part of her concentration to maintain the link, allowing it to flow out as she began to chant the words of power that would shape her magic. She took her time, working slowly, meticulously, giving her undivided attention to every rune on each of the eight beads, one at a time. Her words and mind shaped the purpose behind the power, crafting a shield against malig-nant magic in its many forms. She built controls, set limits, defined parameters. Sweat beaded on her brow even as her body temperature dropped, part of her own energy being sucked into the spell. She maintained a delicate balance between putting enough of her essence into the wards to make them her own while not letting the spell consume her. Seconds grew into minutes, which stretched into hours as she worked.

Though her attention was focused inward, had she looked she would have noticed that Sir Kipling's eyes remained locked on her. As she sank deeper into her spell, he began to glow again with a pure, white light. The light flowed gently through her shield spell as if the barrier didn't even exist, splitting into tiny, almost invisible tendrils that entwined throughout her own magic sinking into the ward beads.

After several hours of weaving word and magic, the spell was finally nearing completion. All she had left was to join the magic of each individual bead to make a unified whole, a barrier with no crack or weakness. Physically, the unity would not be visible. The beads would be woven into a new bracelet once the casting was done, but it would not be the bracelet holding them together. Even if the cords were cut, the ward would be maintained by the strength of the magical bond.

Lily started trembling with the effort, her mind and body fatigued from being so long locked in concentration. She ignored it, maintaining iron control as she poured more and more magic into the bond, more magic than she'd ever used on a single spell in her life. Still, it didn't seem strong enough. Something told her this ward would need to withstand an assault from Gilgamesh himself. So she reached deeper, letting more and more energy rage forth in a torrent almost too wild to control. Somewhere in the back of her mind she knew her small beads shouldn't be able to hold so much power. Yet they held, solid, strong, and...glowing? She finally noticed the white light, but it was too late to do anything about it. To interrupt the casting now would risk a massive explosion of energy that could rip her apart.

She held on, speaking the last few words needed to force the magic into the proper shape as she bore down on her link. It was like trying to stem a flood with just your hands; once flowing, the magic wanted to rage on, bursting the banks of control and overcoming everything in its path. In a moment of panic, Lily feared she wasn't strong enough. But then Madam Barrington's words from a long-ago lesson flitted through her mind: "It is not a matter of strength, but of will. Magic has no conscience, no agenda. It is simply unordered energy. You must order it. You must take control."

With massive effort, Lily sharpened her focus to a razor-edged blade of purpose and cut into the torrent. *She* was in control. Crying out the final word to finish the spell, she locked the magic in place and shut the floodgates with a snap. The effort left her gasping, slumped forward as her chest heaved for air. She lay for a few minutes, exhausted but relaxed after such an intense marathon of casting. Though she'd not moved an inch during the entire process, her clothes were damp with sweat and her muscles ached.

Lily twitched in surprise as she felt a warm, rough tongue lick her forehead, lapping up the sweat. She considered pushing her overenthusiastic feline away but couldn't summon the energy. "You know, it's dangerous to cross a containment circle," she murmured, turning her head to eye Sir Kipling's fluffy face. He took advantage of her now-exposed nose to clean it thoroughly. She scrunched up her face in disgust. "Ew, stop licking me. I need a shower, not your tongue." He didn't deign to reply, focusing instead on his efforts.

With a grunt, Lily sat up and murmured the words to dissipate her containment spell. She ought to sit and meditate for a while, let things settle, but she was too tired. A good, hot bath would suffice.

For the first time since completing the casting, she looked at her ward beads, and the sight sent a jolt of surprise through her. The power anchor rune she'd drawn on the floor had been literally burned into the wood by the force of magic it had channeled. Yet that wasn't the most startling sight. As if they'd had a life of their own, the strands of hemp rope already tied to her amulet had woven themselves together through the ward beads, creating a perfect circle with no beginning or end.

Reverently, Lily picked up the bracelet, almost dropping it in shock as heat from the metal beads seared her fingers. Blowing to cool them, she brought the bracelet closer, her wonder growing as she saw tiny veins of light shining in her mind's eye, interwoven through the hemp and outlining all the runes. It wasn't the warm glow of magic she was used to seeing. This light was pure white, almost too bright to look at. It was the same light she'd noticed interwoven with her magic near the end of her spell. The same light that had shone from Sir Kipling.

She looked up at her cat, who, having given up grooming his clearly ungrateful human, was sitting primly and watching her with interest.

"What have I created?" she asked, fingers reverently stroking the cooling beads as she tried to wrap her mind around what had happened.

"A masterpiece," he replied. "Put it on."

She tried, wondering how it would fit with no clasp. When it slid easily over her hand and settled on her wrist, she assumed it was simply too big and would slide off. But as she jiggled her hand, it didn't budge. It had shrunk to fit comfortably against her skin.

Shaking her head in wonder, she decided her brain was too tired to puzzle over the bracelet's mysterious sizing powers. Right now it was time to go home. With more groans, she tottered to her feet, expending only just enough energy to retrieve her purse and shoo her cat out. Turning off all the lights, she stumbled out of the Basement, headed for her car, a shower, and sleep.

Upon waking Thursday morning, she wished she hadn't. Her tired muscles ached, and they'd tightened overnight. There was only one solution, so she dragged herself to the bathroom for another very hot shower. Afterward, she spent thirty minutes slowly stretching every part of her body. By the end of it, helped along by several cups of *very* strong Irish Breakfast tea, she felt nearly human again.

Throughout her morning routine, her eyes kept straying back to the ward bracelet, marveling at its beauty. It still glowed faintly with tendrils of white light, though the aura would be visible only to a wizard—and only one who was looking for it. The aluminum beads shone as if polished, and even her amulet was looking buffed and smooth, as if the wash of magic had given it a thorough cleaning. She had never seen the lapis lazuli stone the amulet was made of shine such a deep blue or the gold flecks in it sparkle quite so noticeably. Back when she first began studying magic and Madam Barrington had told her what her mother's amulet actually was—a power anchor—she'd researched lapis lazuli to better understand the amulet's abilities. It turned out that lapis lazuli was one of the most sought-after stones in the ancient world, from Mesopotamia to Egypt. At that time its deep, celestial blue was the symbol of royalty and honor, gods and power, spirit and vision. It was the universal symbol of wisdom and truth. Lily had often wondered who had made the amulet, and how far back in her family it had originated. She wanted to ask her mother about it. But, like everything else involving her wizard heritage, she knew her mother would refuse to answer.

Lily had no time to consider it further as she dealt with a busy day at the library. The fall semester was approaching and, even though classes wouldn't start for another few weeks, preparation was in full swing. Sir Kipling was content to stay at home, to Lily's relief.

That evening she got another call from Sebastian with news about their thief suspect.

"I've spotted her there the past three days," he said, voice distorted by a rushing sound that made Lily think he was driving with the windows rolled down.

"Really?" she asked, sitting up from where she'd been slouched wearily on her bed.

"Yup. I just watched at first. She spent a lot of time walking around and looking at everything. And I mean everything: exhibits, walls, ceilings, doors, even the floor. She was pretty discreet about it, but I know someone planning mischief when I see it."

"Because, of course, you do it all the time," Lily pointed out.

"Yeah, yeah, whatever," he brushed her off. "Anyway, today I tried to talk to her. But as soon as she laid eyes on me she took off and led me on a merry chase across campus. I thought about sicking Grimmold on her, but I didn't have any pizza with me. She's definitely a witch, and a good one at that."

"How do you know?"

"Because every time I got close, a random stick that hadn't been there before would trip me, or someone nearby would lurch into me as if they'd been pushed. It's classic poltergeist tactics. She must have one following her around, the little bugger. I wonder what their bargain is. Poltergeists are tricky. You gotta avoid the nasty ones like the plague. But, if you find the right one, they'll cause general mayhem for free. Usually you have to bargain for it to cause *less* trouble.

They're a pain in the butt to get rid of once they've taken a liking to making your life hell."

"Well," Lily said, voice grim, "we'll have to be on the lookout for her Saturday night. Do you have any kind of trick to counter her poltergeist if he shows up? I'll see what I can find, spell-wise."

"Oh, I have plenty of tricks up my sleeve," Sebastian assured her. "So when should I pick you up?"

"What?"

"Saturday night. The gala. When should I pick you up?"

"Oh, um, well, I guess...I mean I could just drive myself."

"Nonsense. You're going to dress up and I'm going to pick you up like a proper gentleman. I may even clean out my car for the occasion."

"You'd better, or I won't be setting foot in it," Lily warned, glad he couldn't see the heat rising in her cheeks. She scolded herself for being so silly.

"Okay, okay. So, what time?"

"Well, the gala starts at seven, so pick me up at six. We'll need to get there early to check over things." And he'll probably be late, she added to herself.

"Six it is. See ya then!"

After she'd hung up the phone, she noticed Sir Kipling watching her smugly from the doorway.

"Going on a date, are we?" he asked, purring.

Lily rolled her eyes. "It's not a date. We're on a mission to stop a dangerous criminal. It just saves gas to carpool."

"If you say so," he said, not sounding a bit convinced.

"Well, I do," she insisted, getting up to make dinner.

In the end, though, she wasn't sure she was convinced herself.

Chapter 4

DANGER WALKS AMONG US

MOSTLY BECAUSE OF SIR KIPLING'S SCATHING COMMENTS ABOUT frumpy old maids, Lily caved and wore a black cocktail dress instead of her normal pencil skirt suit. After all, she reasoned, she needed to blend in with the guests, and it *was* a black tie event. This little black dress was the kind every girl had languishing in the back of her closet, never worn, yet prized for its potential. Lily had bought it back in her freshman year, newly escaped from the watchful eye of her parents and taking her first steps into adult life. She'd had the optimistic vision of wearing it on romantic dates, until she figured out most men were crude, cheap, and utterly unromantic. Not that it had mattered. Her shyness with men had effectively isolated her. On the few occasions she'd considered wearing it, the low, swooping back-line and sexy slit up the form-fitting side had seemed too pretentious. Or perhaps she just hadn't been brave enough. Either way, tonight was the night.

To the dress, she added pearl earrings and necklace—family heirlooms from her mother's mother, a woman Lily had never met nor even knew by name. The silver and black of her ward bracelet complemented the outfit nicely. With a bit of concentration, she enchanted the attached amulet to appear pearly white instead of the normal royal blue flecked with gold. She completed the ensemble with sensible pumps of shiny black. No point in wearing stilettos when mischief was afoot.

"Aren't you forgetting something?" Sir Kipling commented from the bed as she examined herself in the mirror.

"What?"

"Oh, you know, just a little matter of destiny and constant foreshadowing, nothing major," he said sarcastically.

She stared, confused.

Sir Kipling sniffed and jumped off the bed, tail held high. Despairing at the drama of cats, Lily followed him into the living room where he sat down beside her desk, right in front of…"The tablet fragment? I can't take that. It's fragile and, well, dangerous."

"Exactly," Sir Kipling agreed.

Lily glared at him.

"You'll need it," he insisted, his tail twitching.

"But I can't carry around the warded case, it's too big."

"Then ward the thing you have in your hand. It'll fit in that."

She looked down, eyeing the black and silver clutch she held. Her cat's idea was crazy, but this whole evening was bound to be even crazier.

Sighing, she quickly cast some basic wards on her clutch that would protect the fragment from breakage or magical tampering. It was the best she could do on short notice.

Six o'clock came and went with no sign of Sebastian. Lily wasn't worried—she'd given him a good half hour of wiggle time. When he pulled up at 6:23, she almost smiled. Predictably late people were much easier to plan around than unpredictably on-time ones.

Descending her apartment steps as Sebastian clambered out of his car, she caught sight of his outfit and it took an effort not to gape. Somewhere he'd acquired a *very* handsome, honest-to-god tuxedo. Not your run-of-the-mill rental, nor the kind found in discount aisles at outlet malls. It was definitely tailored, with silver cufflinks, a formal waistcoat, and a bow tie to boot. Where in the world had he gotten it? She wasn't exactly privy to his personal finances, but the state of his house, clothes, and car gave the impression he lived in constant danger of going broke. A ghost of a suspicion formed in her mind, but it was so ridiculous she waved it away.

"My goodness, you certainly clean up nicely." The comment slipped from her lips before she could stop herself, and she immediately blushed and dipped her head, not looking him in the eye.

When he didn't reply, she braved a peek, only to discover that he was staring at her in unabashed amazement. More heat rushed to her cheeks but she stubbornly lifted her chin, determined to act normal. It was *not* a date, so there was no need to simper like a girl on her first outing.

"I could say the same about you," he finally got out. "You look stunning." Remembering himself, he lifted his eyes from her body to her face, not bothering to hide his silly grin.

"Hogwash," she said, brushing the compliment away with her stepfather's favorite phrase. That didn't stop a pleased smile from touching her lips. But she quickly hid it and stepped forward to inspect the passenger seat of his car, ready in case anything alive and covered in mold jumped out.

To her amazement, the front seat was miraculously clean. Crumbs still littered the floorboards, and a general mess of personal items cluttered the back. But all the pizza boxes were gone and he'd used air freshener—a lot of air freshener—on the interior.

"Incredible. You actually cleaned your car. I didn't think it was possible."

"Hey," he protested, coming around to open the door for her. "I *do* know how to be a gentleman. I just usually don't go to the effort." Lily shot him a disapproving look but didn't comment.

They set off to the gala, the air between them filled with awkward silence. Strangely, it wasn't just her; Sebastian seemed nervous, too. That was odd, since Sebastian was usually overconfident and cocky. Lily was distracted from pursuing this thought, however, by a sudden suspicion, and she twisted around to peer into the back seat.

"Sir Kipling! No!" she exclaimed.

"Wha—" Sebastian began.

"Turn around, we have to go back." She should have known. That sneaky feline hadn't uttered a single plea to accompany her; it should have been obvious he was planning to stow away all along.

"Balderdash. Tell him to keep going," Sir Kipling said, peeved as he extricated himself from the pile of clothes he'd been using as camouflage.

"No! You can't go to a black tie event. You are a *cat,* not a human. And besides, I never had time to finish your ward collar. You could get hurt."

"What the heck is going on?" Sebastian asked, twisting around to look even though he was supposed to be driving.

"Watch the road!" Lily yelled, resisting the urge to rub her face in frustration, as that would smudge her painstakingly applied makeup.

"What is your cat doing in my car?"

"Going home, that's what he's doing. Turn around."

"I need to go with you," Sir Kipling meowed in protest.

"Why is he meowing like that?" Sebastian pulled over so he could safely turn and stare at his stowaway.

Lily sighed. "It's a long story. And I said turn around, not stop."

"Hey, we're in this together," Sebastian reminded her. "What's going on?"

"We're going to be late!" she insisted, voice rising in both annoyance and an effort to forestall further questions.

"Not if you stop stalling and tell me what's going on."

"Fine," she said, throwing up her hands in defeat. "Something strange happened with an enchanted artifact and now Sir Kipling and I can understand each other. And he's intelligent."

"Excuse me. I was *always* intelligent," Sir Kipling interrupted.

"So...when he meows, that means something to you?"

"Yes." Rubbing her face was out, so she settled for massaging her temples. "He's been poking his nose into everything since it happened last week because whatever changed him told him there was danger coming and I would need his help."

"Okay. So why can't he come?" Sebastian asked, looking confused.

Lily groaned. "Not you, too! He is a *cat*."

Sir Kipling rolled his eyes, an impressive feat for a feline. "Why are we having this conversation again? Have you forgotten the understanding we came to only nights ago? Do I need to glow again?"

"You can do that at will?" Lily asked, distracted.

"No, but I'm sure if it needed to happen, it would."

"What the heck are you two talking about?" Sebastian asked plaintively, looking back and forth between them.

Lily ignored the question, mouth set in unhappy lines as she tried to come up with a legitimate reason to insist Sir Kipling stay at home. His yellow eyes drilled into hers, challenging every objection. "Fine, fine!" she finally said, giving up and turning back around. "Let's go, or we'll be late. I'll fill you in on the way," she said in reply to Sebastian's look of annoyance.

The gala, as it turned out, was a very nice affair. As it was the major fundraiser of the year for the museum, they'd pulled out all the stops. Lily was glad she'd instructed Sebastian to park down the street instead of in front of the museum where his beat-up Volvo would stand out among the sleek BMWs and Corvettes.

Once parked, Lily got out and opened the back door for Sir Kipling, who hopped out and disappeared into the night with a parting meow that he would be close. She waited on the sidewalk for Sebastian, but he was fidgeting with something in his back seat. Annoyed at the delay, she peered around the car and saw him stuff something into his pocket.

"What's that?" she asked.

"What? Oh, nothing." Sebastian quickly withdrew his hand and tried to look casual. "Come on, let's get going, or we'll be late." He stepped up onto the sidewalk and gallantly presented his arm as if he expected them to enter the museum as a couple. She gave him an incredulous look, and he dropped his arm with a shrug, turning to amble up the sidewalk. Following behind, she could see him shooting surreptitious glances up and down the street as if he were expecting someone. He had that nervous look again, and Lily wondered what he was up to.

At the museum entrance she gave their names to the doorman. True to her word, Madam Barrington had acquired an extra ticket for Sebastian. Lily breathed an internal sigh of relief. As they entered, she felt the wards' magic slide over her, allowing her passage. Once inside, they turned left to enter the large reception hall, elegantly decorated in black and silver. Lily had to concentrate on not shrinking back as she entered the hall; there were so many people. She did not like crowds, or people in general, really. Sebastian must have noticed her hesitation, because he took the liberty of grasping her elbow to guide her through the press and around the dinner tables to a mostly clear spot by one of the windows.

"Stay here. Keep an eye out for that witch, or anything else suspicious. Oh, and find out where Aunt B. is so I know which part of the room to avoid." He turned and made to disappear back into the crowd.

"Wait," Lily said, not quite desperately. "Where are you going?"

He winked at her, though his expression was still tight. "I'm going to scope out the refreshments. I'll be back." And with that, he was gone.

Lily took a few deep breaths, forcing her heart to stop racing as she surveyed the sea of strangers before her. They were just people; how bad could it be? Even if there were a lot—a whole lot—of them. As she focused on examining the crowd, she found herself relaxing. There was no need to talk to anyone. All she had to do was observe and analyze. Easy enough. She took in the scene, admiring the clusters of elegant partygoers. Everyone was dressed to the nines, and she was glad she'd worn her black dress. She would have looked like a pigeon among peacocks in her tweed suit.

With a few more calming breaths, she extended a spell to probe for signs of magic beyond herself and the wards. There was Madam Barrington in a far corner, talking to an older man with a lady on his arm. Other than that, nothing. So she stopped looking for magic and started looking for a slight, cute girl with a pixie haircut.

She was so engrossed in her search that when a tall, warm presence approached from the side, she turned absent-mindedly, expecting to see Sebastian returned with drinks. It was not Sebastian. She started slightly, putting a more polite distance between herself and the handsome stranger who regarded her with a winning smile.

"What's someone as pretty as you doing all alone in the corner?" he asked.

"I'm—" she was about to say "looking for a thief," but stopped herself just in time and scrambled to think of an explanation that didn't make her sound insane. "I'm just… well, I'm…"

"—waiting for me to come back with drinks," Sebastian finished for her, reappearing from the press of bodies, holding two glasses. He glared at the other man. "Shove off, she's with me."

Lily gasped in surprise, not only at Sebastian's rudeness but also his presumption. With him indeed, she thought angrily. As if.

His words had the desired effect, however, and the other man turned with an offended scowl and disappeared.

Satisfied, Sebastian turned back and offered her one of the flutes of what looked like champagne. She did not accept it. "I do *not* appreciate your interference," she stated, arms crossed. "What did you think you were doing?"

He returned her irate look coolly, eyebrow raised. "I was simply trying to prevent distraction while you're supposed to be helping me stop the theft of a dangerous magical artifact. Insulting the man seemed the quickest way to get rid of him. Excuse me for doing my job. Next time I'll let you extract *yourself* from the clutches of your adoring fans."

Lily blushed furiously, realizing she'd read too much into Sebastian's gesture. Or had she? Men were so confusing, and right now was not the time to try to figure them out. She decided to drop the subject, replying instead to his still-extended offering of drink. "Thank you, but I don't like champagne."

He smiled smugly. "That's why I got you sparkling grape juice."

"Oh," she said in a small voice. Chagrined, she took the glass and sipped it as she continued to scan the crowd.

"No sign of the girl yet?" he asked, eyes darting back and forth.

"No."

"What about the Bat?"

Lily rolled her eyes. "She's over there, and we should go talk to her."

"How about you do that, and I'll mingle and see if I can spot our wayward witch."

"All you need for that is a mirror," Lily muttered.

"What?" Sebastian seemed jumpy and distracted.

"Never mind. It was just a joke."

"Ah. I'll just go, um, look around, okay?"

She watched him closely as he drifted off into the crowd, wondering what in the world was making him so uncharacteristically nervous. Was it the close proximity to Madam Barrington? Or was it something else? He was usually gung-ho about dangerous adventure, but tonight he seemed...guilty. Yes, that's the word she was looking for. But she had to be imagining it. What would he be guilty about?

Shaking off her suspicions, she braced herself and dove into the crowd, aiming for the far corner where Madam Barrington still conversed with the older gentleman. Arriving, she stood at a polite distance so as not to intrude on their conversation. While she waited, she admired her mentor's floor-length gown. It was vintage 1940s, made of slinky satin dyed the deepest purple, almost black, that showed off her well-kept form. What made it so stunning, however, was the flowing patterns of tiny crystal beading in shades of purple and silver that began at the hem and swept up and around the body, ending at the shoulders where it complemented the deep amethyst color of the brooch she always wore. Old, Madam Barrington might be. Frumpy, she was not.

When the old man and his companion moved off, Lily approached, turning to put her back to the wall and front to the crowd.

"No sign of anything yet," she said, eyes on the guests.

"Nor would there be," Madam Barrington assured her. "During cocktail hour the museum exhibits are still open and the guests will be enjoying the sights. It would be too public to attempt anything until dinner. In any event, the conveyance spell will alert me if the tablet's security is breached."

"Ah, yes." Lily nodded, reassured.

Sebastian didn't reappear until the meal had almost started. He slid into an empty seat at their table as far away from his aunt as possible and didn't make eye contact. Oddly, he wouldn't look at Lily, either, though that might have just been because she sat next to Madam Barrington. Food was served, and they listened to various speeches by the museum director and the Dean of Arts and Sciences. Lily had trouble enjoying her food, feeling they should be standing guard by the tablet instead of sitting around a table enjoying filet mignon and grilled portobellos. But Madam Barrington had made it clear the museum director didn't want them causing a fuss. There was professional security guarding the entrance and that, the director deemed, was enough.

It was possible, of course, that all their worry was for naught. The tablet might not be the thief's target. Lily tried to believe that all the way through dinner to dessert, when Sebastian quietly excused himself and slipped out of the reception hall. She wanted to follow, but a look from Madam Barrington kept her seated. Sebastian was perfectly capable of keeping an eye on the situation by himself. Unless, of course, he had more in mind than watching. But that was ridiculous. She told herself to stop entertaining wild suspicions and enjoy her chocolate cheesecake. She managed it, too, until she felt a brush of fur on her leg that almost made her jump right out of her skin. Looking surreptitiously under the table, she saw Sir Kipling staring at her with wide yellow eyes. He motioned urgently toward the door, then disappeared again, somehow slipping from table to table unnoticed as he made for the exit.

Without a word to Madam Barrington—how could she explain Sir Kipling at this juncture?—she hurried out of the reception hall and into the museum proper. Sir Kipling's tail was just disappearing into the muted darkness of the now-closed exhibit hall. Glancing to her right and noting that the security guard was nowhere to be seen, she passed the stanchion post bearing the sign "Closed" and hurried after her cat. She followed him into one of the side rooms and was greeted with the sight of a silent but furious struggle. Sebastian had the pixie-haircut girl by the wrists, obviously trying to subdue her. She, however, was having none of it, and writhed and kicked like a cat held over a bathtub full of water. Normally, Sebastian could have handled so slight a girl, but he was distracted by a large club hovering over-head—controlled, Lily assumed, by the girl's poltergeist—which was taking swipes at him. Sir Kipling sat just inside the door, watching the spectacle with obvious interest but not lifting a single claw to help.

"Stop it!" Lily hissed, trying her best to be quiet and commanding at the same time. Both humans froze in sur-prise, but the hovering club seized the moment of distrac-tion to try to clobber Sebastian over the head. Acting on pure instinct, Lily flung out her hand, speaking the word for shield with a razor sharp focus that resulted in the club bouncing off of an invisible barrier instead of Sebastian's head and clattering to the floor.

All three of them remained still, listening for the sound of a guard Lily remembered wasn't there. Yet she was too shocked at what had happened to inform Sebastian. She'd just performed battle magic, a dangerous method of cast-ing where the Source responded instantaneously to instinct more than conscious thought. She decided it must have been a fluke; experienced wizards had trouble attempting such advanced casting, so she certainly couldn't have done it.

It was Sir Kipling who broke the silence. "You should probably ask them what they're doing," he commented, sounding amused.

Both Sebastian and the girl looked at the feline, and Lily took the opportunity to grab the heavy club off the ground before it could do more damage.

"What's going on?" Lily asked sternly, still trying to keep as quiet as possible.

"Lovers' tussle, dearie," the pixie girl said with a taunting grin. "Though a stick-in-the-mud like you probably doesn't even know what a lover is, do you?"

Both she and Sebastian opened their mouths to protest, but Sebastian beat her to the chase. "She's messing with you, Lil, ignore her. I'm trying to stop her from stealing the tablet."

"Stop *me* from stealing the tablet? Now that's rich, seeing as how you're the one who took the contract."

"What?" Lily's gut tightened in sudden anxiety and she looked into Sebastian's face, not wanting to believe but feeling doubt nibbling at her resolve. He had been acting mighty suspicious of late. "What is she talking about, Sebastian?"

"I have no idea, Lily. She's spouting nonsense to throw you off. You've got to believe me! I'm the one who warned you about this whole thing in the first place. Why would I steal it? I came out here to check on things and found *her*"—he gave the pixie girl a shake—"creeping toward the Near East exhibit hall."

"Yeah, right," the girl said, glaring at her captor. "I was just hanging around to keep an eye on the tablet. I knew it was in danger from someone on the inside. Why else would they have passed me up when the bid went out? I'm the best there—" She stopped suddenly, realizing what she was saying.

"So you *are* the thief!" Lily accused, relief flooding her body.

"No, I'm not! I'm not here to steal anything. I'm here to *keep* it from being stolen. If I foil whatever bastard got the contract—" she took the opportunity to aim a kick at Sebastian's shin, which he expertly dodged "—it might be up for grabs later. Why would I waste time stealing something I wasn't getting paid for?"

Lily looked back and forth between the girl and Sebastian, torn.

"Look, Lil, you have got to *trust* me." Sebastian looked at her pleadingly. "You know me, I wouldn't do something like this. I wouldn't lie to you."

She looked into his eyes and didn't know what to believe. If she hadn't known his past, if Madam Barrington hadn't told her about...but his reckless decisions and unwise deals had all been to get his parents back, not for personal gain. He had to be good at heart, right? If she could trust a talking cat, couldn't she trust a friend who had watched her back on many an adventure? With that thought, the balance tipped in his favor, and she decided she would rather trust him and be proven wrong, than not trust him and be proven right.

"I believe you," she finally said. "But if you aren't the thief, then why have you been acting so nervous lately?"

Sebastian shuffled his feet, hands still occupied with restraining the girl. "Well, I was, erm, unsure whether or not I, um—"

"He fancies me, honey," the pixie girl interrupted, grinning. "Isn't it obvious?" She glanced up and winked at Sebastian, who looked away. "He was probably nervous about finding out if I was the real thief or not."

Lily frowned, distracted by an uncomfortable flash of heat as she tried to ignore the girl's smug expression and focus on the task at hand. "So if neither of you is the real thief, then who is?"

"I don't know," Sebastian said, jumping on the change of subject with obvious relief. "But once I hand this wild-cat off to the security guard"—he glanced at his captive, who grinned impishly and made a kissing motion with her mouth—"why don't we go check on the tablet?"

"The guard is gone."

"What?" Sebastian's eyes widened. "He was there a while ago when I left the reception hall."

"Maybe he just stepped out for a smoke," the pixie girl chimed in.

"Maybe, I'll have Sir Kipling check—" Lily said as she turned to address her cat, but he was gone. Confused, she poked her head out of the side room into the main exhibit hall just in time to see his fluffy form tear around the corner leading to the Near East exhibit and race toward them.

"She's there, and it's bad," he panted out as he slid to a stop in front of them.

"Who? Where—" Lily began.

"No time, just go. Go!" Sir Kipling meowed loudly and turned again, racing back the way he'd come.

"What in the world—" the pixie girl started to ask.

"Come on!" Lily cut her off as she grabbed Sebastian's arm and towed him, and therefore the girl, with her.

They all raced past dimly lit cases and shadowed art-work, piling into the Near East exhibit room in a rush. The sight that greeted them was startling. In the dim light Lily could see a large circle filled with intricate patterns drawn around the tablet's pedestal. It was hard to see in the dim-ness, but the marks looked dark, wet, and red. Slumped up against one of the giant stone columns was the missing secu-rity guard. Crouched on the floor with a brush, just finish-ing the last lines of the design was—

"You!" Lily, Sebastian, and the pixie girl said in unison.

"Well, look who's here. Times must be tough if they're letting a librarian, a fool, and Sabrina the teenage witch run security," the woman said. It was the same woman Sebastian had accidentally bumped into the first time Lily had shown him the tablet. Then, she'd looked older, frumpy, with art pencils sticking out from behind her ears. Now she looked younger, her long, jet-black hair cascading over bare shoulders above her black sheath dress. She finished the line she was painting, then touched her fingers to it and murmured a few words. The whole design started to glow faintly red. Standing, she wiped her fingers on the guard's shirt and tossed her hair over her shoulder. "You didn't think they'd give the job to just any riffraff, did you? They needed a professional."

"Well, that rules you out," the pixie girl snorted.

"Don't be sore, Tina. I'm sure there's some candy store you can rob for them. That would be right up your alley, wouldn't it?"

"I'm not the one who steals from children," Tina retorted.

"You know her?" Sebastian asked, incredulous.

"Yeah, I know her. Her name is Veronica Paxton and she's the skank the rich guys call when they want something stolen and then want some action afterwards."

"You're just jealous, dear Tina."

"You wish. I'm also not insane. What the heck do you think you're doing? If you've hurt a hair on that guard's head…" she said, eyeing the dark red symbols on the floor.

"Oh, relax. I used goat's blood. This oaf of a security guard was unscrupulous enough to kiss a stranger and got a healthy dose of sleeping potion."

As they spoke, Sebastian was examining the symbols around the pedestal. Suddenly, his eyes went wide. "That's not—"

"That's exactly what it is, pretty boy," Tina said, glaring at Veronica. "This insane excuse for a witch couldn't figure out how to get past the wards, so she's made a summoning circle to bring in the big guns. Something that doesn't care about measly wards. You're an idiot, Veronica, and you're going to get us all killed."

"Not all. Just you. It's all the same to me, but you might want to back up. He's coming." Even as she said it, the circle went from dull red to shining so brightly it was hard to look at. Red light filled the room and the stench of sulfur filled the air.

"Get back! Get back!" Sebastian yelled, pulling Lily with him as he retreated to the door. Lily stumbled after him and felt the club she still held tug at her arm, as if an invisible someone was trying to pull it from her hand. She let go and watched in amazement as Tina did not retreat, but rather rushed forward, the club hovering in the air behind her.

Before she could reach Veronica, however, a rent opened in the darkness, blinding them with its fiery glow. The brightness was momentarily blocked as a huge form stepped out, its scaled outline backlit by blood-red light. The rent vanished, leaving behind a terrifyingly real demon that stood at least eight feet tall, its body rippling with muscle and lethal spikes. Standing on two legs with a thick tail to balance its top-heavy shoulders and huge arms, it looked straight out of a nightmare. Sharp claws curled from each finger and horns ringed its crown above glowing red eyes and a wide mouth full of dripping fangs. Those hungry eyes were locked onto Tina, and, even as Sebastian pushed her behind him, Lily could tell he wanted to rush to the girl's defense.

Just then, sharp, guttural words in a language Lily had never heard before came from the far side of the pedestal. The creature's head turned toward the speaker slowly, as if against its will. Veronica stood, hands upraised, eyes locked with the beast's, and gave it another command. The monstrosity looked at the small, fragile pedestal below it and with one giant hand reached downward. Right before it touched the glass, it met some sort of resistance. But the demon bore down and broke through the invisible barrier, breaking the glass with its claws and extracting the tablet with surprising dexterity for one so large. It lifted the tablet to hand it to its master.

Halfway there, it lurched and stumbled, thrown off balance as the levitating club wielded by Tina's poltergeist connected with a solid crunch to the back of its head. In that moment of distraction, the club dropped, and Lily saw the tablet levitate out of the demon's loosened grip.

"What in heaven's name is going on?" came the stern voice of Madam Barrington from behind Lily. Before Lily had a chance to turn and explain, she saw the tablet drop into Tina's waiting grasp even as Veronica screamed another guttural command. The demon turned toward Tina, lashing out with blinding speed. Its swipe caught her and tossed her to the side, slamming her against a display case and shattering the glass. The girl slumped there, either unconscious or unable to move, yet curled protectively around the tablet still clutched in her arms. Seeing her torn clothes that even now had begun to turn red with blood, Sebastian rushed forward to help.

"I see we underestimated our opponent," Madam Barrington said dryly as she rounded Lily, who was still frozen in shock. Then she spotted her nephew rushing toward the demon. "Sebastian, no!"

Her mentor's startled shout snapped Lily out of her shock. She rushed after Sebastian, ignoring her teacher's cry of protest. The demon was stooping over Tina's inert form, looking as if it might eat her on its way to retrieving the tablet. Lily was close enough to Sebastian to hear him mutter, "Darn it, Thiriel, this had better work," as he closed the distance between him and the beast. As if on command, a staff materialized in his outstretched hand, its ebony length twisted and branching as though it had been cut from a living tree. At its crown was a glowing, green jewel. In the instant the staff appeared, a symbol like a tattoo shone on his right hand, glowing faintly with the same light.

Sebastian took the most effective, if unsophisticated, path of attack. Drawing back his staff, he swung it full force at the demon's face. It connected with a solid crunch and a flash of green, and the demon stumbled back with a howl of fury, clawing at its injuries. Sebastian didn't stop there. He hit it again, this time in the chest, and yelled a phrase in the same language Veronica had used. The demon stumbled back further.

Dipping down to drag his finger through the still-wet goat's blood that shined with an unearthly light, Sebastian drew a symbol in the air in front of him. His fingers left a glowing red trail that, when complete, shone once and then disappeared. The beast howled again.

Taking her eyes from the battle, Lily reached Tina and started dragging her backwards, away from the fighting. The girl moaned in pain, but her wounds didn't seem to be deep; the blood had only soaked her clothes, not pooled beneath her. She still clutched the tablet. As Lily backed up further, Madam Barrington joined her and together they got the injured girl to the door. Sir Kipling appeared out of nowhere and nosed the wounds, inspecting them.

"What in the world is your cat doing here, Miss Singer?" Madam Barrington looked more surprised to see Sir Kipling than she'd been upon the appearance of the demon.

"It's a long story, but he knows what he's doing."

Madam Barrington looked like she wanted to question Lily further but, in light of the situation, wisely kept her peace.

"She'll live," her cat informed her. "It's mostly surface wounds. But they need to be cleaned up."

"Stay here and keep an eye on her," Lily told him, and turned with Madam Barrington back to the fray.

Sebastian was still taking swings at the demon, but the creature had gotten over its initial shock and was dodging them handily and swiping back with outstretched claws. The sight of Sebastian dressed in a tuxedo and wielding a glowing green staff against a hulking, spiked demon was almost comical, if it hadn't been so deadly. As Lily approached again, she could see he was losing ground, and he seemed to realize this as well. She saw the look on his face harden, and she had a split second to wonder what dangerous thing he was about to do.

Having the beast between him and the stone columns, with Veronica to the side screaming commands, Sebastian suddenly backed up. Muttering words too quiet for her to hear, he lowered the crown of his staff until the shining gem came into contact with the glowing lines of the summoning circle. With a flash of green, the circle sputtered and went dark. The sudden loss of light caught them all off guard, and in those precious few seconds it was the demon that reacted first. No longer under the control of the summoning circle, it turned to the nearest living creature—Veronica in this case—picked her up, and stuffed her head-first into its mouth.

Lily and Sebastian both screamed, though his was more of a terrified yell as he stumbled back in horror, dropping his staff in the process. It vanished before it hit the ground and with it went the symbol on his hand. The demon continued to devour the woman, its jaw unhinging and expanding like a snake's to engulf her body. It was over in seconds, and then its head turned in their direction, its eyes now the only red glow in the room.

"Sebastian, Lily, get behind me this instant!" Madam Barrington's command rang out in the silence and she stepped forward, putting herself between them and the approaching nightmare. Madam Barrington began to chant softly, arms lifted and tracing a fluid circle in front of her. The creature approached, crouched and wary like a hunting predator. It took a swipe at the older woman, but its hand met an invisible barrier and it jerked back as if stung. It moved to the side, trying to circle around behind her, but she moved with it, arms raised, still chanting. Impatient, the beast rose to its full height and roared, its cry echoing through the room and seeming to shake the very ceiling. Then it lunged forward, attacking the invisible barrier with all its strength. The barrier held, but its strength flickered for a split second. All it took was the tiniest gap for the demon's clawed hand to sneak through and glance Madam Barrington, tumbling her fragile body to the floor.

"No!" Lily screamed and surged forward even as Sebastian tried to hold her back. But Sir Kipling was quicker than them both. He darted between their legs and crouched in front of Madam Barrington's still form, hissing and spitting at the towering demon. Miraculously, the demon paused, as if confused by the tiny creature's defiance. But then its hesitation made sense as Lily began to see what it saw. Sir Kipling had started to glow again, but this time the glow rose into the air and coalesced above him. It spread outward and upward, growing, pulsing, shining so brightly Lily had to shield her eyes. Even so, she recognized the rough form of gigantic, outstretched wings. Between them was someone, or something, but the light was too bright to make out its shape. The demon shrank back from the glow, cowering in fear even as hate burned in its eyes and it searched for a way around the light.

"Lily, the fragment!" Sir Kipling's desperate meow came from the floor beneath the glow. "Use the fragment and command the beast to leave. Quickly!"

Lily hesitated a second, paralyzed by uncertainty. "But, the spells. They're ancient—too powerful. I'm not strong enough!"

"You're not alone. Just do it!" Sir Kipling yowled back at her.

Wrenching herself from Sebastian's hold, she dashed back to Tina. Prying the tablet from the girl's arms, she rushed toward the demon as she withdrew the fragment from her clutch. She didn't even need to search for the correct fit; the fragment shot from her hand to its proper place as if drawn by a magnet, a line of glowing light fusing the piece to the whole and completing two lines of text.

Not giving herself time to consider what she was about to attempt, or whether she would survive it, Lily began to read. As each word left her mouth, she felt a pressure grow inside. She hadn't needed to concentrate to tap the Source, it was just suddenly *there*, straining and bursting against her control like a flood. It was as if the words she spoke were so potent that the forces inside her wanted to explode into action. Another word, and another; the pressure grew, and she struggled to maintain control. Though the words were unfamiliar, somehow she understood their meaning. The spell was a command, a call of obedience to any being, living or dead, man or fae or beast. It was a command that could not be ignored or resisted.

She spoke the final words, almost screamed them in pain as she fought to control the power. This was worse, far worse than when she'd created her ward bracelet. She felt herself slipping, coming apart, about to lose control.

Just then, her ward bracelet flashed to life with the same white glow that emanated from Sir Kipling. Lily felt the crushing pressure ease, as if the bracelet were siphoning off energy. Now in firm control of the spell, she stepped away from Sir Kipling and his glowing wings so that they were no longer between her and the demon and raised her arm in authority toward it.

Seeing its chance, the beast leapt forward, mouth open and glowing as red hot as its eyes. A stream of fire shot out of its maw toward her and she had no time to do anything, not dodge, not cast a spell. Yet when the stream reached her, the ward bracelet encircling her upraised arm flashed with a brilliance that left spots on her vision, and the fire vanished as quickly as it had appeared. Not giving the beast a second chance to strike, she spoke the words of command, putting every ounce of will behind them. The demon screamed in defiance, resisting the compulsion. But it was losing ground. A glowing red rift opened behind it, and it took a faltering step back even as it leaned forward, straining as if against a gale wind. Then, with a final howl, it was swept into the rift, which snapped shut behind it, cutting off its cry of fury.

The sudden darkness and silence that filled the room was broken by the echo of voices and approaching feet on the marble floor. Obviously the commotion had not gone unnoticed. But Lily didn't have time to worry about that. As soon as her adversary vanished, she released the spell, fighting to hold herself together as the power raging through her subsided. Head spinning and feeling faint, she dropped her arm in exhaustion, barely having the strength to stumble over to Madam Barrington's inert form. Sebastian was there, too, and together they managed to roll her over. She was bleeding from a scratch on her temple but otherwise looked unharmed. Her breathing was steady, if shallow.

"Go get an ambulance, now!" Lily told him. He hesitated. "The demon is gone, Sebastian. Go!"

He rose.

"—wait!" Lily stopped him. "No one will believe the truth, so don't bother. This was, um…a bunch of teenagers with baseball bats. Vandals. And they had a big dog," she added, remembering Tina's torn side.

Sebastian nodded and hurried off. Lily turned to Sir Kipling, who was now sitting, observing them, looking as enigmatic and unruffled as ever.

"Thank you for saving her," she said, her voice husky with emotion.

"Just doing my job. But I'm not the one you should be thanking," he said.

"Then who—"

You did well, little one.

The voice echoed like bells in her head, and she winced, seeing Sir Kipling mirror her grimace. He must have heard the same thing.

"Who are you?" Lily asked in wonder.

One greater than us both has sent me. Continue as you have. If you seek, you will find.

Good grief, Lily thought. This thing was worse than Sir Kipling. She heard a chuckle of bells and blushed, wondering if it could hear her thoughts.

Your task is complete, for now. Yet more will come. Much more. I have put His light into your ward. It will protect you. Companion, the voice continued, and Lily realized it was talking to Sir Kipling, *you have proven yourself worthy. Do you wish to remain as you are, or return to yourself?*

"She's going to need as much advice as she can get, and I can't very well boss her around if she doesn't understand me. I'll stay, thanks." Sir Kipling's yellow eyes looked into hers as he spoke, and she could have sworn he smiled, though of course that was silly. Cats don't smile.

And just like that, the presence was gone, whatever it had been. No more bells, no more glow. She glanced down at her ward bracelet and thought she could still discern tiny threads of light, undulating under the surface of each hemp cord. She smiled. Maybe not completely gone.

A sound behind her brought her back to reality. Turning, she saw people streaming into the room. EMTs were already tending to Tina, who had regained consciousness. Sebastian, instead of returning to Lily and his aunt, was holding Tina's hand in a very familiar fashion. Lily felt a stab of annoyance. Maybe he wasn't a thief, but he was getting awfully cozy with someone who had confessed to that profession. She told herself the fact that Tina was a very attractive girl had nothing to do with her annoyance.

Medical personnel now approached her, and she retreated, giving them room to see to Madam Barrington as others went to retrieve the unconscious but miraculously unhurt guard. One of the EMTs, noticing her weary stumble, helped her sit and wrapped her in a blanket after ensuring she wasn't hurt. When she looked around again, Sir

Kipling had vanished. She wasn't worried. He'd either show up in the back of Sebastian's car or find his way home. Lily didn't doubt him anymore, as he could obviously take care of himself. He was still a cat, yes, but a very special cat.

Hot on the EMT's heels were the authorities: police, crime scene techs, the whole nine yards. Several started roping off areas and bagging evidence, another got her statement, while a third spoke to Sebastian, who was watching the EMTs wrap up Tina's torn side. After Lily gave her statement, the police drifted away to consult with their colleagues, scratching their heads over the carnage and intricate symbols painted on the floor in goat's blood.

Lily happened to glance toward the door and what she saw filled her stomach with butterflies. It was the same two FBI agents who had interviewed her after Pitts. The woman, Agent Meyer, was as stern-looking as ever. But Agent Grant looked positively concerned as he spotted her and hurried over, eyes taking in the destruction. Lily couldn't help but notice how good he looked in his suit. She hoped it didn't show on her face.

"Miss Singer, are you all right? Are you hurt?"

"I'm fine, thank you, Agent Grant," she said, glowing a bit at his sincere concern. "Just worn out from all the commotion. Fancy seeing you here." She attempted a casual chuckle, but it came out a nervous squeak.

"I was about to say the same to you. You do seem to show up wherever anything, um, interesting is happening," he opined, looking pointedly at the crushed pedestal and crimson floor.

"Oh, I had nothing to do with any of that," she rushed to assure him.

"I…see. Can you tell me what happened?" he asked.

"Well, I—I already gave my statement to the police, and I—I just don't know if I can relive the whole thing over again. It was all so shocking," she hedged, trying to look distressed and fragile. It wasn't hard.

"All right," he said slowly, eyeing her. "Would you feel more at ease if we chatted about it over coffee in a few days, once you've had time to recover?"

Lily was taken aback at the request but supposed he was attempting to get more information by putting her in a relaxed situation. Little did he know how much she hated coffee. She was about to decline when she spotted Sebastian sitting on the edge of Tina's cot, where she lay wrapped in bandages and being prepped for hospital transport. Lily's eyes narrowed as she saw he was holding the other witch's hand again. He bent closer to hear something she was saying, then laughed.

Lily pursed her lips and turned back to the FBI agent. "Yes, I would be delighted."

Epilogue

IN THE END, SINCE THEY ALL STUCK TO THE SAME STORY, THERE wasn't much for the police to do. Both the demon—and Veronica, inside the demon—had disappeared without a trace, so no body, no foul. As the sole witnesses to the crime, they all claimed they'd simply heard a racket and had come to discover a group of teenagers vandalizing the museum. They'd tried to stop them, of course, thus their various injuries. As the tablet was recovered unharmed and nothing else was stolen, the only crime committed was damage of museum property. With Mr. Baker running interference and a sizable, anonymous donation made at the end of the fundraiser that covered damages, the museum filed no charges and the matter was dropped.

No one seemed to notice that the tablet had an extra bit on it. Madam Barrington assured her the tablet's curators would take care of separating the fragment from the whole and hiding it again; it was too dangerous to leave the pieces together. At the hospital where they took Madam Barrington, Lily finally explained everything that had happened with the fragment. Though not pleased, her mentor admitted the fragment had certainly fulfilled its purpose. She still refused to say who'd given it to her and was just as confused as Lily at the miraculous powers it had granted Sir Kipling and, by proxy, Lily. She'd never heard of anything of the sort before but was eager to meet the "new" Sir Kipling over tea sometime.

Madam Barrington was released from the hospital that same night with no injuries beyond a minor concussion and the scratch on her temple. Sebastian had stayed to keep Tina company, so Lily saw her mentor home, holding back the burning questions she had for her friend. There was the matter of him taking up the company of a known thief, as well as his mysterious, glowing staff. Lily was dying to know who Thiriel was. The more she got to know Sebastian, the more women seemed to show up in his life. He obviously had more than his fair share of secrets, and his reluctance to share any of them put her on edge.

Sir Kipling was, indeed, waiting for her at home, but they didn't discuss the evening's events. There didn't seem to be a reason to. Following her cat's example, Lily had decided to accept things for the way they were. She would keep searching, however. The strange presence in her mind had said, *if you seek, you will find*, and she was determined to find the truth about her past. Maybe it would lead her to better understand her future.

Knowing well the importance of record-keeping, she spent a significant amount of time Sunday afternoon carefully recording events in her eduba, from the tablet fragment, to Sir Kipling's startling abilities, to the strange magic manifesting in her ward bracelet, and the being who spoke to her. She just wished it had given her answers instead of more questions.

But answers came sooner than she expected. Monday morning as she headed out the door for work, her forehead bumped into something. Looking up, she saw an envelope hovering overhead. She quickly snatched it out of the air and looked around nervously, but no one was about. Going back inside, she examined it. The envelope was a heavy, yellow parchment, its flap sealed with red wax and stamped with an elaborate symbol of a tower combined with a crescent moon and star. She wondered what careless wizard had sent her a letter by magic. It was simply irresponsible, as any mundane could have seen it and investigated. Email, phone, and snail mail worked perfectly fine.

Breaking the seal, she opened the letter. It was written in silver ink, and as she unfolded it fully the letter started reading itself to her, almost like a voicemail. The voice was deep, smooth, and uncomfortably familiar.

> *Dear Miss Singer,*
>
> *I apologize for my delay in sending you this letter. It took me some time to find you. I also wanted to beg your forgiveness for the nature of our first meeting in Pitts. I truly meant to harm no one, only to retrieve the artifact that was rightly mine and had been stolen from my family long ago. Being in the time loop had put my nerves on edge and I was, perhaps, more harsh than I meant to be. I hope Mr. Blackwell has fully recovered.*
>
> *In a gesture of goodwill, I would like to extend an invitation to visit my family's estate in one week's time. I believe we have much in common and there are many questions you would ask that I have answers to. There are also several people I would like you to meet who have been waiting a very long time to see you again. Simply write your reply at the bottom of the letter and it will find its way back to me. I hope to have the pleasure of your company soon.*
>
> *Sincerely,*
> *John Faust LeFay*

Lily's blood ran hot, then cold, and her heart raced in both excitement and dread. This was it. These were the answers she'd been looking for. The truth. She remembered the last thing the fragment of Annabelle's soul had said to her: *ask the fae*. But what if she'd really said, *ask LeFay*? Who was this man and why did he want to talk to her, much less answer her questions? He sounded sincere in the letter, but she couldn't forget the disdain he'd shown or the hungry curiosity in his eyes when she'd seen him last in the time loop. And who were these people who wanted to meet her… again? Why did this man seem so familiar? Whoever he was, he was the first person who had ever shown any interest in revealing, rather than concealing, information.

Without giving herself a chance to think, lest she lose her nerve, she grabbed a nearby pen and scribbled, "Yes, please," in the blank space at the bottom of the letter. Immediately, the letter levitated, neatly folding itself back up, though the seal remained broken. Then it vanished.

Lily wondered what she'd gotten herself into. The truth might make her free, but at what cost? There was only one way to find out.

Ask John Faust LeFay.

INTERLUDE

WITCHY TIMES

THE ELEVATOR DINGED AS IT PASSED EACH FLOOR, MOVING SO slowly Sebastian had time to rock back and forth on the balls of his feet three times in between floors. Hospitals made him nervous. They were where you went when things weren't right, when people got hurt. Or were dying. He usually avoided them like the plague. Even driving past one brought back memories of the night his parents died.

But that had been a long time ago, and today he was going to see someone very pretty and not at all dead. Even more exciting, she was a witch—the first one he'd met who wasn't trying to kill him, curse him, steal his clients, or turn him into a small, furry animal. Well, there had been that poltergeist she'd sicked on him, but that had been a misunderstanding.

Having finally reached the fourth floor, the elevator emitted one last ding and slowly opened its doors. Sebastian held back, letting the Sunday afternoon press of visitors exit first to ensure he wouldn't be jostled, thus endangering the vase of flowers he carried. He had no idea if Tina was a flowers kind of girl, but it seemed a safer bet than a stuffed bear or chocolate. To throw in his own flair, he'd put a bit of fae glamour on them so they would slowly change color, like one of those fancy lava lamps.

Exiting the elevator and seeking out her room, he reflected on how much Tina reminded him of himself. Last night when he'd accompanied her to the hospital, he'd overheard one of the nurses asking for an emergency contact. Tina had just shaken her head. She was probably very independent and would be reluctant to accept help. But he had to try. Finding the correct room, he took a deep breath and knocked on the open door. "Flower delivery service. Anyone home?" He poked his head in, giving a grin and a wave to the petite girl sitting upright in the room's hospital bed.

Tina gave him a disapproving scowl that did nothing to hide the twinkle in her eye. "Seriously? Flowers? You totally should have brought me a burger. This hospital food is complete crap."

"Well, I didn't just bring flowers. I also picked up some old clothes that should fit, since they threw away your other ones. I mean, hey, you look great in a hospital gown, but I doubt you want to wear it home." He winked, stepping into the room and positioning the flowers carefully on a bedside table where their vibrant, changing colors couldn't be missed. "I also might be persuaded to smuggle in real food. For a price, of course."

Tina crossed her arms. "A price, huh?"

"Yup. A date. Once you're better, of course," he added hastily. Though his smile was confident, he had to resist the urge to wipe his sweating hands on a pants leg.

"Mm-hmm," Tina responded, mouth pursed and eyebrow raised as she considered his demands. "Well, you didn't rat me out to the police, and you *did* save me from a demon—"

she paused, brow furrowing as she stared at the blue flowers. "Weren't those yellow when you brought them in?"

Sebastian grinned like a Cheshire cat.

"How did you do that?" Tina asked.

"I'm a witch," he said airily. "Mystery is sexy, so excuse me if I decline to explain."

Tina laughed. "You wish. And yes, we can hang out as soon as I escape this hellhole."

"Hey," Sebastian said, expression growing concerned, "don't go running off before they discharge you. You've got to give yourself a chance to heal. If I recall correctly, you bruised three ribs, had a minor concussion, and got stitches. If I catch you sneaking out I will turn you in with a completely clear conscience."

Though she looked disgruntled, Tina waved a hand in dismissal. "Chill. I won't. The nurse said they'd be discharging me today anyway. It sounds all scary, but I'm fine, really. I only needed a few stitches, and I think they threw in the concussion stuff to make me stay overnight."

"Still, you'll need to take it easy for a while. You need a ride home later?"

Tina avoided his gaze, fiddling with the sheet in her lap. "I can get a cab or something."

"Hey, come on. If you don't want me to know where your house is, that's cool. I can just drop you off at your car. How's that?" he asked, catching her eye and giving her a knowing look.

Tina regarded him for a moment, then nodded. "Okay. I just hope they haven't towed it yet. You know how rabid campus police can be."

Sebastian nodded. He remembered one time, while visiting Lily at her office in McCain Library, an Agnes Scott security guard had tried to give him a parking ticket. She'd been pretty, and he'd enjoyed talking his way out of it. A smile threatened to touch his lips as he recalled his boast to Lily that he'd used witchcraft to evade campus security. Lily had given him a withering look and gone on about how one should use magic only for good. He pointed out that his visits were good for her. She'd threatened to throw a book at him.

Dragging his thoughts back to the present, Sebastian made sure Tina was settled, then set off in search of a nurse to discover when Tina would be discharged. With a bit of haggling and a few hours wait, she was finally declared fit enough to return home. Sebastian helped her to his car and they headed to the Emory University campus. To his surprise, she was completely unfazed by the state of his car. It became clear why when they finally arrived and he saw that her car was just as dented and cluttered as his. And, sure enough, a parking ticket was tucked under the windshield wiper. He suppressed a smile as Tina pulled it out and tossed it on the ground.

As she maneuvered her bruised body into the driver's seat, he transferred the flowers he'd given her to the passenger side, then bent down to look her in the eye. "Are you going be okay driving by yourself? How do your ribs feel?"

"I'm fine." She waved him off, grimacing at the movement.

He frowned but knew she wouldn't accept any more help. "Mind if I get your number? So I can take you up on that date sometime." He winked.

Mouth curving into a mischievous smile, she cocked her head. "I guess it wouldn't hurt, lover boy," she said, scribbling some numbers on a scrap of paper and handing it to him. "Here ya go."

"Thanks, *chica*." He started to stand up, then bent down again. "One more thing. You don't have any idea who put out that job on the tablet, do you?"

Tina stared at him, expression unreadable. Finally, she sighed. "Well, since I've got about a snowflake in hell's chance of getting that job after yesterday's fiasco, I guess it doesn't matter anymore if you try to steal the job."

Sebastian laughed. "It's not like that at all. I already told you, heists aren't my thing. Whoever this guy is, he sent someone to steal my friend's tablet and almost got us killed in the process. He and I have some unfinished business."

"Hmm, I see your point. I wouldn't mind getting a few punches in myself. But I can't help." She shrugged apologetically. "Sorry. I got no idea who he is. The middleman, Anton, he runs a tight operation. I couldn't get a word out of him, and I'm a lot prettier than you are," she added with a grin.

"Only according to straight guys," he countered, matching her smile. "Anyway, Anton and I have some history. I might be able to get something out of him."

"Good luck with that," she said, and started the car.

Sebastian stood up. "I'll figure it out. Drive safe and heal fast." He shut the door and stood back, watching as she drove away.

As far as the public was concerned, Anton Silvester was an art dealer with a prestigious gallery in downtown Atlanta. But while his gallery walls were filled with expensive canvases, some visitors weren't there for the art. It was commonly known in certain, closed circles that if one needed anything involving magic, Anton would see it done. He was a middle-man, sub-contracting out jobs to appropriate players in the magic world, both witch and wizard. He knew more about magic than any mundane Sebastian had ever met, including himself. Though efforts to delve into his associate's past had proven fruitless, Sebastian assumed he came from a wizard family and acquired his knowledge through proximity and self-study, much like Sebastian himself.

Unlike Sebastian, however, Anton was in his fifties, rail thin, and sported a rakish goatee and mustache that matched the black of his curly hair. Those who saw his gaunt build and assumed him weak were in for a rude surprise. His exceptional intellect, extensive knowledge base, and ruthless devotion to business made him a player to be reckoned with. Sebastian liked the man and thought Anton liked him, too, since the art dealer openly insulted him. People he didn't like got the veiled insinuation of idiocy treatment, unless they were paying clients, of course. Clients were treated with impeccable courtesy.

Sebastian waited until Monday evening to visit, slipping through the glass front door on the heels of a well-dressed couple intent on the artwork. He hung back and pretended to browse the canvases while waiting for the gallery to empty. When the couple finally left, he drifted toward the rear where Anton stood, typing something into a sleek computer terminal recessed in a wood-paneled wall.

"What is your unsightly visage doing in my gallery, Sebastian? You are completely ruining the atmosphere," Anton said dryly without even turning to look at his approaching guest. "Those rags belong in a dumpster."

"Hey," Sebastian protested. "Some of us have to blend in with the crowd, you know? Armani suits don't exactly fit Atlanta's average demographic. And besides, our culture stereotypes witches as freaky, marginalized outcasts. People pay you more when you don't confront their prejudices. A well-dressed witch is threatening. Unless they have breasts, of course. Then it's just sexy."

Anton finally turned around, a sardonic smile on his face. "Insightful, crude, and to the point, as always." He stepped forward and briefly clasped Sebastian's hand. "And what insignificant drivel have you come to subject me to today?"

"I love you, too, Anton," Sebastian said with a grin, unfazed by his associate's expressions of long-suffering. He slapped Anton on the back, then draped his arm over the man's bony shoulders as he glanced around, ensuring the gallery was empty. "So, you know that museum job?"

"What of it?" Anton's posture did not stiffen. He was a master at appearances, much too professional to reveal any emotion he didn't want his observer to see. He was so good, in fact, that Sebastian didn't bother checking his truth coin around Anton anymore: he'd never caught the man in a lie. There were many ways to not tell the truth that didn't include lying, and Anton was exceptional at it. Most likely because he dealt with wizards and witches on a regular basis who had lie-detecting capabilities, like Sebastian.

"Well, as we both know, it went south," Sebastian answered. "I may have, possibly, gained some insider infor-mation about the mark that could prove useful to your cli-ent. But I want to talk to him directly."

"I'm sorry, that won't be possible, Mr. Blackwell. I assure my clients' confidentiality. Discretion is my most valuable asset."

"Oh, come on. Don't be a—"

Anton put up his hand, cutting Sebastian off. "Let me save you the need to waste my time. The contract has been withdrawn, therefore the point is moot. Now, if you would kindly remove yourself from my gallery, your very presence degrades the value of my artwork."

"Yeah, yeah. I'm a disgrace to society and all that. Thanks for the compliment. Since the job has been withdrawn, maybe you can get me something else. You got an address or contact information for the gal who got the job, Veronica Paxton?" Sebastian mentally crossed his fingers. Since Veronica had taken the contract, perhaps she had information on the client. It was worth it to search her house. She wouldn't mind, after all. She was dead.

Anton turned, extricating himself from Sebastian's hold and examining him with a raised eyebrow. "And why would I provide such information? I guarantee my contractors' anonymity as well as my clients'."

"Because I can tell you something *very* interesting about her. The information I have makes your confidentiality pointless." Sebastian crossed his arms, waiting to see if Anton would take the bait.

"Intriguing," Anton said, a glint in his eye. It was the look of a wolf scenting a particularly juicy rabbit. "Very well, Sebastian. If your information is compelling, I will give you what you want. If not, I will give you a reasonable bonus for your trouble, say three percent, on your next contract."

"Deal." Sebastian held out his hand and they shook on it. "Veronica's dead."

That took Anton by surprise, though only the tiniest widening of his eyes gave any indication. "Do tell," he encouraged.

"I was there, saw it all myself. She couldn't get past the caretaker's wards, and I guess she was feeling cocky, because the idiot summoned *a greater demon*. Needless to say, her demonology wasn't up to snuff and she lost control of it.

That's when the beast she so foolishly summoned—to put it delicately—had her for lunch."

"Indeed." Anton said, eyebrow inching higher and higher with each of Sebastian's words. "And once it had, hmm, terminated Miss Paxton, it meekly returned to the depths of hell, did it?"

Sebastian didn't bother hiding the cheeky grin that crept across his face. "I might have helped it along a bit, but that's all I can say. I only agreed to give you information about Veronica. She's dead. Gone. Kaput. So, do you have an address for me?"

Anton stroked his goatee, thoughtful. "Perhaps. How do I know you're telling the truth?"

"Seriously? When have I ever lied to you? And anyway, I'm not stupid enough to tell such an easily debunked lie and damage our working relationship. You know I'm not stupid; ergo, I'm not lying."

With a slight smile, Anton turned and went to his computer terminal. "I find your logic sound, even if you are an insufferable cur." He did some sort of database search, writing down what he found on a piece of paper which he handed to Sebastian then waved him away in dismissal. "Now, begone. I have affluent, impressionable sheep to sell art to, and your mere existence gives me a headache."

Tipping an imaginary hat, Sebastian bowed himself out, grinning inwardly. Only once he was out on the street did he glance at the slip of paper in his hand. It bore an address, which meant he was going on a field trip.

The address led him to a historic apartment building in Midtown, north of downtown Atlanta. Being the second largest business district in Atlanta, not to mention a center for cultural attractions and noteworthy architecture, it was one of the most affluent neighborhoods in the area. The five-story, red brick building was on a relatively quiet street, at least compared to the hectic bumper-to-bumper bedlam that was the rest of Atlanta during rush hour. He'd followed a circuitous series of alleys and back roads to avoid the traffic. Parking his car a few blocks away, he walked past the building, observing to get a feel for the area and see if anything tripped alarm bells in his head. Nothing seemed out of place, though he did spot a man in a leather jacket leaning against the wrought iron fence blocking parking access to the apartment building across the street. The man simply stood there, staring at the same building Sebastian had in his sights. So, was someone watching the building because they knew Veronica was dead? Or because they didn't? Whichever it was, he preferred to remain unknown, so he slipped around the street corner, looking for an entrance to the building out of the man's line of sight.

Having entered through a side door, Sebastian took the old-style, grille elevator to the third floor and knocked on the door for apartment number 312. He assumed Veronica lived alone, but he couldn't be sure. It was safer to knock first.

To his great surprise, he heard footsteps approach. He barely had time to rearrange his features into a casual, unassuming expression and stick his hand in his pocket, fingers curling around his coin, before the door opened. The woman before him was blond, beautiful, and well off, judging by her designer clothes and shoes. She also looked as mundane as they came, and there was no sign of anything remotely occult from what he could see of the apartment through the open door. Her expression was a mix of uncertainty and polite greeting, not at all the kind of shifty suspicion he expected from an associate of a criminal like Veronica.

"I'm sorry, can I help you?" the woman asked when Sebastian said nothing, still thrown off by her appearance.

"Oh, yes, yes. I apologize, please excuse my rudeness. I just had no idea Veronica didn't live alone. My name is John," he said, extending his hand to shake hers, which she reciprocated. "I'm a work associate. We've been working together on a project, but she hasn't been answering her phone for a while. I was worried, so I thought I'd stop by to see if she was home." As he spoke, he noticed the woman's brow crease in concern.

"I'm sorry...she's not here." The woman's marked hesitation gave Sebastian an opening.

"You seem worried. Have you seen her recently? Is she all right? Do you know where she might be?"

"No, I haven't seen her." She bit her lower lip. "Would you like to come in for a moment? I feel so rude, making you stand there."

"Thank you, but only for a moment. It's important I speak to Veronica as soon as possible."

"Of course," the woman agreed, moving aside to let him in. She led him through a short hallway that opened into a high-ceilinged combination living room and dining room. Large windows let in ample sunlight which glinted off the polished wooden floors, obviously antique, yet expertly restored. Oriental rugs broke up the smoothness of the floorboards and the decor was both tasteful and expensive. Nothing in the apartment suggested her line of work, though she seemed to like traveling, from the number of photos of her in exotic locations. In some of the pictures, there were smiling children with her. He wondered if this woman did aid work. Whatever she did, it was without

Veronica, who didn't appear in any of the pictures. "Please, sit," she said, indicating the sofa. "Can I get you anything? Tea? Coffee?"

"No, no. That's completely unnecessary. If you could just help me find Veronica, that's all I need. When was the last time you saw her, Miss...?" He let the question hang.

"Sara. My name is Sara. I'm sorry, I'm just a bit flustered. Veronica was gone for the weekend on a business trip, but she's usually home by Sunday night. We don't share date books, by any means—she has her life and I have mine—but it's not like her to come home late from a trip."

"I see. Well, this is definitely concerning. Have you reported her missing?"

"No, nothing like that." Sara shook her head, expression even more troubled. "I'm sure she's fine. She probably just had a late flight."

"Perhaps..." Sebastian said slowly, heaping on the concerned skepticism. "But it really is important that I speak with her immediately. Can you think of anywhere she might be? Does she have her own office or another house where I might call?"

Sara shook her head, hands tightly clasped. "I think she works downtown, but I don't know where her office is. She always slept here when she was in town, always paid her half of the rent on time. We don't see much of each other, but that suits us fine. We're just roommates for convenience, you know, to share expenses. There might have been an occasional drink we had together, but we weren't close."

As Sara spoke, Sebastian's coin remained cool. This was one of the most trusting, forthright individuals he'd ever met. He was almost worried for her. Nobody should be that open to complete strangers. Not even Lily was so foolish. But maybe that was why Veronica had chosen Sara. Perhaps she preferred the double life and needed Sara to maintain an outwardly mundane appearance? Whatever the case, Sara obviously had no idea her roommate was a demon-summoning, thieving witch. Despite there being no love lost between himself and the woman who tried to get her pet demon to eat him, he felt a pang of pity for her roommate. She seemed genuinely concerned about Veronica, who was quite irreparably dead. He wanted to tell her but knew he couldn't.

When she finished talking, Sebastian sighed. "Well, if there's nothing you can tell me, I'll leave you in peace." He stood. "You're sure there's nowhere at all you can think of where she might be?"

"I'm sorry," Sara said. "Veronica never talked about work—" she suddenly stopped, expression turning thoughtful. "Actually, there was this place we stopped by one time. She said she had to run up and get some things. I assumed it was a boyfriend's place, or maybe storage. Here," she grabbed a piece of paper and wrote down a street name. "I'm sorry, I don't know the unit number. But the entrance is at this intersection, second door from the corner."

"I'll check it out," Sebastian said, taking the piece of paper. "Thank you, Sara, you've been quite helpful. In the meantime, keep your eyes open. If anything happens, call the police. And I would report Veronica missing if you don't hear from her in another day. You never know what might have happened."

Sara's brow furrowed even more. "What do you mean? Is Veronica in trouble? What kind of work did you say you do?"

"I...don't think it's my place to speculate. I was simply giving general advice. Hopefully Veronica is fine. I'll be sure to have her to call you if I see her, all right?"

"Of course. Thank you." Sara showed him out, and they bade a polite goodbye. But her face was still troubled as she shut the door, and Sebastian wondered what would happen to her. Veronica would never come home; no body would ever be found. No one would know what had happened, except him, Lily, and his aunt. He ought to say something, tell someone. Surely Veronica had a family somewhere, a person who would weep for her.

No, he thought. It was none of his business. Better to stay out if it. Veronica had suffered the consequences of her own actions. He'd done nothing wrong, simply defended himself and his friends. He didn't owe her or her memory anything.

He exited the apartment complex the way he'd come. Peeking around the corner, he grimly noted the leather-jacketed man was still there, watching. Well, it was none of his business. He tried to clear it from his mind as he made his way to his car, resigned to another maze of back roads and traffic from hell.

Veronica's hideout—or whatever it was—turned out to be a mere three miles southeast, right outside Little Five Points. Sebastian felt slightly uncomfortable, as this location was edging in the direction of Lily's home near Agnes Scott. But he reminded himself that Veronica was dead and therefore no threat to his friend.

Surveying the building, he realized it was an old warehouse repurposed into studio apartments. It was an ideal place for a witch—no one questioned what an artist did in her studio. Mounting the steps for the second door from the intersection, he saw that it opened into a stairwell servicing multiple units. There were people about, so he went straight inside as if he belonged there. Slowly ambling along the hallway and up each flight of stairs, he surreptitiously examined the studio doors, all senses on high alert to detect which one might be Veronica's. Someone like her, he suspected, would favor the top floor where there was less traffic.

As he reached the top landing, he was pleased to see only two doors to choose from. One looked perfectly normal, but the other...something seemed off. Sebastian used his foot to shift the welcome mat and, sure enough, symbols warding against demonic attack were painted onto the concrete floor beneath. These were not the same runes Lily used. Witches couldn't manipulate magic like wizards could. There was, however, more than one way to skin a cat. Not that he would ever skin a cat. He imagined Sir Kipling's disapproving eyes on him at the very thought. Crouching down, he ran his fingers along the symbols, studying them and trying to dredge up buried memories of when he dabbled in demonology—to his great regret, as it turned out.

From what he'd read and experienced, two other types of magical beings existed besides wizards: fae and demons. Well, technically three, if you counted angels. No one really believed in them anymore, but after what he'd seen Sir Kipling do at the museum... Demons didn't usually shrink back from cats. Cats didn't usually glow, either, for that matter. But he'd let Lily figure out what in the world her talking feline was up to. He'd stick to fae. Fae magic was unique. He'd never heard of anyone being able to use it directly, and he did only because it had been given to him. Burned onto his hand, actually. Nobody could use demonic magic, not witch or wizard. But anyone could summon them and, properly trained, force them to do their will. Thus, demonology, a dangerous—suicidal, really—area of witchcraft. The wards underneath Veronica's welcome mat were ones only a witch who regularly brought demonic attention to herself would need.

Straightening, Sebastian took a quick glance around and, seeing nobody, put on tight leather gloves and got out his lock picks. He made quick work of Veronica's locks, including two deadbolts. This was one paranoid woman. It was with some trepidation, therefore, that he inched open the door, alert for booby traps or whatever else the crazy witch had left for uninvited visitors.

After a careful search of the studio, he'd found no booby traps, but plenty else. Primarily, there was a sophisticated alarm system that blinked an angry red at him from its mount on the wall of her office. The absence of any noise, however, made him certain the alarm was simply meant to alert the owner of an intrusion, and no one else. Veronica didn't strike him as the kind of person who'd want security company personnel barging into her secret lair. And, since she herself was dead, he had little to worry about.

Surveying the rest of her apartment, he concluded that Veronica must have been an odd mix of professional and amateur. Or perhaps superstitious was a better word. She looked professional when it came to the mundane aspects: her wardrobe showed impeccable taste, and all her equipment looked top of the line. Yet, when it came to witchcraft, he saw an odd mix of true craft—the stuff that actually worked—and all the bells and whistles you used to impress your superstitious clients so they'd pay you more. Things like pentagrams, salt, crosses, garlic, the whole works. It seemed Veronica thought having everything just in case was the way to go.

Working methodically, he searched the studio a second time, looking for hidden files or compartments and putting everything back exactly as he'd found it. After a good hour, he stood in the middle of the apartment, hands on hips. He'd found not a scrap of material about demonology or Veronica's client. Well, there was always her shiny, top-of-the-line laptop. Being the paranoid type, perhaps she preferred to hide files on jobs and clients behind digital encryption. Maybe that's also where she stored her demonology material, though you didn't often find such archaic knowledge digitized.

He sat down at her desk and opened the laptop, trying his hand at a few random passwords just for the heck of it. None of them worked, of course—he was no hacker. He might know someone who was, however, so he unhooked Veronica's equipment, packed it in a nearby computer bag he'd spotted, and headed out of the studio, careful to lock it behind him.

It looked like Tina was going to get a call from him sooner than she expected.

He drove until he was a safe distance from Veronica's hidey-hole, just in case anyone was watching it, before pulling over to call Tina. Tension crept into his shoulders and he caught himself holding his breath as the phone rang, once, twice, three times.

On the fourth ring, there was an answer. "Uh-huh?"

"Hey Tina, it's Sebastian."

Silence. Then, "You know, tiger, I didn't give you this number so you could stalk me. Don't ruin the good thing we got going here."

"Yeah, sorry about that. That's not why I called. I know you're probably in pain and grumpy anyway, what with being slugged by a demon. But I've got something you're going to want to see."

"Is that so?" Tina sounded skeptical, but open-mindedly so.

"Yup. Veronica's laptop."

"What? No way!" Tina said, demeanor taking a one-eighty. "How did you find it? That's sick. Totally sick, man."

Sebastian grinned against the phone, wishing he could see Tina's face. She was probably impressed. "Oh, I know people, and I'm good at finding things. I tracked down Veronica's little witchy lair and it was just sitting there. It's password-protected, though, and I'm better at hacking girls' hearts than computer parts. You any good at cracking code?"

"Girls' hearts, huh? Aren't you the poet." Tina sounded amused. That was nice. Lily wouldn't have appreciated such humor.

"Only for you, sweetheart. So, hacking?"

"Yeah, I've got skills. But I'll only help on one condition."

"A piece of my heart?" Sebastian joked.

He heard a soft chuckle. "I can get that anytime I want," Tina said. "No, I get a copy of her hard drive once I crack it."

Sebastian thought about that. It was unlikely anything on that drive could prove harmful to himself or Lily, and he wasn't worried about Tina. She wasn't the dangerous one, as long as you didn't come between her and her mark. She also seemed smart enough to stay away from demons, should Veronica's drive contain anything overly dangerous. "Sure. You got a deal. I've got it on me now, can I bring it over?"

There was a longer silence this time. Finally, Tina sighed. "Sure, whatever. But if you start showing up uninvited, you'll be getting some unexpected visits from dear Percy."

"Got it. Percy the poltergeist, I assume?"

"Yeah. One nasty son of a bitch even without my help, so I'd stay on my good side if I were you," Tina said, voice casual.

"So noted. I promise to always bug you over the phone before I bug you in person."

"Yeah, whatever. Here's my address," she said, giving him the street, which he wrote down on a discarded pizza box in the passenger seat.

"Great, thanks. I'm on my way," Sebastian said, starting his car.

"Hey," Tina interrupted. "Since you're already out, pick up some beer and pizza. I need junk food to get my mojo on."

"You got it, boss," Sebastian said, and hung up.

As Sebastian pulled up to Tina's apartment, he felt the hair rise on the back of his neck. He was being watched.

"Right. Percy, I know you're there. Stop being creepy and go tell Tina I've got her beer and pizza, okay? Now get lost." Something invisible tweaked his nose, hard, making his eyes water, and he heard a cackling laugh that quickly faded. Stupid poltergeist.

Computer bag slung over his shoulder and hands full of junk food, he got out of the car and carefully looked around before crossing the street. College Park, right beside the Atlanta International Airport, wasn't the nicest neighborhood in town. You weren't guaranteed to get mugged, but it was a close bet. He rang Tina's doorbell and the door opened as if on its own. As he passed through, something smacked him on the back of the head.

"Percy," he growled, gritting his teeth. That miscreant was getting on his nerves. Climbing a set of steep stairs, he finally got to Tina's apartment and stood for a moment, looking around. Surprisingly, and yet not, it looked much like his own. Pizza boxes—minus the moldy pizza—lay everywhere, along with empty beer, energy drink, and coke cans. The walls were plastered with band posters, some familiar, some not. The main room was decorated with lava lamps, black curtains, a neon green, furry rug, and more CDs than any one human ought to possess. As with most real witches he knew, her apartment looked fairly mundane except for a few odd quirks that indicated she knew more than she was letting on. In his house it was the specially aged pizza and cups of mixed drinks he left on his windowsills and outside his door at night—payment for various fae favors. His neighbors thought he was just a slob, feeding stray cats alcohol as a joke. That was fine with him.

Tina's place looked deceptively normal, until you peeked into the kitchen and saw the boxes and boxes of broken glass—perhaps Percy had a penchant for breaking things—and noticed that, despite the fact that no animals were in evidence, all of her couch cushions looked like a dog had been at them. A dog with very sharp teeth.

Obviously forewarned by Percy, Tina emerged from what must have been her bedroom, dressed in a faded tank top and boxer shorts. It was immediately obvious that she wore nothing *under* the tank top, but then, she did have bandaged ribs, so maybe it wasn't just her way of trying to throw him off. He fixed his eyes on her face, resisting the urge to stare a bit lower down.

"Gimme the pizza and the computer bag," Tina ordered, hands outstretched. "Beer goes in the fridge. There should be something cold in there if you're thirsty."

Sebastian handed off the food and computer, stowing the six-pack in the fridge and snagging himself a coke before venturing into Tina's bedroom. Unlike the living room, this room's walls were plastered, not with posters, but with maps, diagrams, and photographs. With curtains drawn against the late evening sun, the room was illuminated only by her computer screen and several more lava lamps. Apparently, Tina had a thing for lava lamps.

She'd already shoved a pile of papers and trash out of the way, clearing a spot on her desk where she set up Veronica's laptop. Stuffing a piece of pizza into her mouth, she typed away furiously, staring at the blinking white cursor of a boot screen. He was glad all the gobbledygook running across the screen meant something to her, because it might as well have been Chinese for all he could tell.

Snagging some pizza for himself, he opened his coke and settled on the bed, watching Tina's fingers fly over the keyboard. Armies of letters and numbers marched back and forth and the computer beeped at odd intervals. Sebastian was entranced, fascinated by this whole unique language, known only to computers and people who studied them. He wondered if Jas knew any of it.

Attention fixed on Tina, Sebastian's grip on his coke loosened and he almost didn't notice when it started to levitate out of his grasp. Just before it cleared his hand, however, he came back to himself and grabbed it out of the air. "Hey! Stop it, you little sneak, that's mine!"

"Shush," Tina shot over her shoulder. "I'm trying to concentrate. Percy is being exceptionally well behaved, so shut up and deal with it."

Sebastian snorted to himself, glaring around the room as if he could somehow spot the mischievous spirit. To pass the time, he tried to formulate a defensive strategy to protect himself from Percy's version of "good" behavior.

The pizza was long gone when Tina finally straightened and pumped her fist in the air "I'm in!"

Sebastian rushed to her side. "Wow, that was fast."

"It was nothing." Tina shrugged off the compliment. "The floozy had all the best security software but wasn't smart enough to have it customized. All the standard stuff is an open book if you know where to look. Never trust anything you can buy online, that's what I always say." As she spoke, she plugged an external drive into the laptop's USB port and started duplicating Veronica's hard drive.

"I'm gonna need a copy of that," Sebastian said, returning to the bed. "I want to return the laptop to Veronica's apartment, so if police come looking they won't be suspicious someone broke in."

"That'll cost you, lover boy. External hard drives don't grow on trees," Tina told him, still staring at the computer screen as she began searching through Veronica's files.

"Hey, I brought you this goldmine, and it took you barely thirty minutes to hack it. I think a free copy of the drive isn't asking much."

"It is if you wanna stay on my good side." She turned and winked at him, her profile—including her chest—sharp against the light of the computer screen. Sebastian swallowed involuntarily and looked away, just in time to see a pillow fly at him. It hit him full in the face, and he fell back on the bed with an "oomph!" of surprise.

Tina cackled, almost falling backward in her own chair. "Good one, Percy."

"No, not good!" Sebastian spluttered, struggling upright. "Will you tell that darn thing to lay off?"

She cocked her head, examining Sebastian with an evaluating eye. "You wanna know something? I go on dates with guys so Percy can torment them. It's part of our deal. And you know what? It's hysterical. They have no idea what's going on, but they try to stick it out because I'm hot, you know? The really tough ones come back for a second date, but nobody lasts past that. You, though..." she got up and came over to the bed, standing in front of Sebastian and reaching out to twirl a lock of his hair around her finger. "You're cute, and not an asshole, yet. I think I might like you. So I told Percy to back off. But poltergeists never really do what they're told, you get me? You can either deal with it, or get lost."

"Yeah, okay. I'll deal with it," Sebastian said, greatly distracted by her proximity. Fortunately, the level of the bed combined with his height and her petite frame meant they were almost at eye to eye, instead of his eyes being closer to chest level. He had a brief thought, wondering if this was what Lily felt like. The being constantly annoyed thing, not the height thing. He tried to clear his mind, thoughts of Lily, Tina, and Tina's chest making a very bad combination that he had no desire to dwell on.

Tina chuckled softly. "Too bad I have bruised ribs, or I might have you pay me with something other than cash. Maybe later, huh?"

"What?" Sebastian said, still distracted. "Sure. Wait, no! I mean, maybe. Well, what I'm trying to say is—"

"What, getting cold feet?" Tina asked, running a hand through his hair. That was very, very distracting. "Let me guess, there's someone else?"

"Noooooo..." he answered slowly, brain still trying to catch up. "Not exactly." Even as he said it, Lily's face popped into his head, but he pushed it aside. She was way too good for him.

"Well, then, maybe when I'm better, and you take me on that date, we can come back here. I promise Percy'll leave you alone."

"I—we'll see," was all he could manage.

"Sure, babe, whatever," Tina laughed again and returned to her seat, once again scanning lists of files. "Hey," she said after a while, "you're looking for any dirt on the client, right? I think I found something."

Sebastian came to bend over the computer with her. He scanned the document she'd opened. It wasn't much, but there was a name: Rex Morganson - Wizard. Well, that was comforting, he thought. He wondered how Veronica had gotten ahold of that information and how reliable it was. The name was likely just a cover, but it was still something to go on. "Could you copy this and everything relating to it onto a thumb drive for me? I'm sure it'll take a while to copy the whole hard-drive, so I'll come back for the laptop tomorrow."

"Sure thing," Tina said, eyes glued to the screen, already zipping through more lists of documents while one hand rummaged in a drawer for a thumb drive.

Once she'd gathered a few more files together, copied them, and handed over the thumb drive, Sebastian said a hurried goodbye and made a beeline for the exit. He suffered more harassment from Percy on his way to the door but was left alone once he exited the building. Heaving a sigh of relief, he headed home to examine the files and start calling in favors.

He called Tina the next evening, checking to make sure the drive was copied before heading over to pick up the laptop and return it to Veronica's apartment. On the way, he contemplated the fruits of his labor over the past twenty-four hours: if he'd had a fruit basket, it would have been empty. Everyone had either never heard of Rex Morganson or were so scared of him they shut down as soon as they heard his name. It was decidedly frustrating. If Tina hadn't dug anything else up in the past day, he would try Anton again.

Plans made, his mind drifted and inevitably lit on Tina. He'd been wondering since last night at her odd bargain with Percy. Poltergeists, by nature, were not indiscriminate troublemakers. Most often, a person was wronged in life and their spirit came back to haunt a specific place, specific person, or even a specific *type* of person after death, instead of moving on in peace. What if their odd bargain implied that both Percy and Tina had been in abusive relationships or were perhaps abused as children? What if Percy was a nickname for Priscilla, or Prudence, and he was a she? Perhaps she was even murdered by a male she trusted. Their odd arrangement could be a sort of proxy revenge, lashing out at men for what had been done to them. It could be why they worked so well together.

He shook his head, pulling into a parking space on Tina's street. It was all speculation, of course, even if it did seem to fit. He wouldn't know unless he was foolhardy enough to ask Tina directly. For the time being, he liked a poltergeist-free existence too much to risk it.

It took little time to run up to Tina's apartment, exchange cash for hard drive, and collect the laptop. He was getting better at anticipating Percy's attacks and so was only slightly annoyed by the time he left the apartment. Unfortunately, Tina had found nothing else relating to Veronica's last client, or any demonology material. The former didn't surprise him, but the latter left him confused. If it wasn't in her laptop, and it wasn't at her apartment, where was it? Despite the lack of material useful to him, however, Tina had found plenty to interest *her*. She barely spared him a glance while he was there, though the brief glance he did get was accompanied by a crooked smile and a suggestive wink. He found himself both anticipating and dreading the day when she was fully healed.

Finally, he was out and on his way to Veronica's lair. He wondered if anyone had realized she was missing yet. Had Sara reported it to the cops as he'd suggested? The thought made him press a little harder on the gas. He wanted to return that laptop before anyone came snooping, looking for Veronica.

The moment he mounted the top flight of steps to the studio apartment, he knew something was amiss. Heart sinking, he stepped forward, avoiding the shredded welcome mat and gently pushing on the door. It opened without resistance, revealing an apartment that had been completely ransacked. It looked like someone had turned the apartment upside-down, shaken it a few times, then put it right side up again. Every single item had been moved, turned over, or thrown across the room. Pillows had been cut open, chairs overturned, and glassware smashed. Obviously whoever had been there had been frustrated and desperate, not to mention careless. Even the refrigerator had been unplugged and pulled out. Judging by the still-cool food inside, Sebastian was not far behind the perpetrator.

There wasn't much point returning the laptop now. In fact it would look suspicious if it were found, sitting pristine and undamaged amid all the wreckage. He'd have to throw it in a dumpster somewhere, or better yet, have one of his fae friends hide it in another dimension. Let a mundane detective try to figure that one out.

Even as these thoughts ran through his head, standing amid the wreckage, another thought kept poking at him, derailing his musings. What had the perp been looking for? Nothing appeared to be stolen, only smashed to bits. It might have been the laptop, but with it missing so obviously from the desk, computer case and all, anyone would have logically assumed Veronica had it with her. Nobody would have thought it hidden somewhere in the house. So if not the laptop, what else?

A thought struck him, and with it came a cold wash of dread. He bolted out of the apartment, taking the stairs down three at a time at breakneck speed.

The only thing of value remaining had been her book or books of demonology—potent summoning rituals to command demons of immense power. And if someone had already determined it wasn't here, there was only one place left to look: Sara's apartment.

On the outside, everything about the apartment looked normal. It was past rush hour, so only a few cars trundled past and he saw few pedestrians. The man in the leather jacket was gone, and Sebastian didn't waste any brain space wondering if that was a good thing or a bad thing. After giving the area a thorough sweep, he proceeded around the building to enter at the side, as he had before. Creeping carefully up the steps, he listened hard and flared his nostrils, every sense on high alert. On the first two floors all he heard were the normal rustlings and murmurs of people relaxing after a day of work. But halfway up the stairs to the third floor, he started smelling sulfur. Sebastian cursed inwardly. He should have seen this coming, been proactive.

Mounting the stairs as silently as possible, he crouched by Sara's door, pressing his ear to the wood. What he heard made his blood boil: harsh whispers in the demon tongue over a string of muffled screams and sobs, as if the victim's mouth had been stuffed with cloth. Knowing the assailant thought himself alone, Sebastian carefully checked the door, hoping he'd left it unlocked. He had.

Sebastian stood and took several deep breaths, calming himself. This was not going to be fun, mostly because he had no idea what was behind that door. Yet he couldn't wait for the cops. He had to go in all guns blazing. But who said he had to do it alone?

"Elwa Pilanti'ara, Elwa, Jastiri'un," he whispered, almost too quietly for human ears to hear. Fortunately, the ears he wanted weren't human. "I have some serious ass for you to kick, double our normal payment, just get your butts over here *now*. Keep the ugly human occupied, protect the pretty one, and I'll take on the demons. Got it?" He heard a faint squeaking laugh, but that was all. Well, at least Pip had answered the call. Who knew where Jas was. It would have to be good enough.

Extending his right hand, he drew on that part of him that wasn't truly part of him, the fae magic he'd been given. It rested like a lead weight at the back of his mind, a burden to carry, an irritant on his psyche, but so very, very useful. The pain was a small price to pay to use that which no human was meant to touch. Immediately, the back of his right hand seared with pain, the black tattoo on it shining for all to see. Usually it was hidden by fae glamour, but when he summoned the staff Thiriel had given him, he couldn't hide the mark.

The black, twisting, ebony staff crowned by a green jewel materialized in his grasp, and he gripped it firmly with both hands. The jewel was glowing brightly, its magic thirsting for demon essence. Fae and demon were not friends, to put it mildly. If one wanted to be particularly effective against demonkind, making friends with fae was the way to go. He had a brief thought, wondering if Lily had taken an even more effective path, if indeed she'd been aided by angelic power. But angels hadn't been seen or heard of for centuries, so he wouldn't hold his breath.

"Ready, Pip?" Sebastian whispered, grasping the door handle. He felt something tug a lock of his hair, and that was answer enough. Silent as a panther, he cracked open the door and slipped inside, hoping to take his opponents by surprise. The sight that greeted him almost stopped him in his tracks. A portly man in blood-red robes was bent over Sara who lay, bound, on the living room floor. It looked as if she'd put up a good fight, because the surrounding furniture had been smashed and overturned. He saw a gash on her forehead that bled sluggishly, and her eyes were wide with abject terror, her screams muffled by the cloth stuffed in her mouth. Worse, two lesser demons were couched over her, holding her struggling form still while the witch chanted, painting demonic symbols on her breast in her own blood. He'd ripped open her blouse to get access to the bare skin, and Sebastian could see Sara's chest heaving up and down, almost hyperventilating. This witch was preparing to summon a third demon to possess Sara and, Sebastian assumed, force her to tell him where Veronica's demonology manuscripts were. There was no time to waste.

Taking three swift yet silent strides, he was upon the group and waded in swinging. Pip went straight for the man's eyes while Sebastian took aim at the demon on the right, the larger of the two. But the demon was quicker on the uptake than the oblivious witch, and it glanced up in time to dodge Sebastian's blow, the ebony staff whistling by bare inches from its face.

No longer held down, Sara started flailing. The red-robed witch fell back with a scream, hands upraised to protect himself against Pip's gouging attacks. The smaller demon, temporarily out of his master's control, saw his chance for blood and bent over Sara, pulling her toward him as his eyes glowed in anticipation. Sebastian put an end to that demon's plans for dinner with a golfer's upward swing to the face. The staff crushed and gouged the scaly flesh so that black blood bubbled forth, hissing as it dripped to the floor. The demon fell back, screeching in fear and pain.

Sebastian was just starting to feel proud of himself when the bigger demon, having retreated, now leapt on his back. It reached forward, claws cutting into skin as it tried to get at his face. Dropping his staff, Sebastian fell backward and landed with a crunch on top of the demon. It screamed, loosening its hold to struggle against him. In a flash he'd rolled off and flicked his wrist, putting all his strength behind a downward arch of the staff that had instantly reappeared in his hands. The green gem at its crown blazed as it hit, its sharpened tip sinking into the demon's chest while the surrounding twist of pointed branches bit into the creature's skin. With a last howl of agony, the red light in the demon's eyes dimmed. Sebastian scrambled back, eyes searching for the smaller demon even as he hunched his back against what he knew was coming.

The dead demon exploded, sending shattered bits of crystallized sulfur throughout the room. The hail pelted Sebastian's back, biting through his thin cotton shirt. He ignored it, letting go of the staff so that it disappeared back to the fae realm. With the smaller demon nowhere in sight, Sebastian surmised it had fled through the open door, obviously deciding wisdom was the greater part of valor. Then again, it was a demon; they weren't known for bravery or loyalty. All demonic threats neutralized for the moment, he delivered a swift kick to the groin of the witch still rolling on the floor, trying to fend off Pip, then crouched by Sara.

Sara was still struggling and gasping, eyes wide and staring as if she didn't yet understand it was all over.

"Hush, hush! Sara, calm down, you're safe," Sebastian said, trying to untie the knots around her wrists. He gave up and flicked out a pocket knife, swiftly cutting through her bonds and then pulling out her gag. Now free, Sara threw herself on Sebastian, sobbing uncontrollably and gasping for air.

"Oh—oh—god—my—god—th—thank you," she said between sobs.

As much as he understood her trauma, Sebastian only had time to give her a swift, reassuring hug, before he pried her off. "I'm sorry, but time is short. We're going to call 911 and they're going to come take care of you, but first I have to make sure you'll be safe."

He got up, passing the witch who still lay on the floor groaning and clutching his groin, and poked his head out the front door. Nobody was about, so he closed and locked it and went back to the witch. "Enough, Pip, leave him alone. Go outside and keep watch. Warn me if anyone, or anything, comes." The pixie gave a disappointed squeak but obeyed, leaving the witch's bloody face and wiggling through the crack under the door.

Taking the rope that had bound Sara, Sebastian roughly tied the witch's hands and feet. Then he hauled the man into a sitting position and slapped him several times across the face to get his attention. And because it felt good. Gazing at the witch's garish red robes, he categorized this thoroughly repugnant piece of slime as one of those nut jobs who enjoyed dressing up like some geek at a convention when doing magic. It was an insult to magic. And geeks.

"Banish the demon, that little one that got away. If you don't, I'll let my pixie friend come back and cut off your balls. She'd like that."

The witch stared at him, eyes wide with terror, but still with enough spine to be stubborn. Sebastian put a knee to the man's groin and leaned in. The witch screamed. "Okay, okay! Stop!"

"Not until you do it," Sebastian growled.

Sobbing, the man gasped out a few phrases, and Sebastian saw a pendant around his neck glow briefly, then turn black.

"Good," he said, leaning back again on his heels. "Now, what were you doing here?"

"That bitch, Veronica, she stole my book. I was just—just trying to get it back." Still breathing hard, the witch attempted to look self-righteous.

"Figured," Sebastian said, disgusted. "Did you summon any more demons? Are there others about?"

"N—no! I swear. Who are you?" the witch asked, eyes wide. He was obviously afraid, yet Sebastian could see the hatred running deep. This man was a coward, but a vengeful one.

"No one you need concern yourself with." He let go of the man's collar, and the witch fell back with a thump and a yelp as his head made painful contact with the hard, wood floor.

Sebastian turned "Sara, do you have any tape?" The woman, lying propped up on one elbow where he'd left her, held her cloth gag to the gash on her forehead. Nodding shakily, she pointed to a cabinet drawer. Sebastian found a roll of duct tape and thoroughly gagged the witch, then wrapped it around the man's hands, knees, and ankles, just in case.

All threats neutralized, he crouched again by Sara. "I know you're scared and you don't understand what's going on, but I need you to concentrate for me, just for a moment. Did Veronica ever give you a book for safekeeping? Probably leather? Maybe with strange symbols on it? I know she probably told you to keep it safe for her, but Veronica is—" he almost said dead, but stopped just in time: Sara didn't need any more trauma at the moment. "—gone. I don't think she's coming back. But that book is trouble, and if you don't give it to me, people will keep coming after you. Will you please tell me where it is, so I can get rid of it?"

Sara's eyes teared up and she looked ready to cry. "I don't know. She never gave me anything, or else I would have already given it to those monsters who—who—"

"All right, calm down. I'm not going to hurt you." Sebastian patted her on the shoulder, then turned away, resisting the urge to grind his teeth in frustration. Then had an idea. Speaking softly, he called out to Pip. "Hey, can you feel anything demonic in this apartment?"

The tiny pixie joined them via the crack under the door and zipped around the apartment like a hummingbird, nosing in every corner. Sara's eyes grew wide as they followed the pixie's progress, but she said nothing. Finally, Pip gave an excited squeak from an adjacent room and Sebastian followed the sound.

He entered what looked like Veronica's bedroom—his guess because there were no pictures in it, neither of Sara nor Veronica. Pip was dancing excitedly on a section of floor at the foot of the bed. "Ah, so it's under there is it?" Sebastian asked. Pip squeaked and flew in a tight circle.

Lifting up the rug, Sebastian ran his fingers along the wood and found a tiny crack. With the help of his pocket knife, he levered up a section of the floor to reveal a leather-bound volume covered in blood-red symbols. Even without touching it, Sebastian could feel its demonic power. It oozed from every corner, making his skin crawl. He took it gingerly, holding it in his right hand, which made his tattoo shimmer and tingle uncomfortably. Pausing to replace the board and rug, he returned to the living room, showing the book to Sara. She looked horrified at the sight.

Turning to the bound witch on the floor, he held the volume up so it could be clearly seen. "Is this what you were looking for?" The witch nodded, a greedy light in his eyes. "Good. Because I'm going to destroy it." At that, the man began yelling through his duct tape gag, wiggling vainly like a worm. "Yup," Sebastian continued, "I'm going to burn it to ash. This woman here doesn't know me, my name, or where I live. So if I ever hear that you or anyone else has touched a hair on her head, I'll track you down and kill you myself. Got it?" The witch glared at him with hate-filled eyes, and Sebastian knew he was making an enemy. He didn't care. Raising a foot, he stomped down on the man's groin. "I said, got it?" The man's eyes rolled back in his head, and he didn't respond. Well, Sebastian thought with a shrug, that was good enough.

He crouched down and cut off the many pendants hanging from the man's neck, removed all the rings from the man's fingers, and searched his pockets, collecting a few other odds and ends. Putting it all in his own pocket, he turned one last time to Sara, who had collapsed onto the couch. "As soon as I leave, call 911. Tell them you fought off this man yourself. I wouldn't mention the demons if I were you, they'll lock you up in a loony bin. This guy assaulted you in your own home, tied you up, and was going to rape you. That should get him behind bars for a while. I'm sorry all this happened just because you roomed with Veronica. It would be safest if you forgot she existed and never spoke her name again." He turned to leave, but Sara reached out to stop him.

"Wait! Who are you? What are you?" The look in her eyes was desperate, and he could only imagine how she felt, having her whole world turned upside-down in barely an hour. She needed something to give her closure. Unfortunately, he couldn't give it to her.

"It's safer for you to not know, I'm sorry. But I promise I'll...keep an eye on this place for a while, in case anything comes back to bother you. Now, call 911, and please, don't mention me." He turned and swiftly left the apartment, not giving her time to reply. He had no idea if she would respect his wish, but there wasn't much he could do. He'd done what he'd thought was right, and there was no easy way to fix things.

Pip joined him as he hurried down the stairs. "Good job, Pip. You earned your keep." Pip squeaked and tugged on his ear, a sign of affection from the pixie. "Oh, stop it." Sebastian grinned. "You just say that because I give you enough alcohol to kill a horse. Now get gone. I'll have the usual waiting for you tonight." Pip's squeaking laugh quickly faded, and Sebastian shook his head in wonder. For having the body mass of a mouse, pixies sure could hold their liquor.

It was too late that night to visit Anton, so Sebastian spent the evening destroying everything he'd taken off the witch. None of it really wanted to be destroyed, but with a combination of fae magic, a hammer, and a small fire out back, he managed it.

Despite his victory, he slept badly that night, waking at odd intervals to what he thought was the sound of police sirens approaching the house. But it only turned out to be Pip and her friends having a party over several glasses of Captain Morgan on his windowsill. Those ridiculous pixies were actually small enough to swim in the glasses, which they did with great glee. One of these days an inebriated pixie would drown, and then he'd be in trouble.

He turned over and tried to go back to sleep. Fae retribution could get in line with all his other worries that kept him up at night, the foremost being Rex Morganson and the crazy, demon-loving witches he seemed to attract. Sebastian finally fell asleep, but his slumbers were plagued by nightmares of demons holding down a screaming Lily, tearing out her heart.

The next day he parked by Anton's gallery, frustrated. He'd tried calling Lily multiple times over the past few days, just to make sure she was okay, but it had always gone to voicemail. That was understandable; she didn't always answer her phone. But he'd tried calling ten times since that morning and she hadn't answered a single one. She was avoiding him. He punched the steering wheel and immediately regretted it. As he put away his phone and unbuckled, he decided to drop by her office as soon as he was done here. It was time the two of them had a talk.

Sebastian had timed it so that he entered the gallery during a lull and no customers were about. As amusing as Anton's bitching was, Sebastian didn't have time for it today. He made a beeline for the back where he found Anton at his stand-up desk beside the computer terminal, writing in a datebook.

"A word, Anton. I promise it won't take long," he said in way of greeting.

"Any length of time is too much for one as tiring as you, Sebastian," Anton replied without looking up.

"Then I'll get right to the point. Rex Morganson was your client for the museum job. What can you tell me about him?"

At the name, Anton got very, very still. He looked up slowly, hands dropping from his datebook and behind the desk. He stared at Sebastian for a moment, then smiled quite pleasantly. Sebastian's inner alarm bells went off. He was not a client, so a pleasant smile was bad.

"Certainly, Mr. Blackwell. Please, step back in my office and we can have a word."

Nervous, but not sure what else to do and still keep Anton talking, Sebastian opened the door at the back of the gallery that led to the offices and loading dock—not somewhere customers were allowed. Unsure which door off the dimly lit hall was Anton's office, he turned to ask and was greeted by the sight of Anton holding a gun on him, face as blank as a slate.

"I'm sorry Sebastian, but you've broken the rules. I can't have that."

"Whoa, whoa! Wait a minute, what's going on here? What rules?" Sebastian said, raising his hands in surrender.

Anton's face remained passive. "The FBI visited me last night and had some very...uncomfortable questions. Questions I did not like. Questions about Mr. Morganson. Now how would the FBI have known that name? I certainly did not give it to them. How would they have known to ask me? And here you are, asking the same question." He tutted. "You spoke to the authorities. That is not allowed, you know."

"Wait, stop." Sebastian extended his arms forward, palms turned toward Anton in a placating gesture. "You've got this completely backward. First of all, you know I would never talk to the cops, much less the FBI. I'm not that kind of guy. What would I gain? Second, I got that name off Veronica Paxton's laptop which I might have possibly taken a passing peek at when I was at her place. But all she had was a name, I swear! If I had to guess, this guy Rex is a crook and the FBI already had him in their sights. I have no idea why they would come to you, but you're not exactly an unknown player. Seriously, man, put the gun down."

Sebastian counted his breaths, blood pounding in his ears as he held motionless and tense, running escape scenarios though his head in case Anton didn't back down. Finally, Anton lowered the gun. "Your logic, as usual, is convincing, if only enough to prevent your summary execution. But you are snooping, and I do not appreciate it, not at all. This man you speak of does not appreciate snooping, either. Yet, he is not fond of you as I am, which is why I tell you this: approximately three weeks ago, when he contacted me regarding the job Veronica failed so spectacularly, he inquired about you by name as well as any known associates. I informed him my rules of confidentiality prevented me from supplying the information he sought. But, to quote you, you are not exactly an unknown player. It would be best if you disappeared for a while, Sebastian, both for your safety and my sanity. It might also be wise to warn your...associates."

He fell silent, but Sebastian didn't reply, still trying to wrap his mind around this sudden development. "You may leave through the rear," Anton said, gesturing with the gun in a not-quite-threatening fashion. Turning slowly, Sebastian saw an exit light shining at the end of the hall. He started walking, glancing back over his shoulder and seeing Anton's silhouette against the light from the gallery. As he reached the exit, he heard Anton's voice once more. "Oh, and Mr. Blackwell, if you ever ask me about one of my clients again, I *will* shoot you. Good day."

With that, Sebastian heard steps receding and a door click shut, cutting off all light except for the red glow of the sign above. Sighing, Sebastian pushed out onto the sunlit alley and headed back to his car.

"Hey, Terry! How's it going, man?...Great, glad to hear it. Look, I've got a job for you. There's this dude, Rex Morganson. I need a face to go with the name. You think you can find out who he is?...Good...Yeah, I think it's a cover, but finding out is your job... Pardon?...Yeah, as soon as you can...I don't care if you're busy, bill me for a rush fee, whatever. Just get it done fast, okay?...Thanks."

Sebastian hung up and started his car, heading toward Agnes Scott. He had a bad feeling in his gut and hoped to goodness he was wrong. But in case he wasn't, someone had to warn Lily, and that someone was him.

Episode 4

THE TRUTH SHALL MAKE YOU FREE

Chapter 1

The Pitfalls of Well-Meant Interference

"**S**TOP WIGGLING!" LILY SAID, EXASPERATED. "IT WON'T SIT right if you keeping twisting around like that."

"But it feels strange," Sir Kipling complained.

"Of course it does, silly. You've never worn a collar before. Give it a few days and you won't even notice. There, finally." She finished fastening the ward collar around her cat's neck and sat back on her heels to admire her handiwork. The collar was made of a slender strip of tooled leather decorated with rune-carved aluminum studs. The ID tag was a small aluminum plate attached flush to the collar instead of dangling from the front. Sir Kipling had insisted on this, pointing out that a dangling tag would make noise.

"It still feels strange," he said, sitting to scratch at the collar.

"Don't do that." She reached out to reposition the collar so that it mostly disappeared underneath his long fur. "Does that feel better?"

"Humph. Perhaps. I still don't like it."

"Well, it'll keep someone from taking you to the pound if you get picked up—"

"—as if I'd let anyone lay their hands on me—" Sir Kipling muttered.

"—and the wards will keep a wizard from scorching your nose off for being a nosy, annoying know-it-all," she finished.

Sir Kipling sniffed and started cleaning himself, obviously ignoring Lily now that she had stopped saying anything useful and was merely teasing him.

"You'll thank me later," she promised with a smile as she got to her feet. "Now, be good. I have to get to work."

"Be good," her cat grumbled. "I'll be good when you stop accepting invitations from mysterious wizards of questionable intent."

"Will you quit bothering me about that?" Lily sighed, gathering up her purse and keys. "I'm going, and that's final." After accepting the invitation to meet John Faust LeFay and his friends, she'd gotten a second levitating letter saying he'd send his chauffeur to pick her up on Friday. She'd written back, insisting she drive herself to his estate and asking for his address. She had yet to receive a reply.

"You should tell someone where you're going. Someone like Madam Barrington."

"It's none of her business. It's not anyone's business, actually. Including yours."

"It will be my business when they discover your cold, dead body and I have to find myself a new human," Sir Kipling retorted, giving her a perturbed look.

"Why are you being so difficult? You've never even met the man."

"Well, he's rather murderous, according to your own description—"

"—that was an accident—"

"—and I'm a cat. I know these things."

"Well, you're wrong. I'll be fine. I can take care of myself."

Sir Kipling didn't reply, just stared at her with that look cats give you when they think you're being supremely idiotic. Lily pursed her lips and turned away, heading out the door to work.

It was almost three by the time she finished her last bit of paperwork. She was leaving early today to meet with Agent Grant over coffee—well, tea, in her case. Waiting until Wednesday had given her enough time to "recover" from Saturday's ordeal at the museum, plus given her space to think about what to say. She'd considered calling it off—after all, she'd agreed on the spur of the moment, annoyed at seeing her "friend" Sebastian getting cozy with a girl he'd just met, even if she was a witch like him. But the more she'd considered Agent Grant, the more he'd intrigued her. So she'd decided to keep the appointment.

Lily paused as she gathered up her purse, her mind drifting automatically back to Sebastian. She realized she'd started putting air quotes on "friend" in her own head when she thought about him. She shook herself. It was silly, really. His relationships were none of her business. It just irked her so...

"Hey, Lil! I was hoping to catch you...oh, you're leaving early today?" a voice said behind her. She spun, surprised, and glared at the "friend" himself as he lounged in the doorway, blocking her exit.

"How many times do I have to tell you, this is a *women's college*. You aren't supposed to be here." She said it more harshly than she'd meant, but perhaps that would get him to leave her alone.

"Well, I wouldn't have to break the rules if you'd answer your phone," he replied, unperturbed.

Lily avoided his gaze. She *had* been ignoring his calls. "I'm very busy and late for an appointment. Can't this wait?"

"If I didn't think you were saying that as an excuse to avoid me, then yes, it could. But this is important. I'm sure you can spare five minutes."

She opened her mouth to protest, but he kept talking.

"I've been doing some digging into who was behind the museum theft. Something just felt fishy, and I thought it would be good to for us to track them down. Keep them from causing any more mischief."

"Is that so?" Lily said, arms crossed.

"Yeah," Sebastian paused and raised an eyebrow at her tone, but she motioned impatiently for him to keep going. "So Tina and I found—"

"Ah-ha, so you've been hanging around that girl again? You know she basically confessed to being a criminal. She's trouble, and you get into enough of that without her around to make it worse—"

"Will you shut up a minute and listen?" Sebastian's sharp voice cut through her indignant tirade, and she snapped her mouth shut, heat rising to her cheeks.

"I don't know what you have against Tina. Yeah, maybe she's had it rough. But you've got to take what you can get on the streets. She's been helping me dig up dirt on this guy we're tracking. I think her heart's in the right place."

"Are you sure it's not something lower down you're worried about?" Lily snapped, and immediately regretted it. What was she doing?

Sebastian's nostrils flared, but he smoothed his features and flashed her a casual grin. "I never worry. But I'm not stupid. So far, we've confirmed that, whoever this bozo is, he's definitely a wizard, and pretty powerful, too. People seem to know who he is, but no one will tell me a thing about him. They're all scared. I did find out, though, that the bid didn't go out until *after* we got back from Pitts. That's pretty short notice. I mean, contractors usually give a couple months' notice, and this was barely a few weeks. It's not like no one knew the tablet was there before. It'd been on display for almost two years. So what changed? I think it has something to do with that Mr. Fancy Pants we ran into in Pitts. Maybe he didn't get as stuck in Nowhereville as I'd hoped."

At the mention of "Mr. Fancy Pants," Lily started. She tried to hide her surprise, but Sebastian was on it like a hawk on a rabbit.

"What? Have you heard something?"

"No, I haven't. Thank you for all this fascinating information, but I really am late for an appointment."

"This is important, Lil. We've got to find out who this guy is. He's going to cause more trouble, I can feel it."

"Sorry. I'm leaving Friday and will be gone for a week. But I'm sure *Tina* can help you. She seems to know everything there is to know about criminals, after all."

Sebastian's gaze sharpened. "What are you doing for a week that's more important than finding a dangerous wizard?"

"The library is closed between semesters. I'm taking a vacation. Not that it's any of your business."

"You? Vacation? Yeah, right," he scoffed. "You love this place *and* you're a workaholic. I bet you haven't taken a vacation since you started. Come on, what's really going on?"

Annoyed, Lily wanted to tell him to mind his own business, but Sir Kipling's vociferous objections came back to her. His insistence that she tell someone where she was going resonated with her common sense, sending her wall of stubbornness tumbling down. Of course, Sebastian's theory that John Faust was the mastermind behind the museum heist was pure speculation. Still, it wouldn't hurt to be cautious. In a moment of weakness, she spoke.

"I'm going to meet...someone. Someone who has information about my family."

Sebastian's eyes narrowed. "Who? Are you sure it's safe? I should probably go with you, just in case."

That raised Lily's hackles. "It's really none of your business. I can take care of myself just fine without you, thank you very much."

His brow creasing in concern, Sebastian pushed off the doorframe and came forward to put his hands on Lily's shoulders.

"Hey, Lil, come on. What's gotten into you? If it were safe and normal you wouldn't be trying so hard to hide it, so I know you're up to...hey, is that perfume you're wearing?" He paused suddenly, sniffing. "You never wear perfume. Are you going on another one of those blind dates?" He grinned, eyes twinkling at the anticipated opportunity for teasing.

Lily raised her chin, goaded into replying. "Yes, as a matter of fact I *am* going on a date. It's with that FBI agent you saw at the museum. The handsome one," she added.

Sebastian guffawed. "That government stooge? You know he just wants an excuse to nose into your life and get dirt on you for Pitts and the museum, right? They're sneaky bastards, the FBI. I'd avoid him if I were you." He said it casually, but Lily detected a frigidness behind his smile.

"Well, you're not me," she said, and pointed at her office door. "Now, out. I'm already late and I need to lock up."

"But we're not done—"

"Yes, we are. Have fun playing investigator with your new best friend. I'm sure she's oh, so trustworthy. She won't get you into trouble at all. A pillar of the community, that one."

Sebastian's expression grew closed. "Well, if that's the way you feel, I hope you have a pleasant *vacation*." with a snort, he stalked out of her office.

That went well, Lily thought with a sigh. Locking her office door, she hurried to her car. Though tempted to worry about it, she forced it from her mind. He'd eventually get over Tina and all the rest. Then things would go back to normal. Him, getting into trouble. Her, getting him out. Right now she had to focus. She didn't believe what Sebastian had said about Agent Grant, but that didn't mean she was going to let her guard down.

Coffee Press Café was a very urban-looking little coffeehouse. It was situated on a tree-lined street in a reclaimed district where old buildings had been adopted, cleaned up, and repurposed for chic cafés, boutiques, and a stray antique store or two. Agent Grant was waiting for her, of course. She offered a breathless apology then ducked her head and accompanied him inside to select their drinks. It was challenging to not steal sideways peeks at him as they waited in line. Though not in uniform, he still looked just as handsome. He wore his dark jeans and brand-name t-shirt with the quiet confidence and muscled build of someone who knew how to take care of himself. She might have forgotten he was FBI if it weren't for the watchful way he took in everything around them, and—she squinted—were those iron lines on his t-shirt? She smiled inwardly.

Once she'd ordered the least awful–tasting tea and a biscotti, she settled down at a small table near the front window and waited for Agent Grant to retrieve their order. He joined her a few minutes later and flashed her a warm smile as he got situated. They sat in awkward silence while Lily stirred her tea, thinking desperately for something to say that wasn't completely idiotic.

Agent Grant saved her the trouble. "I see you're not a coffee drinker," he said, one side of his mouth quirking upward in an almost-smile.

"No. I find it rather disgusting," she replied, then blushed, hoping she hadn't offended him. Silently berating herself, she bemoaned her traitorous brain that seemed to shut down anytime she was in the presence of a handsome man. Well, except Sebastian. His irreverent attitude and aptitude for getting into trouble had become familiar enough that she was immune to his charm.

Taking a long sip of something that smelled bitter enough to be straight black coffee, Agent Grant's eyes danced. "It is an acquired taste, I'll give you that. I don't go in for all the frou-frou drinks, the mochaccinos and frappes. I'd inject myself with coffee bean extract if I could and skip the whole drinking process." His tone was lighthearted, obviously meant to help her relax, which it did.

"Agent Grant, did you just say *frou-frou*?" Lily asked with a smile. "Surely such language violates some code of manliness you FBI agents are sworn to." There, that was witty. She was getting better at this.

He laughed. "Please, call me Richard, or just Rick, if you prefer."

"Richard..." she said the word slowly, testing it out. It was a good name. Solid. Respectable. Like the man who wore it.

"Well, when you say it like that, it sounds like you're checking it for misspellings," he said, eyebrow raised and that twinkle back in his eyes.

Lily blushed and raised her cup of tea, taking several sips to give her something to do as she stared out the window.

"So..." Rick began again, obviously trying to restart the conversation he'd inadvertently derailed.

"I suppose you want a statement about last Saturday?" Lily asked briskly, trying to focus on business. Anything to get her brain functioning again.

He leaned back in his chair, examining her. "Not really, no. Unless you have anything to add to what you told the police."

"I—well—no, I don't. I told them everything. But I thought that's why we were here," she said, confused.

"Technically, yes. But mostly it was just an excuse to see you without my partner hanging around." He smiled at her, this one warm and a not a bit embarrassed. "I'll put in my report that you repeated what you told the police and that will be the end of that."

"Oh," Lily said in a small voice. "But aren't you supposed to be figuring out what happened?" She immediately regretted what she said, mentally kicking herself. Here was an FBI agent *not* prying, and she was poking the sleeping dragon with a stick.

Rick raised an eyebrow, a bit of his previous watchfulness returning. "We know what happened, at least as much as we'll ever know unless the police track down the vandals who did it and get signed confessions. Is there something we're missing?"

"No, no, nothing," she assured him, trying not to look away, knowing that would seem suspicious. But looking at him was worse. His gaze seemed to go right through her, and that made her nervous. She was positive he wasn't the least bit magical. He was as normal as a mundane could get. But the way he examined her made her skin crawl as if he were using a scrying spell on her.

He must have sensed her unease, because he leaned forward, expression softening. "Don't worry, Miss Singer. I'm sure you never hurt anyone, or anything. Personally I don't think you're telling us everything. But everyone has secrets, and you're entitled to yours, as long as they're nothing illegal." He winked and leaned back. "In the big picture, the FBI's job is to prosecute federal offenses, and none were committed. End of story. I'm here because I'd like to know more about you, for my own sake." His smile was now uncertain, giving just the right impression of interest mixed with hesitancy.

Lily looked away, envious at how easily he seemed to control his emotions, but also a little wary of it. She didn't know much about the FBI, but "end of story" didn't seem to be in character for a government organization. Was there something else going on? Or was she just terrible at reading body language and social cues, as usual?

Finally, she looked back and tried a small smile. "There's not much to know. I organize books, drink tea, and read about history. It's all rather boring."

"I like boring," Rick said, grinning widely. "It beats getting shot at. What kind of history do you study?"

Perking up at the question, Lily told him about her bachelor's thesis on ancient Mesopotamia and her study of the classics. Soon, they were having a lively debate about the virtues of Greek versus Roman philosophy and she'd forgotten all about being shy or awkward. Rick, though no expert on ancient civilizations, was well read and had a sharp mind for debate. They talked as her substandard tea, forgotten, grew cold, and she completely lost track of time. Finally, a ringing sound interrupted them and Rick apologized, stepping away to answer his phone. He came back, explaining that duty called and they would have to finish their debate another time. They exchanged phone numbers and Lily wrapped up her forgotten biscotti in a napkin to take home and enjoy later. Though it made her blush, he insisted on walking her to her car. When she pulled away, it was with the picture of his tall, solid form waving in her rearview mirror.

The rest of that week wasn't nearly as pleasant as her meeting-turned-date with Agent Grant. A large shipment of books for the upcoming semester had somehow gone astray and she had a dreadful time tracking it down. She was kept busy scheduling last-minute orders in case it didn't arrive, and rearranging the reserves with all the professors' new selections for their classes—changed at least three times before she finally put her foot down, of course. Finals for summer classes had been the last week of July, so all the books on reserve had to be rotated out to make room for the fall semester books. Though classes didn't start until the last week of August, it was essential to get the stacks and archives organized well before that to make sure the incoming students had everything needed ahead of time.

Lily's week was especially hectic because she had to get everything organized and lined up by end of business

Friday. She'd taken the next week off, in case she had reason to extend her stay at John Faust's estate. If things were less informative than she anticipated, she could simply cancel her vacation time and come back early. But, if everything worked out, she'd have significant research to do to keep her busy. Penny, her assistant, could oversee the process of actually moving the approved books next week, and Lily would double-check everything once she got back. Penny was an excellent assistant when she had clear instructions to follow, and she never seemed to get bored with moving things around—or else bossing the work-study students who were usually assigned the actual grunt work. Lily was apt to get distracted when she saw an interesting title, and so she stuck to organizing the databases and making the rotation plans. The only actual moving she ever did was when some of the fragile documents or valuable books from the closed archives needed to be handled, or when they were sending or receiving such documents to and from other libraries.

To make matters worse, Sebastian kept trying to call her. On Thursday, after she ignored the first call, he kept calling once every minute, obviously in an attempt to annoy her into answering. So she turned her phone off. When she turned it back on, she deleted the five waiting voicemails without listening to them. After that, he made only a few more half-hearted attempts. She got so used to ignoring him that she almost missed a call late in the day from Rick. Scrambling for the phone, she managed to pick up on the very last ring, and so her voice was rather breathless when she answered.

"Yes? Hello?" Not the cool, collected, and thoroughly unruffled impression she'd hoped to give.

"Hello Miss Singer. I'm not interrupting anything, I hope?"

"No, not at all," she hurried to assure him. "It's just, I had set my phone down, and had to rush to pick it up and... well, anyway, what can I do for you?"

"Well, I had hoped we might spend a little more time together, if you'd like. I apologize for rushing off yesterday. It comes with the job, unfortunately. I wanted to make it up to you by offering dinner sometime. I know a nice little diner on Ponce De Leon called Majestic. Would next Friday work?"

Lily's heart rate picked up. She was being asked on a date—a real date—by a handsome guy who seemed halfway decent, could argue Greek philosophy, and didn't wear pocket protectors. Was this really happening?

"Hello? Are you still there?" Rick's voice echoed over the radio waves of distance between them and Lily was jerked back to reality.

"Sorry, yes."

"Yes, you're still there? Or yes, you'd like dinner?" he asked, and Lily could hear the amusement in his voice.

"Both. But I'll be gone on vacation next week, so it will have to be the week after."

"Oh, vacation? Going anywhere nice?"

"Um, not really. Just staying close to home and relaxing. I like to keep things simple." The truth—that she was going to meet a mysterious wizard and delve into the secrets of her past—was much more information than Rick needed to know. Now, or ever.

"Well, enjoy your vacation, Miss Singer. I'll see you in two weeks. Is it all right if I pick you up about six?"

"I...yes, that's fine," she said, about to refuse but changing her mind. Ponce De Leon avenue was close to home. She could always get a taxi back if the date went awry, as they usually did. She had terrible luck with men.

"Great. I'll see you then. Have a good evening."

"Thank you. You as well." She hung up and took a deep breath, letting it out slowly. She'd carried on a normal conversation and had successfully been asked on a date. It felt like something she should celebrate, but she didn't drink wine and wasn't one to yell triumphantly or pump her fist. In any case, she still had mountains of work to do.

When she finally returned home after staying late at the office, she was relieved to find another spelled letter waiting for her, this time with directions to the LeFay estate. A bit of the tension she'd been carrying around all week loosened. John Faust was obviously courteous and understanding, as evidenced by his willingness to change plans to accommodate her. That was a good sign.

There was just time to make dinner and pack for her trip before bed. Sir Kipling followed her from room to room, listing reasons she shouldn't go or why she should, at least, take him with her.

Finally, she got fed up. "Look, Kip, I'm going, and you're not. That's final. Will you please leave me alone and let me pack?"

"I'm supposed to keep an eye on you," he meowed plaintively. "How am I supposed to do that if I'm here and you're there?"

"Someone has to look after the house while I'm gone. I need you here."

"Poppycock."

Lily raised an eyebrow. Where had her cat learned such a word? "Fine. Look at it from this perspective: people don't normally travel with pets. They especially don't take their pets to strange places uninvited. It's unhealthy for the pet and rude to the host."

"I'll be fine, and I'm sure Mr. LeFay is a cat person. All smart people are."

"Maybe I don't want you around. Maybe I don't want this LeFay man to know I have an intelligent familiar who can communicate. If you're so concerned about his trustworthiness, we should keep you a secret."

"Excellent plan. So I'll go with you and lurk about unseen."

"No!" Lily threw up her hands. "Mundanes might not notice you, but this is a powerful wizard we're talking about. I don't want to risk it. You're staying here."

"You're being foolish."

"And you're being annoying, so we're even."

"I'm serious."

"So am I." Hands on hips, Lily glared at her cat, and he glared right back. Unfortunately for her, he happened to be far better at glaring than she was. She chalked it up to his being a cat and relented. A little bit. "Look, how about this. I'll put a location spell on your collar and my bracelet. That way we'll always be able to find each other, no matter where we are. So, if something goes wrong you can bring help."

"And how will I know if something goes wrong, pray tell?" he asked, glare easing only a microfraction.

"I don't know. How do you walk through walls and be invisible?"

"I don't. I'm a cat. Enough said."

"Then use your 'cat magic.' I'm sure you'll figure it out. Now, will you please leave me alone? I have to finish packing."

With one last glare, he stalked off, leaving her feeling alone and uneasy. She pushed the feelings away and finished her preparations. This was important. It might be her only chance to find out the truth. Maybe it was a bit risky, but she'd figure it out. She had to.

The next morning, Sir Kipling wouldn't speak to her. So she did her spell in silence, casting a location link between bracelet and collar. The spell would give the bearers a feeling of direction, like a compass, pointing the way to each other. You didn't have to tap the Source to feel it, so it would work for mundanes—or cats, in this case—as well as wizards. Once finished, she gathered all her things and left the house without a word of farewell.

Before getting into the car, once at a stoplight, and again when she got to the library, she carefully searched her car, ensuring that Sir Kipling hadn't stowed away somewhere discreet. He was nowhere to be found. Obviously he'd decided it wasn't worth bothering, knowing she'd find him and take him back.

The day went by quickly and, before she knew it, it was five o'clock. She half expected Sebastian to waylay her again as she locked up her office, but he was nowhere in sight. With a feeling of relief, she headed to her car, excitement growing inside at the thought of the adventure she was about to embark upon.

She pulled up short as she exited the library and found Sebastian leaning against her car, waiting for her. He was rolling that silver coin over his knuckles again, and she remembered the symbols on it she'd wanted to examine. Apparently he remembered, too, because as soon as he noticed her, he pocketed it and stood straight, looking apprehensive.

As there was no avoiding him, she simply went to her car, keeping her mouth shut and her eyes straight ahead. Perhaps if she ignored him he would go away.

"Look, Lily...are you okay? Usually when you're sure you're right, you waste no time putting me in my place. Why so secretive all of a sudden?"

"There's no secret," she replied tersely, trying to get past him and to her car door. "It's just none of your business."

Surprisingly, he didn't make a scathing reply. He seemed to be making an effort to remain calm and respectful, keeping his razor-sharp sarcasm in check. "Okay. But it's pretty normal for someone going on a trip to leave a point of contact for their hotel or wherever they're staying, in case their pet gets sick while they're gone or there's an emergency at home. Maybe it's not my business, but you've told *someone* where you're going, right?"

"Of course I have," she said. It wasn't really a lie. She'd cast that location spell, after all, so Sir Kipling would know where she was...in general terms. "Now, will you please move so I can leave? I have a schedule to keep."

Hands in pockets, he moved away from the car, brows angled in concern. "You know I'm just trying to help, right, Lil?"

"Well, stop. I don't need your help," she said, brushing past without looking at him. "Have a nice weekend." Swinging her purse into the passenger seat, she got in and closed the door, shutting out whatever he was about to say. She tried not to look at him as she pulled away, but she couldn't help seeing his hunched shoulders and pained expression. As if he'd just been punched in the stomach. Fixing her eyes straight ahead, she didn't glance at his image in her rearview mirror, though she could see from the corner of her eye that he remained frozen in place, staring after her as she drove away.

159

It turned out John Faust's estate was much closer than Lily had imagined, a mere hour northeast of Atlanta—well, three hours if you started at five o'clock, when everybody else was leaving Atlanta, too. Throughout college and the years since, when she'd spent countless hours thinking about who her real family might be, she never imagined the information she sought would be so close. Because, of course, this mysterious wizard had to have information about her family. He'd said he had answers to her questions, and that was the question that had burned in her heart since she'd discovered she was a wizard herself. Obviously, as a powerful, connected member of the magical community, John Faust had the information she sought. Perhaps wizards kept their own genealogies. Maybe he knew her family personally. The thought was an exciting one, after so many years of fruitless questions.

If only she'd had a name to go on, she might have found out who her family was by now. But her mother had never breathed a word about her past. It was a black hole of silence in their household. Lily had never found any public record mentioning her mother, not a marriage license, birth certificate, nothing. She hadn't started looking seriously until she'd left for college, so there'd never been a chance to search the house for records; she hadn't been home since. Oh, she sent Christmas cards and birthday presents. But she hadn't laid eyes on her family in seven years. It wasn't that she didn't love them. She just didn't fit in. They spent their time farming, she, reading. They got excited about tractor pulls and county fairs, she, exotic teas and historical manuscripts. After the furious fight with her mother the year she left for college, she couldn't bring herself to go back and reconcile. It was just easier to stay away.

Shaking off the feeling of loneliness such thoughts always brought on, she concentrated on the directions John Faust had given her. There'd been no address, just a step-by-step guide for someone leaving Atlanta and traveling north on Highway 19. Once she'd passed the worst of the rush-hour traffic, the drive went smoothly, and she even rolled down the windows to enjoy the early August evening. The scenery was peaceful, and she tried to use the time to figure out who John Faust could possibly want her to meet. A famous historian, perhaps? Maybe a mutual friend of Madam Barrington's? Her mentor's silence on the wizard community in general had always annoyed Lily, but she'd long since discovered it was useless trying to pry information from her she didn't want to divulge. Her teacher would have made an excellent spy, with those tight lips of hers.

Soon enough, she was nearing the end of her road trip. The directions said to follow Highway 19 to the north end of Lake Lanier, a large, man-made reservoir north of Atlanta. The next step was to turn east onto Route 318, which ran into the neighborhoods along the west side of the lake. She was supposed to follow it until it ended, so she kept an eye on her map as she drove. The road wound through mostly woods, though she frequently spotted houses through the trees or came upon open yards. Finally, she drove onto a peninsula of land, passing boat docks and parking lots for waterside activities. The road went over a neck of land onto what was almost an island, or at least would be during high water. It seemed deserted. She drove slower and slower as the road wound into thick woods, a mixture of deciduous and evergreen growth. Though the sun was still visible on the horizon, under the trees it was unnaturally dim, so she switched on her headlights. Finally, she reached a dead end. Confused, she scanned her map. As far as it was concerned, the road had ended. There was no house or buildings of any kind. She peered ahead at the guardrail and bright yellow sign that read "dead end." A lone crow cawed in the distance, and Lily shivered involuntarily.

Turning her car around with difficulty on the narrow road, she started driving back very slowly, searching on both sides for a driveway she'd missed. It was the bridge she spotted first. Looking through the trees where the road came close to the shore, she saw a dark line against the water. Following it with her eyes, she finally spotted the turnoff. Once she'd found it, she couldn't believe she hadn't seen it the first time she drove past. It was there in plain sight. Yet she could have sworn there'd been nothing there a moment before.

Relieved, she turned onto it and drove onward, trees bending down close over the driveway. Abruptly, the trees thinned and a sliver of evening sun broke through the foliage, almost blinding her. That's when she felt the magic. It hit her like a wave and she was amazed she hadn't felt it earlier. In front of her a bridge stretched across the water for a hundred yards, closing the gap between the peninsula and a true island that sat surrounded by deep water. The magic didn't even start until the island shore on the other side of the bridge, but she could feel it all the way over here. It was blatant. Obvious. Someone didn't care if anyone magical knew where they were. Mundanes, on the other hand, would never find the place unless they knew exactly where to look.

Halfway across the bridge she felt the urge to turn back. It was an external, not internal urge, and she recognized it for the spell it was. Pushing onward, she finally reached the high gates at the other end that barred her from proceeding onto the island. Perched on one wrought iron peak sat the lone crow she'd heard earlier. It was so big she wondered if it wasn't a raven. But it couldn't be, as they didn't live this far south. It examined her with beady eyes, then croaked and took off, winging away over the island.

Nervous at the forbidding gate, it took Lily a moment to notice the panel to the side, illuminated in the setting sun. She pulled her car close and pressed the call button on it.

"Please state your name and business," said a cool, mechanical voice.

Hesitating, Lily leaned in and said, "Lily Singer. I'm here to see Mr. John Faust LeFay."

There was a slight pause, then, "Thank you. You may proceed." The gates swung open, and Lily drove forward. As she passed through she felt multiple wards, very strong ones, slide over her like heavy silk fabric. They examined her and ultimately let her pass. Someone around here liked their privacy, she thought. The place was warded like the magical equivalent of Fort Knox.

The road passed back under thick foliage that blocked out what little sunlight was left. It wound through the trees for another hundred yards or so until the tree line ended abruptly, giving way to manicured lawn and gardens. She felt more wards, spells for seeing, for warning, for hindrance. As she approached the house, she spotted what looked like a tennis court off to one side and a horse stable in the distance. The house was surrounded by a smaller, more ornamental wall, and its beautifully wrought gates stood open as the road left the lawns and passed through to a circular drive with a fountain in the middle. Resisting the temptation to hang out of her window and get a good look at the enormous building before her, she pulled all the way up and parked by the wide front steps before clambering out to gaze in wonder at the LeFay family mansion.

It. Was. Huge. She'd never been to England, but she felt this place could give any of the royal palaces a run for their money. It was built completely of stone, its south-facing facade a mixture of yellow glow and grey shadow in the evening light. Directly in front of her was the main building, three stories tall with an impressive portico sheltering the front entrance. To either side were smaller, two-story wings which curved around as if embracing visitors with outstretched arms. The stonework was elegant, mostly smooth, but with carved edges and ornamental peaks here and there that added a feeling of ornate grandeur.

She was so absorbed in her awestruck examination that she didn't notice the front door being opened. It wasn't until she heard the questioning "Ahem?" that she looked down and noticed the man dressed in a crisp black-and-white butler's uniform, holding the door open for her.

"I'm so sorry!" she apologized. "Give me just a moment to grab my things."

"No need, Miss," the man said. "They'll all be brought up to your rooms for you."

Even as he spoke, a second man emerged and descended the steps. As he approached, she realized with a start that he wasn't a man at all. He certainly appeared human, but she could partially see through the shimmer of a glamour spell hiding his true form. Underneath he was quite clearly a mechanical construct, straight out of *Ergonomics of Advanced Thaumaturgy*. Such constructs were supposed to be very hard to make. She'd no idea any still existed. Her books talked as if the art had been lost and disused for years. But then, she wasn't exactly an expert on current wizard's culture.

"Come, Miss. He'll collect your things. We don't want to keep the master waiting."

Bewildered, Lily almost stumbled up the front steps as she tried to keep an eye on the thing pulling luggage out of her trunk. She decided to let him do his job and focused on not tripping, finally making it to the top.

The finely dressed butler ushered her in with a bow and she stepped inside, trying to hide her awe at the vaulted ceiling and giant chandelier of the grand entryway.

"Ah! Here she is at last!" A refined female voice with a faint British accent spoke from the left. Lily turned to see a slender woman in a fashionable skirt and blouse approaching. The woman looked to be in her mid- to late sixties and had shining black hair, piled high in an artful arrangement of pins and hairspray that was reminiscent of the 1960s. Her heels clicked on the marble floor as she came forward, arms outstretched and an expression of appropriately restrained joy on her face.

"Lily, darling! You have no idea how long I've waited for this moment. Look how you've grown! You're a perfectly beautiful young woman. Come here, let me see you."

Frozen in shock, Lily couldn't even recoil as the woman reached her and grasped her upper arms in a viselike grip. Turning her this way and that, she inspected Lily's face before leaning in to kiss her firmly on each cheek and embrace her tightly.

"Mother! Good grief, let her go. You're going to squeeze her to death." A man's voice spoke behind them, deep and rich. Familiar. The same voice that had spoken out of the several enchanted letters she'd received over the past week.

The woman pulled back and looked over Lily's shoulder. "Nonsense. I'm entitled a little enthusiasm, aren't I? After twenty-three years?"

Lily felt a firm hand on her shoulder that pulled her away from the woman's clutches. Jarred into action, she recovered enough to step back even further, putting space between herself and the two strangers who acted entitled to her physical proximity. She wasn't used to physical affection, much less a hug from a complete stranger.

"Ex—excuse me, but what is going on?" Her voice caught slightly, rough with surprise, but she tried to maintain a semblance of courtesy despite the indignity of their greeting.

The woman looked just as surprised as Lily felt, and she spoke quickly, cutting off whatever John Faust was trying to say. "What do you mean, dear? Didn't John tell you? Good heavens, John, shame on you."

"Mother, don't, I—"

But the woman kept right on speaking, voice rising in agitation. "Why Lily, dear, don't you recognize me? I am your grandmother after all."

A roaring grew in Lily's ears and her skin became clammy with sweat. She felt suddenly weak all over, lightheaded. She couldn't process it. Her grandmother? That wasn't possible. That would mean...John Faust...was her...

She fainted.

Chapter 2

THE STORIES WE TELL

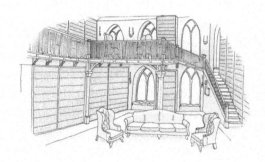

L ILY ROUSED TO A DISTINCTLY UNCOMFORTABLE TICKLING IN HER nose and she jerked her head reflexively, trying to escape it. Of course, since she was lying down, head propped against something soft, all she achieved was a sort of sideways twitching motion.

"Ah, she's coming round, Sir."

Scrunching up her nose at the smell of ammonia, Lily opened her eyes to see the butler standing over her. He held a small, old-fashioned glass vial full of what appeared to be yellow salt. She put two and two together.

"Smelling salts?" she asked dazedly, mind still struggling to focus. "I had no idea people used those anymore."

Another face loomed into her field of vision. The woman with The Hair. Wait...that was her grandmother. Or, she'd said she was. And that was when...

"Goodness, dear, are you quite all right? You gave us such a fright, collapsing like that. Are you unwell?"

"No...no, I..." Lily shifted, trying to sit upright as she examined the posh drawing room around her. It was full of expensive antiques, mostly Victorian in style, and lit by two chandeliers, smaller than the one in the entry hall but impressive nonetheless.

Hands helped her from behind, and pillows were placed to support her back as she attained an upright position in the camelback settee where she'd been laid. Now alert, she took stock of the people gathered 'round.

The Hair woman—she couldn't bring herself to even think the word "grandmother"—had pulled up a chair and sat close, hovering with a frown of worry. Before the settee stood John Faust, straight and commanding in a gray suit and wearing an expression of concern as casually as he did the suit. Beside him stood an older man, his salt-and-pepper hair combed neatly to the side and wearing a cardigan vest that matched the color of his hair. His protruding belly and kindly, if passive, face were in sharp contrast to John Faust's aura of sleek power. Cautiously, Lily opened her senses just enough to tell that all three were wizards, though the two elders' magic was a pale shadow compared to John Faust's blaze of glory.

"Might I fetch you a drink, Miss?" The butler's voice distracted her, pulling her eyes from the group of strangers staring at her.

"Yes, please. Water would be fine," she said, grateful that he, at least, was not a wizard. She wondered what he thought of all this magic around him. Surely he knew?

"At once, Miss." The man left, disappearing through the drawing room doors and leaving her in awkward silence.

The silence didn't last long. "Well, this is all a bit unsettling," the woman said, reaching forward to grasp Lily's hand with both of her cold, bony ones. "But we're happy you're here, safe at last."

John Faust finally spoke, his gaze as piercing and intense as she remembered from their first meeting in Pitts. "I sincerely apologize for my mother's behavior, Miss Singer. I had hoped to allow us time to get to know one another before making you aware of our...relationship." The way he said the word, as if savoring every syllable, sent a shiver down Lily's spine—whether from excitement or apprehension, she couldn't tell.

"It is a sensitive and emotional matter, I am aware," he continued, "and one for which, I suspect, you have long sought answers, as have I. All will be explained, but first, please let us make you comfortable. I had dinner prepared. Would you like some wine? Or perhaps brandy?"

"Oh, no, please. That's very kind, but I've already eaten. I'd really just prefer to know what's going on." Being with so many strangers had her responding with automatic politeness when all she really wanted to do was demand to know what the heck was going on.

"Now, sweetie, don't be silly. Dinner and a nice glass of—"

"Mother, she said no." John Faust's clipped voice cut across the woman's words. "I think Miss Singer needs a bit of space. This is all rather shocking, I'm sure you understand. Why don't you and father go have dinner—I'll take care of our guest."

The woman looked ready to protest but instead pursed her lips and stood, finally releasing her clutching grip on Lily's hand. "Don't let him keep you long, Lily dear. I've waited twenty-three years to see my granddaughter. We have a lot of catching up to do. Come, Henry." The last statement was aimed at the silent man behind John Faust, who turned to follow her clicking heels out the door, passing the butler, who entered carrying a glass of water.

"Here you are, Miss." The butler handed her the glass and she drank slowly, feeling more relaxed already now that The Hair woman was gone. "Do you feel well enough to stand?" the butler asked, taking the now-empty glass.

"I'm fine, thank you," she insisted, shifting to rise on her own before anyone could offer help. Despite her words, she did still feel faint. But she ignored the feeling as she stood, squaring up to the mysterious wizard who had started this whole chain of events and turned her world upside-down. They regarded each other in silence for a moment as the butler, a veteran of nonverbal communication, made himself appropriately scarce.

Now alone in the room with her father—because, of course, that was all he could be, that elusive familiarity reinforcing what her gut had already told her—she gazed long and hard into his eyes, searching for she knew not what. She'd waited so long for this day, this moment. And yet it had come upon her so suddenly she had no idea what to do or say. Feelings warred inside, distracting her thoughts and interrupting any attempt to form a sentence. Excitement, fear, hurt, longing, curiosity, anger, all of them jostled for attention and she felt exhausted just trying to sort them out.

His eyes never left hers, watching her watch him with an intensity that was simultaneously terrifying and thrilling. The desire in them was carefully controlled, but obvious. What did he desire? To know her, she assumed, and felt the same desire reflected in her own gaze. She'd spent her lifetime wondering, searching, wanting answers. Yet, she sensed something deeper in that desire, a hidden facet she couldn't begin to guess at.

The only way to find out was to ask. John Faust remained silent—content, it seemed, to let Lily make the first move. She felt a sudden fond connection to the man, recognizing herself in him through their shared preference to observe and evaluate rather than initiate. She wondered if her reckless curiosity had also come from him.

"Father." Lily tried out the word, her low voice hesitant. She saw the spark of desire flare in his eyes, obviously pleased at her use of the word. For some reason that put her off, and she withdrew into her shell, letting politeness take over.

"Mr. LeFay," she began again. "Thank you for inviting me. The house and grounds are breathtaking. I look forward to seeing them better tomorrow."

"Please, call me John," he said, wise enough to not insist on a familial title he hadn't yet earned. "You are more than welcome. It is your home as much as mine." He spread his arms wide in welcoming, his expression becoming less calculated as it was overcome by sincere emotion. "I can't express how pleased I am to see you, to have you here. I know we are strangers to each other now. But I hope, I believe, that will soon change. You are my future, my legacy, that has been lost to me for so long. To find you again...it is more than I could have hoped for."

Ah. So that's why he looked at her with such intensity. The realization made her relax a bit, even as the weight of what he'd said settled heavily on her shoulders. She still struggled to grasp the situation. If this man was really her father, that meant she was heir to...all this. This house, this island, this magic. The immensity of it frightened her. She'd never imagined that *this* was what had lain hidden in her past. What other momentous truths awaited her discovery?

"Lily? May I call you Lily?" John Faust asked, hesitant. Lily realized she'd been awkwardly silent, lost in thought, and nodded automatically in reply. She didn't feel on first-name basis with this man, but he *was* her father...

"Lily, would you walk with me? We have much to discuss. Perhaps I could show you some of the house while we talk."

She nodded again, eager to be moving and getting a feel for her surroundings, even if it meant more awkward conversation. John Faust led her out of the drawing room and across the grand entryway. Behind her she could hear muted conversation and the clinking of silverware, indicating where the dining room was. As they traversed the vaulted space that was the central nexus of the house, she could see a grand ballroom through double doors on her left. They opened between two sweeping staircases that rose, curving upward along the wall, to the second floor. Another parlor-type room opened ahead and to the right, its windows looking south out the front of the house and onto the fountain outside. Straight ahead John Faust led her, through another set of double doors and into a hallway that bisected the eastern wing of the house. Doors opened on either side along the hallway, revealing studies and sitting rooms.

"First," he began as they walked, "allow me to fulfill my neglected duty of introductions. As you know, I am John Faust LeFay, heir to the LeFay line. You met my mother, Ursula, and my father, Henry. My family has lived here, at the LeFay estate, since the late 1950s when it was built in conjunction with the damming of Lake Lanier. As a family, we are only recently come to America from England. I was the first in my family to be born here. Most of my childhood was spent in English boarding schools and later at university, but I returned after graduating from Oxford.

"We live a quiet life. Father oversees the family business and our estates here and in England; mother tries to run everyone's life and complains about the failings of American culture; and I—" he paused at the end of the hallway and turned to look at her with his piercing gaze, "—I seek answers."

Lily raised an eyebrow, curious, but reluctant yet to voice an opinion. She was also distracted by the finery surrounding her, from the wood-paneled hallway lined with exquisite art in gilt frames to the antique French Aubusson rug she stood upon. She wondered absently if it was Louis XVI era or Napoleonic.

A knowing smile hovered on John Faust's lips as he watched her survey the house. Catching her eye, he extended his arm in polite invitation to precede him into the next room. Lily stepped through the doorway and was immediately captivated. They'd entered a magnificent library. Its ceiling extended upward through the wing's entire two-story height. Stairs led to a large landing on the northern side of the house, which then curved around to became a walkway along the west wall, providing access to the second story. Floor-to-ceiling shelves covered the walls, some of which were bathed in the fading glow of the setting sun, gleaming through enormous windows facing south and east. From the cushioned window seats set into the wall to the antique sofas, dark wood shelves, and old-book smell, Lily was in heaven. Based on her experience, she estimated a library this size contained upwards of eight thousand books.

Ignoring her host, she wandered the length of the room, running her fingers over rows of book spines and stopping occasionally to read a title. They were all shapes and sizes, many of them old, some leather-bound. Their titles ranged from history to politics, fiction, nonfiction, and more. She wished she could forget John Faust's presence and simply luxuriate in the exquisite company of all these books.

With a fair amount of effort, she reined in her desire. She'd come here for answers and doubted they would be found in any of these tomes. Turning her back to the quickly darkening summer evening, she smiled at John Faust.

"This is a wonderful library. I would be quite content to never leave it."

He smiled in return, though his smile didn't quite reach his eyes. "Of course. Which is why I thought this would be an ideal place to converse, as far away from my mother as possible."

"She does seem quite, um, exuberant," Lily offered tentatively.

"Overbearing and controlling are the words you're looking for," he returned with no hint of shame. Taking a seat in one of the cushioned chairs, he motioned for her to do the same. "She's a strong-willed and opinionated woman. Such traits could be disastrous, but combined with intelligence they are a credit to the family name. You just have to learn how to say no."

Lily chose a seat on an antique couch opposite her father, its tufted cushions embroidered with silk threads in the shape of branching limbs covered in flowers. She fingered the threads, finding comfort in their elegant, smooth lines as she let the atmosphere of the library calm her. It reminded her of her own domain at the McCain Library, and she finally felt settled enough to begin sorting out the confused tangle inside her.

"So...you said before that you seek answers. What did you mean by that?" she asked, voicing the first question that came to mind.

"That question has more answers than there is time in the evening," John Faust chuckled. "But to put it simply, I seek knowledge that has been lost and conduct research to add to the knowledge we already have. As I'm sure you've realized from your own studies, there is much about our wizard heritage that has been destroyed or simply vanished into the mists of time. I seek to discover and add to it."

Lily leaned forward, curiosity drawing her out as it always did. "That sounds fascinating. What are you researching? What are your sources? Do you have any original documents?"

A genuine smile touched John Faust's face. "Slow down, Lily. I can see you share my thirst for knowledge. Soon, I'll show you my study and workshop. There is so much to learn, so much I want to teach you. Now that you've returned, however, we have plenty of time for all that. For the moment, I'll say that my primary area of research is our family history, the LeFay line. We are descended from some of the greatest wizards of all time. I want to uncover their wisdom and use it to ensure the survival of wizardkind."

"The survival of wizardkind?" Lily asked, cocking her head.

"Yes..." John Faust said, pausing contemplatively as he gazed at her. "It is a multi-faceted situation that you would better understand once you know your own history."

Lily's heart began to beat faster, and she leaned forward even more, her apprehension swallowed up by her burning desire to know the truth. "Tell me."

John Faust sat back in his chair, hands resting lightly on its arms, his onyx ring shining dully in the fading light. The chair's winged back cast a shadow on his face that was only partially dissipated by the lights high above. His eyes glinted brightly amidst the shadow, always watchful, as he began.

"Your mother and I met at university. Oxford is one of the few schools left with wizards in residence. I believe there are only two, now, since Dr. Grootenboer retired. Upwards of a hundred and twenty, I believe she is, though she didn't look a day older than eighty the last time I saw her.

"Freda...your mother," he added when he saw Lily's look of confusion. "Obviously she changed her name, or else I might have found you long ago. In any case, Freda was only at Oxford for a semester, but it was an eventful one. She was so bright, so intelligent and full of life. We spent many hours together, and I enjoyed showing her around the city. We took trips to London and my favorite countryside spots. England is a beautiful and magical place, when the sun shines in any case." He shook his head, as if trying to dislodge old memories. "It was one of the happiest times of my life. Once she left I had to endure a whole year before I graduated and was able to join her in America.

"Our relationship was not looked upon with favor. Freda's family is of French and Italian descent, and they disapproved of English wizards on principle. My parents were pleased at Freda's pedigree—she's an almost direct descendant of the Flamel line, after all. As you know, certain wizard families have chosen to intermingle with mundanes, diluting their blood and, for all intents and purposes, abandoning their heritage. Freda's family was not one of those; their blood was still pure. Yet, they did not maintain a social status worthy of wizards. My mother in particular was not satisfied with their social standing—they were in the restaurant business, for goodness' sake. Not exactly the English heiress my mother had envisioned for me."

Working to keep her face passive, Lily refrained from voicing her disapproval at such a medieval attitude. She supposed it was how he'd been raised to think. But that was no excuse, surrounded as they were by a modern, enlightened society.

"Yet, we persevered," he continued, "and against all odds were wed and came to live here with my parents. You were born soon after. It was the happiest day of my life, knowing our legacy would continue." With the sun now completely set, the lighting in the library seemed to shine more brightly and Lily could see the fond smile on John Faust's face. "You were the most precocious, troublemaking child. Quiet and observant, but unable to keep your hands to yourself. If it wasn't bolted to the floor or suspended from the ceiling, you found a way to get hold of it."

Lily blushed, looking away from those vivid blue eyes that never once wavered from her face. She remembered very little from her childhood. Her earliest memories were of her mother and of growing up in Alabama. She felt there should have been more, that this house ought to feel familiar. But her early childhood was as blank as river-washed slate, empty of even the vaguest impressions or feelings, almost as if they'd been erased or locked away.

"After you were born, your mother changed," John Faust said, voice fading and eyes drifting, gazing into the past. "To this day, I haven't the slightest notion what prompted it, but she became secretive. She stopped using magic and became irritable when it was used around her. Though you showed an amazing aptitude even as a toddler, she wouldn't allow magic anywhere near you. Beyond a few standard tests for wizard children I performed to ascertain your abilities, she refused to let me teach you anything or cast any spells on you. Even when you were sick she insisted on a mundane doctor, of all the foolish things.

"Finally, when you were almost two, she took you and disappeared without a trace. She left a note claiming she no longer felt safe and not to look for either of you. I can only suppose she grew so paranoid and afraid of magic that she became obsessed with protecting you from it. I've wondered for over two decades what could have caused so drastic a change. She was such a skilled wizard and helped me with my research before you were born." Eyes distant, John Faust shook his head sadly.

"We contacted her family, but they had not heard from her and had no knowledge of her alarming transformation. We considered informing the police, since Freda had technically kidnapped you according to the law. But I loved her and only wanted her and my little girl back. I did not wish to cause more grief. So I continued my own private investigation, year after year, always hoping but never finding a trace. Until now, that is."

John Faust shifted, leaning forward in his chair and folding his hands in front of him. He gazed at them in contemplation, speaking as if to himself. "When I saw you in Pitts, I was so taken aback by how much you looked like your mother that I didn't know how to respond. You acted as if I were a complete stranger, and I did not *know* you were my daughter, I only suspected. So I kept silent. I didn't even know what name you went by. I might never have found you, seeing as how you pushed me through a wrinkle in the time loop before I had a chance to speak to you." Looking up at her from under his brows, he smiled wryly, almost proudly. "A quick bit of thinking, that was. It took me a long while to find my way out again, and by then you were both long gone.

"But, all was not lost. Do you know why?" he asked, sitting back up and fixing her again with his intense gaze.

She shook her head mutely.

"You said his name. The Blackwell boy. You spoke his first name. I could not find you, but I could find Sebastian Blackwell. The family is well known to me. Historically, the Blackwells have striven to remain hidden, but apparently that legacy was not passed on to Sebastian. He was easy to find, even in a city as big as Atlanta. Apparently he fancies himself a witch, though no *real* witch advertises himself. Only the charlatans do that." Lily bristled at his implication, wanting to jump to her friend's defense, despite the fact that she'd called Sebastian a fool as well as a charlatan on numerous occasions. Yet, she remained silent, guessing by his tone that John Faust would not be convinced of any of Sebastian's merits anytime soon.

"After I found Mr. Blackwell, it was a simple matter of elimination. He doesn't have many associates, and none as respectable as you. As soon as I saw your name on the Agnes Scott staff listing, I knew. Freda was always partial to the name Lillian.

"So I sent you a letter and hoped you would respond. And here you are. Home at last, where you belong." He fell silent, face inscrutable, though his eyes never left her.

A long silence followed. Not awkward, exactly, simply expectant. John Faust gazed at her, relaxed yet watchful like a cat, waiting for her to make the next move. Lily looked away, not wanting to hold that gaze. It felt as if he could perceive her innermost thoughts and feelings just from a look, and she didn't like her defenses being swept aside so easily. Of course, that assumed *she* knew her innermost thoughts and feelings.

Frankly, she didn't know what to think. His story, though enlightening, did not surprise her. Her mother, whom she knew as Mary, had always seemed like a normal woman. She'd been a loving and caring mother, and Lily could make no complaints. The only oddity was her rabid aversion to discussing her past. During Lily's teenage years, when she'd begun to feel her difference more acutely and to start searching for a reason why, Mary had been immovably resistant to her doing anything out of the ordinary. She hadn't allowed fantasy books or movies in the house, forcing Lily to explore that facet of pop culture on the sly at school or the library. So John Faust's explanation of what had happened rang true, though it left her just as clueless as him as to why.

Then there were her feelings toward John Faust himself. She still couldn't quite internalize that he was her father. She'd always assumed her father had been some sort of criminal or terrible person, for her mother to cut off all contact and refuse to discuss him. Yet here he sat, a wealthy, courteous, well-spoken individual. Yes, she still felt some misgivings from their encounter in Pitts. But his actions were understandable, given his perspective. He was an intense, intimidating man. That wasn't his fault, simply his personality. She wanted to be angry with him for being absent from her life, yet it hadn't been his choice. It was her mother's actions, not her father's, that had deprived her of a relationship with him. Alternatively, she wanted to be angry with her mother. But she'd been angry with her mother for so long that she no longer felt much toward her except emptiness and loss. She couldn't even be angry with her stepfather, who had always been kind to her, even if he did favor her stepbrothers and sisters. She'd always been the odd one out, the one who didn't fit.

Now she was discovering her true family, a place where she did fit. Yet, she found little satisfaction in the answers she'd sought for so long. Knowing was a relief, but if this was where she belonged, why did she still feel so out of place?

"What is my birth name?" she finally asked, breathing the question in an almost hesitant whisper that eased into, rather than shattered, the silence.

"Lilith Igraine LeFay," her father responded. He said the name with a reverent tenderness that shook her to the core, while the power he put into those three words sent tingles dancing across her skin. She felt...something. Not familiarity so much as history. She was not Lily Singer, the person she'd always thought she was, but rather a stranger named Lilith. Her head hurt just thinking about it, and she suddenly felt too emotionally drained to deal with it all.

"I think...I've had enough for tonight," she said, standing slowly.

John Faust stood as well. "It's a great deal to take in, I know. I'm sure you're tired. Let me show you to your room and we can speak more tomorrow."

"Thank you," she said, hoping her relief wasn't too evident.

They exited the library and took a staircase off the hall to the second floor. This story was no less finely adorned, but the rooms were geared more toward comfort than display. They passed numerous bedrooms and sitting rooms, a reading room and study. Finally, he opened the door to a room whose decor looked more modern, though still elegant. A sleek chest-of-drawers stood by a finely carved dressing table and stool. The canopy bed, though large, was outfitted with plain sheets and had only two sleeping pillows, instead of the pile of embroidered, decorative fluff that usually littered guest beds. On the bed lay her suitcase, purse, and shoulder bag.

Entering the room, she suddenly remembered the man who wasn't a man that had gathered her bags from the car.

She turned to John Faust. "Did my eyes deceive me, or do you have constructs for servants?"

His mouth quirked and he seemed pleased. "Actually, yes, we do. There are several my parents brought from England who've been in the family for centuries. I've added a few of my own, of course. They cook the food, clean the house, keep the grounds, things we would otherwise have to hire mundanes for, and that wouldn't do. The only human servants are my father's butler and my mother's maid, both initiates."

"Initiates?" Lily asked

"Ah, apologies. I forget that, not being raised in a traditional wizard household, some terms we use may be foreign to you. Initiates are what we call members of wizard families who were not born with the gift. They are more common in diluted lines, but even the most pure families have them. Part of my research involves understanding what this magical gene is and why some have it while others do not. Suffice it to say, initiates are those who know and keep our secrets. They are our aides, servants, butlers, and managers."

Lily nodded, thinking of Mr. Baker at the Clay Museum.

"Should you need anything, cast this spell," John Faust demonstrated, a simple command of attendance, "and the nearest construct will see to you. I'll teach you their names later, so you can call each one at will." He then turned and pointed to a small pull cord by the doorframe. "Mr. Fletcher, the butler, manages the household and attends my father, but will respond if he is needed. Simply pull the bell. The bathroom is through there," he pointed to a door in the corner, "and should already be stocked with all the necessities. Have a restful evening and I will see you in the morning." He gave one of his polite smiles that didn't reach the eyes and turned to leave the room. As he began to close the door, he turned back. "I forgot to mention. It would be unwise to wander the house at night. It is very large and has unexpected turns and staircases. Also, there are magical protections on the house and grounds that respond...adversely to intruders. Until you become familiar with everything, I recommend you stay in your room. Should you need anything, simply call and a construct will assist you."

"Thank you. I'll keep that in mind," Lily said.

He finally left, closing the door softly behind him. Relaxing fully for the first time since she'd arrived, Lily wearily unpacked her essentials, changed, and fell into bed. She fell asleep quickly, tired as she was, but awoke several times in the night, momentarily panicked at the unfamiliar surroundings. Each time, she thought she heard distant moaning echoing through the house. But it was so faint and erratic she couldn't tell where it was coming from, or even if it was real, rather than a figment of her tired and restless mind.

She was woken by a brightness beyond her eyelids and a rustle of cloth as of heavy curtains being flung back.

"Goodness, Lily! Still abed at this hour? That won't do at all." The refined yet bossy voice of Ursula assaulted her ears. Lily sat up, blinking in the glare of morning light that streamed in through the curtains Ursula had just thrown open. The woman continued, "We have many things to do and only today to do them. I wish you'd been able to come sooner, but what's done is done. Hurry now. Breakfast is already laid."

Looking around blearily, Lily saw one of the constructs, this one with the seeming of a female. It hovered fretfully about Ursula as if commanded to attend but not knowing what to do, since Ursula had already done it.

"I...what things?" Lily asked, question interrupted by a splitting yawn.

"Why, new clothes, of course." Ursula seemed surprised. "I commend you on your taste. Vintage has a certain...nostalgic charm to it, I'll admit. But the quality is sadly lacking."

"I thought John—"

"John had to leave early on urgent business," Ursula cut her off. "But don't fret, you'll have plenty of time with him later. Today, you're mine." She flashed Lily a smug smile that would give even Sir Kipling a run for his money. "I have everything arranged. Just pop downstairs as quickly as you can and we can be on our way."

With that, Ursula swept out of the room, followed by the still-fretting construct.

Bewildered and annoyed—she'd been hoping for a quiet morning in the library, just her and her eduba—Lily got out of bed, washed, and dressed in prompt fashion. Not hurrying, exactly, but not dawdling. She was, after all, curious to see what was going on, even if dealing with Ursula was like standing in the face of hurricane winds. She assumed Ursula had planned this shopping trip as a bonding experience with her newly discovered granddaughter.

Lily navigated without too much trouble to the first floor, the smell of bacon and eggs helping to guide the way. Peeking through doors that opened off the west-wing hall, she first found the formal dining room. On the right— toward the center of the house—it opened into the grand ballroom, while the left-side door opened to the kitchens. Following her nose, she found a small breakfast room across the hall from the kitchen. No doubt this was where the family ate on less formal occasions.

Entering, she immediately noted Ursula's absence and relaxed somewhat. At the head of the table sat Henry, hidden behind a spread of newspaper. He tilted it downward at her entrance, gave a nod, and retreated again behind it. The repast laid out on the white tablecloth was simple but delicious. Besides bacon and eggs were sausage, some sort of fried bread, and porridge. Lily noted the conspicuous lack of grits or biscuits and gravy. She supposed the elder LeFays brought their English cooks with them when they immigrated to America. There was also, to her great relief, a large pot of steaming tea. She made a beeline for it. From the smell, it was a rich blend of English Breakfast.

She ate hurriedly, not sure how much she would get through before Ursula reappeared. It was hard to focus on the food, however, when distracted by the fine china and silver of the breakfast service. She itched to turn some of it over and find the maker. Though no expert on antiques, Lily could hardly avoid developing a taste for them when shopping for vintage clothing at boutiques and antique stores.

Soon enough, Ursula came sweeping into the breakfast room, saw Lily's half-empty plate, and announced they couldn't wait a moment longer if they were to return in time. Dragged from the dining room, she followed Ursula out to the front steps and noticed her car was nowhere in sight. Perhaps one of the constructs parked it in the garage? As she examined the surrounding buildings, she spotted another lone crow, or perhaps raven, atop one of the house's spires. It sat unnaturally still and almost appeared to be watching them.

The crunch of gravel distracted her and she looked down to see a young man pulling up in a sparkling BMW. He jumped out and hurried around the car to open the door for Ursula. Putting birds from her mind, Lily followed her grandmother while murmuring a word of thanks to the chauffeur. He pulled smoothly out of the driveway and toward the estate entrance.

Once on their way, Lily asked Ursula about the chauffeur in surreptitious undertones, since John Faust had said the butler and maid were the only human staff. Ursula waved a hand in dismissal. "Oh, he's one of Fletcher's nephews. The boy wanted to study at an American university, so he drives for us in the summer. Henry has a mind to train him as Fletcher's successor, but the lad's a tad young for that, and I told Henry so. But never mind all that. We have so much to catch up on. It's delightful having another female in the house amid all the dull males. John is always in his workroom, and Henry, of course, is away taking care of business during the day. We'll have so much fun, just the two of us, I'm sure. Now, tell me *everything*. Your life, your house, your position at that library, your magic—John said you take after him in skill, of course, but who has had the privilege of teaching my lovely granddaughter? And men, are you seeing anyone?" She said all this in one long, gushing stream of words, barely pausing for breath and not leaving any opening for Lily to actually answer her questions. Not that Lily wanted to. What a busybody, she thought, asking about her love life. As if she would discuss it with a stranger, even if they were related.

Yet, as long as it took her to think these things, Ursula's brief pause was over and the hurricane winds were back. "Well, I suppose we'll have all sorts of time to chat later, now that you're back. What's really important is today and tomorrow. Of course I told everyone who's anyone you've returned, back from university at last and ready to be introduced to society. John told me you have a degree in history, which is acceptable for a lady of your status, if rather bland.

He also said you're the head archivist at Agnes Scott. It's a respectable college, but very small. We won't mention that to anyone, especially not that you've been *working* for a living. Goodness, no! We'll just say you've recently returned from university and took extra time to intern as an archivist to aid in your history degree. No one need know the particulars. It will be a scandal that you didn't attend Oxford, but that can't be helped. I've indicated you have a delicate disposition and so chose to attend a prestigious private university in the States rather than travel overseas."

"Wait, you've told who what?" Lily interrupted, barely believing her ears as indignation overcame shyness.

"Why, everyone, dear," Ursula said in surprise. "The DuPonts and the Johnstons and the Chandlers...but of course you wouldn't know any of them, not the way *that woman* raised you." Ursula spoke the words with such obvious disgust that Lily blushed, though whether from anger on behalf of her mother or shame, she didn't know. "But we won't mention any of that. It's in the past, and that's where it ought to stay. Just change the subject if anyone is impolite enough to ask. It's expected."

"I don't understand. Who would be asking, and when?"

"Why, your debutante ball, of course! You can't imagine how exciting it all is. Twenty-three years John has been looking..." Ursula paused to sniff, and dabbed at her eyes with a handkerchief that quite literally materialized in her hand. When she was finished, she simply dropped it with a flourish and it vanished again. "We've kept the whole affair as quiet as one can, you know. But it hasn't been easy. It was such a scandal when *that woman* disappeared with you and we had no notion if you were even alive or dead. The ball is a coming-out, or homecoming celebration, if you prefer. You're a bit old for it, of course. Most girls have their debutante before university, but again, that can't be helped. It will be a quiet affair—well, not too quiet, of course, you must meet all the most important people in these parts—but on such short notice I could only get ahold of a few dozen, instead of the hundred or more you really deserve. Everyone will want to see you and talk to you, the heir to the LeFays. I was so disappointed when John wouldn't remarry, of course. But he wouldn't have it. Too engrossed in his work and looking for you."

Lily finally found her voice, or at least half of it. "A— ball?" she fairly squeaked in alarm.

"Of course, dear. But not to worry, I've arranged tea with the most important ladies this afternoon, so you can become acquainted. Mrs. DuPont and Mrs. Johnston are the matriarchs of the two most important wizard families in these parts—after the LeFays of course—and it's essential you make a good impression. We'll need to pick out a suitable wardrobe for you, and of course a gown for tomorrow."

"I...apologize," Lily stammered. "If John Faust had warned me I could have—"

"Nonsense, dear. Nothing you could buy on a library salary would have been good enough. We shall outfit you with the most fashionable clothes, of course. It's only proper, as I've missed twenty-three years worth of spoiling! You wouldn't deprive me of that, would you?" she asked in an off-hand way, as if the answer were obvious.

Lily didn't know what to say and so didn't say anything. It was easier than trying to resist. Even though she was distinctly uncomfortable with it all, it was reasonable. Her grandmother *had* missed twenty-three years of interaction with her. If her stepfather's parents were anything to go by, it was a grandparent's purview to spoil their grandchildren and shower them with delighted gushing and cheek-pinching at every opportunity. At least Ursula hadn't made a move toward her cheek. And debutantes *were* normal for high-society girls, even if she was altogether too old and had no desire to be thrown a party. She wasn't sure she even wanted to be a part of her father's world. Yet, it was the heritage she'd long sought. How could she turn away now? Tea wouldn't be so bad. Perhaps she could make a token showing at the ball and then go hide in the library. These thoughts reassured her. She remained silent throughout the drive, giving vague, subdued answers to every question Ursula peppered her with.

Their shopping trip was a whirlwind of high-end stores and fittings, trying on clothes that cost more than she made in a month. She attempted to remain engaged and bond with her grandmother, who seemed to be trying hard—in her own clueless, overbearing way—to include her. Or rather, control her. The treatment rankled her, but she stayed quiet; they were only clothes, after all. She often thought of the quiet Henry, wondering if Ursula was why he was so reserved.

When they finally got home around three—trunk stuffed full of bags upon bags of items—Lily was burned out and ready to go hide in her room. But Ursula would only allow her a brief hour to freshen up, relax, and change into some of her new clothes before coming back down to greet their guests for four o'clock tea. Only the prospect of a proper English tea and her curiosity at meeting other wizards kept her going. Otherwise she would have just hidden, and damn the consequences.

The tea was *excellent*. Lily had rarely tasted such wonders as the constructs prepared, but then, if you'd had hundreds of years to perfect your cooking, of course you'd be good. In addition to the delectable spread, silver needle white tea was served—an expensive tea Lily had heard about but never tasted. It was delicate and refreshing, with infusions of cucumber and fruit that made for a sweet, silky aftertaste.

Unfortunately, she couldn't say the same about their guests. Mrs. DuPont was as proud as her name sounded, and Mrs. Johnston as boring. Both were wizards but, like all proper and upstanding citizens of the mundane world, they were used to operating without magic for most normal, everyday tasks. To Lily, it seemed they actually went out of their way to avoid using it if it meant doing any extra work themselves. When Mrs. DuPont's tea was too cold, she summoned one of the constructs with a haughty wave and sent it back to the kitchen for more, when a perfectly simple heating spell would have fixed the problem in seconds.

Lily survived the ordeal by retreating into her shell and letting Ursula do the talking. Though they addressed her politely, both ladies eyed her throughout, measuring and examining every stitch, every hair, every motion she made or word she said. It was like being on trial. She couldn't understand why they were so interested. An uncomfortable feeling in her gut, however, told her there was more going on than her tired and socially awkward brain was catching onto. She'd simply have to wait and ask John Faust about it later.

After the guests left, Lily retreated to her room, flatly refusing to emerge for dinner with the excuse that the day had tired her out and she felt faint, so would take dinner in her room. It felt good to finally say no, and it was a minor enough matter that Ursula gave way. It was also surprisingly pleasant to realize she had constructs at her beck and call that would cook, serve, and clean up every meal. It was nice to kick back for once, though she knew she'd eventually itch to cook, herself.

Dishes cleared away and stomach full, Lily rested on her canopy bed and reflected that John Faust had still not returned from his "urgent business." That was disappointing. He had yet to show her his workshop and she'd been dying to see it all day, resisting the impulse to do a bit of exploring on her own.

She was lying there, staring at the fading sunlight on the underside of her canopy, when she heard scratching at her window. It went ignored for a time, since a tree by her bedroom window at home made a similar sound when a wind came up. But then she realized there were no trees near the house and no wind. As she considered whether to drag herself from bed to investigate, a quiet, almost furtive meow made her sit bolt upright.

Scrambling to the window, her mouth dropped open at the sight of Sir Kipling balancing precariously on the ledge, ears laid back, a scowl of annoyance pasted across his feline features.

"Stop imitating a fish and open the window," he hissed at her through the glass.

Still in shock, Lily fumbled with the window latch trying to puzzle out how in the world Sir Kipling had appeared two stories up, on an island, in a lake over a hundred miles away from home. She finally flipped the latch the correct way and heaved the window open enough for her cat to slip in. Peeking outside furtively, she ensured no one was staring up at them before shutting the window again.

"What in the name of heaven and earth are you doing here?!" Lily sputtered in a whisper, gesturing wildly with her hands in place of yelling at the top of her lungs.

"Rescuing you, of course," Sir Kipling informed her, jumping up on the bed and beginning to vigorously wash himself.

Well, Lily thought, this is just fabulous. I'm being rescued by my cat. What next?

Chapter 3

OF MOTHERS AND MEN

SIR KIPLING AND LILY SAT OPPOSITE EACH OTHER IN THE BATHROOM off her guest bedroom—Lily with her back against the tiled wall, Sir Kipling sitting on the toilet. The door was locked and the water was on in the sink to create cover noise. The last thing Lily needed was someone hearing a cat in her room and coming to investigate.

They glared at one another.

"First of all," Lily began once it was clear she wasn't going to beat Sir Kipling at their glaring contest, "what gave you the crazy idea that I need rescuing? Second, how in the world did you get up here, or even on this island? And don't you dare say you can fly or teleport. I don't think I could take that."

"Nothing quite so melodramatic," her cat replied. "Though I would give a lot to be able to fly. Then I could wipe the smug look off of those squirrels' faces who keep taunting me at home. No, it's all quite reasonable. After you left I tracked down your friend Sebastian. It took me the whole night to find him. Through a crude series of guessing games, I finally got him to understand that I could take him to you, and we set off together. He was as eager as I to rescue you from your own madness. As to how I got up here, I climbed. It's what cats do."

Lily closed her eyes, took a deep calming breath, and tried to think of what to say. She was exasperated but oddly gratified that Sir Kipling had come after her despite the coldness of their last parting. "The walls are solid stone," was all she could think to say.

"I have claws. And I cheated," he admitted.

"You what?"

"One of the not-humans working in the gardens had a ladder against the side of the house to trim the hedges. When he wasn't looking, I climbed up to the stonework on the second floor and hid. There are quite a few useful nooks up here."

"Okay, okay." Lily raised her hands in defeat. "So you didn't fly or teleport. But that still leaves me as mad as heck that you...wait a minute, Sebastian is here, too? Where is he? I can't believe you two! You're going to get me into such trouble." She buried her head in her hands, furious and at her wits' end.

"Actually," Sir Kipling said, examining his claws. "He's not here. Not on the island at least. You might want to know that there are considerably powerful protections around the perimeter that bar the passage of mundanes, among other things. He didn't feel safe trying to scale the gate in daylight, so I came alone to scout the area and warn you."

"Warn me of what?" Lily almost exploded, remembering just in time to lower her voice. "Warn me that my grandmother is a controlling maniac and my father is probably a millionaire? Oh, I'm sorry, did you not get the memo? That's right, Mr. I Know Everything, John Faust LeFay is my *father*. My flesh and blood. And I'm not Lily Singer, as it turns out," she said, feeling slightly hysterical. "I'm Lilith Igraine LeFay. Heiress to the LeFay line and all this." She spread her arms wide, having gotten up and started pacing. "Is that what you're rescuing me from? Is that what you'd rather I not know? What you and Sebastian would prefer to keep me from, so you can have me all to yourselves and your little games? Well, too late." She reached the end of her outburst and stood, rigid, fists clenched and breathing hard as she stared at Sir Kipling.

He was silent for a long time, his golden eyes fixed on her, motionless except for the slight twitch of his fluffy tail. "Well," he finally said. "That complicates things."

"I'll say it does," she snorted, slumping down again against the bathroom wall.

"It's also rather unfortunate," he added.

"What?" Lily stared at him, her glare back.

"Well, you will be less inclined to listen to anything negative towards Mr. LeFay if he is your father instead of a random stranger."

Lily rolled her eyes. "What nonsense has Sebastian been filling your head with?"

Sir Kipling took a moment to clean one paw with his extremely pink tongue before answering. "Namely, that since he last spoke with you he found evidence that the criminal mastermind behind the Clay Museum robbery is none other than John Faust LeFay."

"That's ridiculous," Lily said immediately, ignoring the jolt of worry that clenched her gut.

"Is it?" Sir Kipling asked. "I would say it has at least a seventy percent chance of being true. Besides, I'm inclined to believe Sebastian. He's never been wrong about such things before. Why would you suddenly lose trust in his advice if not because you don't wish to believe it?"

"Because it's ridiculous!" she said, leaning her head back and rubbing her face. It gave her an excuse to avoid Sir Kipling's inscrutable yellow eyes.

"It seems to me that the only ridiculous thing in our vicinity is sitting in front of me."

"Oh, shut up," Lily grumbled into her hands, then finally looked up. "I'm sure Sebastian doesn't *know* anything. It's probably just him and his new *girlfriend* poking around and getting into trouble. I appreciate your concern, even if it does make you a pain in the posterior. But I'm fine, and you and Sebastian need to go home and mind your own business."

Sir Kipling looked at her long and hard. Determined to wait him out, Lily wondered what was going on in that feline head of his and if he had caught on to her bluff. For she was not, in fact, fine. She was confused, annoyed, and frightened. But all those things were normal if you'd just discovered you had a family you never knew existed—and quite a family at that. There were a few doubts buried deep inside, but she ignored those. Somehow she would find a way to make this work. If only she and John Faust could be somewhere alone and undisturbed, spending their days researching magic. How glorious that would be. She didn't need Sebastian and Sir Kipling around causing trouble until she was a little more sure of her position here.

Apparently Sir Kipling was fooled, or else he allowed her to think he was. "Very well," he finally said. "You're still being foolish, but I can see that no one will profit from my presence here. I can promise nothing in relation to return-ing to Atlanta, however. As of yet, they have not invented cat-driven cars. My ride might decide to be stubborn, as he is wont to do."

"Well, then out-stubborn him," she insisted, uncurling herself and standing up. "You do it to me often enough."

"Only because you are especially weak-willed and susceptible to logic. Most of the time, anyway."

"Weak-willed?" Lily spluttered. She wasn't weak-willed, she told herself. She just changed her mind when necessary.

"Yes. But Sebastian has a decided invulnerability to logic. He is much more impulsive, and once he has an idea in his head, naught will turn him from his course. You are his friend and he thinks you're in trouble. I suspect I'll have more luck convincing him to clean his house than leave you here."

"That bad, huh?" she asked, exasperated. Why did males always have to be such a pain? Though still furious, she couldn't deny she felt slightly more generous toward him at the thought of his stubborn loyalty. And if he was here, he wasn't with Tina. "Just keep him out of the way, will you? I'll probably be here all next week. I need time to get to know my family and figure out how this changes things. After a few more days he'll see I'm fine and go home."

Sir Kipling stared at her skeptically but flicked his ears in agreement. He jumped down from the toilet and came to rub on her legs, leaving long, grey hairs on her expensive stockings.

"Stop that," she scolded, picking him up to "save" her stockings even as it ensured a liberal layer of grey hairs on her blouse. She held him tight for a moment, letting all her fear and uncertainty drain away in the soothing rumble of his purr and the soft comfort of his fur. He endured the squeeze patiently, then craned his neck to land a lick on her forehead, despite her attempt to avoid him.

"You always ruin it," she grumbled, setting him back down on the floor and then turning the faucet off.

"A simple yet effective survival technique," he purred smugly.

Peeking out the bathroom door to ensure her bedroom was empty, she let Sir Kipling out and went to open the window. "How are you going to get down?" she asked.

"I'll manage," was all he replied as he hopped up onto the windowsill. Lily noticed the sill was only slightly above a stone ledge that wound its way around the edge of the ornamental stone carvings that decorated the side of the building.

"Now," he said, turning, "make my life easier, if you please, and stay out of trouble."

"Me?" Lily asked, incredulous. "Don't you mean you? I always stay out of trouble."

Sir Kipling narrowed his eyes. "Yes, I mean you. And if you need me, I'll probably be around. The mice on this island are particularly fat and lazy." With that, he hopped down onto the ledge and disappeared from sight around a stone carving.

Despite her indignation, Lily was sad to see him go. Closing the window quietly, she undressed and went to bed as the loneliness crept back in. In the middle of the night, she was roused again by the ghostly moans, and this time she stayed up deep into the night, listening and thinking.

The next morning she woke all on her own, bleary-eyed and still tired from her nighttime vigil. Dressing and padding down to the breakfast room, she found Henry and John Faust at the table this time, both absorbed in their respective reading materials. For a brief moment, she smiled internally. If this was a family who read at the table, she would fit right in.

Quietly taking a seat opposite her father and to the left of her grandfather, she buttered some toast and heaped eggs and sausage onto her plate from silver platters in the middle of the table. After a polite amount of time was allowed for her to make headway on her food, John Faust put down his book and gave her a small smile.

"Good morning, Lily. You slept well, I hope?"

"Yes, thank you," she lied. "It sounds as if someone else did not, however." She cocked an ear as a refined, feminine voice floated through the open doors. It raised and lowered in pitch, probably complaining about something to a flustered construct.

"My mother is bit of a wreck whenever we throw a party. You understand we are relatively understaffed for such a large estate. This mansion was built to comfortably house an extended family, each with their own retinue, in addition to all the housecleaning and groundskeeping staff. We make do with our constructs, but mother goes through the menial labor ones so quickly."

Lily raised an eyebrow, silently asking for elaboration.

"The most easily made constructs," he explained, "need clear, simple, and consistent commands—though even they require a long and involved process to create. I make mother a housecleaning construct, and she ignores everything I've told her about its use and tells it to do things willy-nilly, confusing the poor thing. Eventually the magic breaks down under the stress and I have to recast all the runes. She does the same with many of the other constructs I make her. Only the family constructs, the ones made for our ancestors, seem to wear her with grace. They were created to be much more multi-use, which is why they've lasted so long. Unfortunately, I can't seem to replicate them. Construct-making is an art, and wizards who've mastered it are understandably reluctant to share their methods. Certain wizard families have had a monopoly on construct-making for centuries, and believe me, they make a fortune. I've done the best I can with the simple methods found in general tomes. I don't have time to study it more deeply, despite the grey hairs it gives mother."

Trying to hide her smile at his irreverent, if fond, attitude toward Ursula, Lily concentrated on eating. She felt at ease amongst the quieter members of her family and loved the way John Faust readily and thoroughly explained things to her. Madam Barrington always limited what she shared to the essentials Lily needed to know to master magic and casting, as if she were afraid of saying too much.

When she was finished, John Faust put down his book. "I expect you'd like to see my workshop?" he asked, a smile on his lips and a gleam in his eye.

Lily nodded. "Very much so."

"Follow me." Nodding to his father, who nodded back at both of them, he rose and led Lily out of the breakfast room and down the west hall. Apparently his workshop occupied the end room of the west wing, mirroring the location of the library on the other side of the house. Drawing close to its door, Lily felt *very* strong magical wards pushing back which let her through only reluctantly as John Faust murmured inaudible phrases under his breath with each advancing step.

There were several small rooms on either side of the hall close to the end. Their doors were shut and warded so strongly that Lily felt the impulse to shrink back from them. She wondered what they contained.

With a series of commands and, lastly, a large brass key, John Faust unlocked the end door and led Lily through. Upon stepping inside, she was even more awed than she'd been by the library. The room's basic architecture mirrored the library's, and there were books here as well. But only half of the shelf space was occupied by tomes. The rest was filled with odds and ends, devices, sculptures, strange artwork, artifacts, and many more things besides. A roll-top desk overflowing with haphazard stacks of paper sat against the west wall between two windows. In the middle of the southern portion of the room stood a very large worktable covered in tools and materials, the results of frequent crafting and rune carving. Because of its position it had the best natural light. In addition, dozens of light globes floated all around the room, making it even brighter.

Turning to the right, Lily saw that the whole north wall under the landing was covered with innumerable pieces of parchment pinned to its surface. The papers bore an assortment of pictures, diagrams, and scribbles in languages she didn't recognize, though she picked out the dimmu runes easily enough. A thrill of excitement coursed through her at the thought of all the things waiting to be learned in this paradise of knowledge. She would have to remember to show her father her eduba and see if he could help her unravel all its mysteries.

Still looking around, she glanced up at the landing and saw the curving top of a largish device which framed a chair. The chair was old-fashioned, as if it came from a dentist's office in the 1940s. Tables around the chair were cluttered with bottles, papers, books, and strange devices she couldn't make out from her position. She could, however, see that the landing walkway on this side of the house led not to a door opening onto the second floor, but a blank wall, as if the door had been removed and the gap walled up. That made the heavily warded door on the ground floor the only entrance to John Faust's workroom.

Lily walked further into the room, fascinated by everything around her and turning this way and that to take it all in. On a side table next to a reading chair sat the most realistic-looking sculpture of a raven she'd ever seen. Every feather was intricately carved. She reached out to touch it, but it suddenly twisted its head to eye her. Starting in shock, she almost fell backward into John Faust's arms.

"Steady, Lily," he chuckled. "I promise, it doesn't bite."

"Is it...real?" she asked, bewildered. Was this the lone bird she'd seen hanging around the estate? But that one had been alive...or had it?

"Of course not." John Faust came around to stand by the bird. "Though I appreciate the compliment. This is Oculus, my finest work, even if I did have to bribe and threaten to acquire some of its more complex spells. It helps me keep an eye on the estate. The island is quite large, and mundanes are always trying to come ashore for picnics and hiking. The wards are a reliable defense, but a pair of roaming eyes is always useful."

Peering closer, she was finally able to separate the seeming from the actual construct. She hadn't noticed it before because it fit so snugly, the magical illusion only adding a rustle of feathers and a beady glint of life to each shining pupil. Everything else about it was so lifelike already. Well, now she knew why it had always been alone. Mundanes might be fooled by the seeming, but animals would know the difference and shy away.

She stepped away from the raven while simultaneously trying to keep an eye on it, a feat that backfired when she bumped into something that rattled. Turning and shrinking back in surprise, she realized it was a human skeleton. A real one.

"That," John Faust said with a fond smile, "is your great-great-grandfather, Algernon Blackwood." Lily started, noticing how close Blackwood was to Sebastian's own surname, Blackwell. But John Faust didn't notice her surprise, staring as he was at the grinning skull. "Born 1869, he died in 1985 and donated his remains to scientific research. He has continued to be very useful to the family, even in death. I've used tissue and bone samples from him to make quite a bit of headway in my research on what makes us wizards."

Lily shuddered involuntarily, revolted despite her curiosity. She preferred to stick to books and manuscripts. "Why are you researching that? What do you hope to accomplish?" she asked instead, trying to distract herself from that grisly visage.

"It's quite simple, really," John Faust said, taking a seat in the cushioned chair by the raven. "Wizardkind is dwindling, not only in number but also in power. It's been happening for hundreds of years, and no one has thought to do anything about it. Or else those who did had neither the resources nor the knowledge to find a solution."

Looking around, Lily found her own chair and sat on the very edge, hanging on her father's every word and trying to ignore Oculus's beady-eyed stare. It remained still and silent but watched her every move.

"It's worse now than it ever was, unfortunately," he continued. "Mundane science has reached such a peak that many wizard families use their magic less and less. They see less value in it and even consider it a shame or hindrance. They want to assimilate, be like everyone else. Science has lulled us into a false sense of security that there's no more need for magic and the danger that accompanies it. We are a dying breed, daughter. But I am determined to not let us become extinct.

"The first step is to preserve the family lines and promote large families. Unfortunately, I'm working against years of tradition. Historically, large wizard families fell prey to infighting and disputes over every imaginable thing. Oftentimes it would cause disruption in the community and there was the risk of witch hunts. Of course, they were simply an excuse to squash anything out of the ordinary, whether magic, witchcraft, or just someone with odd habits. To remain hidden, it was considered proper to have no more than two children, three if the first two were girls. And, of course, because of what magic could accomplish, wizard families were often the most powerful and wealthy in the community, and the upper class has always had low birth rates.

"But in our modern times, there is no longer a stigma against magic. The whole world is open to us and mundanes barely bat an eye at the supernatural. They are comfortable in their disbelief, surrounded by a culture that bombards them with their fantasies, making them unable to differentiate between real and imagined. There is no reason now not to have large wizard families, except our own laziness and pride."

"But...father," Lily began timidly, "Don't you have only one child?" She couldn't bear to look him in the eye when she asked the question, afraid of what his answer might be. So she pretended to examine the nearest bookshelf as she waited for his answer.

It was long in coming and sounded tired. Defeated. "I never got over your mother. I tried, but I could never bring myself to remarry, much to your grandmother's frustration. She certainly paraded enough eligible women past me, but...I just couldn't..." he sighed. "So I've devoted myself to research, trying to discover what makes us the way we are. Perhaps there's a way to increase the frequency of gifted births among each family. Even among pure lines, some are born without it. If I can only discover..." He trailed off.

Glancing at him, Lily saw his expression had gone cold and distant as he stared at the floor in fierce thought, seeming to have forgotten her presence. She coughed lightly. He looked up and his face transformed abruptly, turning warm and welcoming as if a switch had been flipped. "Forgive the ramblings of an old man," he said, and stood up. "I am always studying many things, of course, as well as searching for lost documents and artifacts that might give us insight into ancient methods and spells. Our line especially, the LeFays, has quite a history. In the mists of our past lie many secrets that, I am sure, will prove profitable once I uncover them." His eyes glinted as he said this, and Lily felt a twinge of unease.

"Enough about me," John Faust declared, extending a hand in invitation. "Tell me of your studies, your strengths and weaknesses. What do you know and what can I teach you?"

Forgetting about her unease, Lily smiled and began describing her areas of study. Her father was both impressed at her skill and disappointed at what he called the "vast gaps of knowledge in your mental library." She felt the urge to defend Madam Barrington's teaching methods but was checked by her own resentment. She'd known for years her mentor was holding things back, supposedly for her own good. John Faust held nothing back. He told her everything she wanted to know and answered every question in thorough detail. They worked for hours together, practicing spells and discussing magical theory until somewhere a clock struck four. But the quiet chime was drowned out by a piercing, magnified cry of "Liiilllyyy" echoing through the house.

"Goodness," John Faust said, "I hadn't realized how long we've been here. You had better submit yourself to your grandmother's ministrations." He smiled wryly and she thanked him, hurrying off toward the increasingly hysterical call. As she passed through the door, she felt wards snap shut behind her. Something ominous about the doors on either side of the workroom entrance made her shudder. She quickened her pace, racing down the hall and almost colliding with a construct as it exited the kitchen.

Her grandmother, standing in the grand foyer, turned at the sound. "There you are, Lily!" her voice boomed out, much louder than normal. "Good heavens," she said, still overloud as she muttered a few words of Enkinim and her voice returned to normal.

"Didn't you hear me calling?" Ursula asked, speaking rapidly as she stalked over. "It was quite impolite of you to make me scurry all over the four corners of the earth. But never mind, you must be quick. My maid will dress you, but before that you must look at the guest list. You should know who'll be attending. It won't do for you to seem the country bumpkin with no connections in high society. Not that you are, of course. But *that woman...*" she snapped her lips shut into a tight line, then forced a smile on her face. "Never mind all that, dear. Come, let's get you upstairs."

Taking Lily's bicep in a firm grip, she marched up the grand front staircase, Lily in tow. Once in the guest bedroom, Lily was shooed off to the shower. Every minute or so, Ursula's voice outside the bathroom door urged her on with a, "Hurry up, dear. They'll be here soon." She then endured being dressed while Ursula fussed over the clothes, her makeup, and her hair. Everything had to be *perfect*, the woman declared at regular intervals while her maid and a construct with a female seeming labored over Lily's appearance. They ignored her protests that she could do it perfectly fine herself.

As she was poked and prodded, Ursula slowly listed off each guest, taking time to divulge every juicy detail. Soon her head was whirling and she couldn't remember a single name, much less who was whose ex or which men broke a million and which ones "weren't quite there yet, so best not encourage them." She started getting the uncomfortable feeling that her grandmother expected her to actually speak to the young men she'd invited, as if Lily had romantic interest in privileged, rich prigs. Even if debutante balls were historically used to find suitors, that was an old tradition. Surely her grandmother wasn't expecting that, was she?

Finally, it was all over, and Lily stood staring at a stranger in the mirror. The dress was brilliant white silk, with a close-fit bodice that hugged her curves. It was embroidered with Swarovski crystal beading in pale golden hues that curled in twists and waves all over her torso and breast. The beading swirled down to blend into the cascades of fabric that swept about her feet. Several petticoats and yards of stiff tulle made her skirt arc gracefully out at the bottom as if she were floating on air. It was a gorgeous dress, but the neckline made her distinctly uncomfortable. The bodice extended up in a V to cup the edges of her shoulders, but it dipped further in the front than she was used to, revealing more cleavage than she actually had thanks to the modern technology of push-up bras. In the back, the V plunged to just past her waistline. The overall effect was much more glamorous and seductive than she had ever been or ever wanted to be. The cool brush of air on all that bare skin made her feel exposed.

The one place she'd put her foot down was when Ursula wanted her to take off her ward bracelet because it didn't "match" the outfit. Lily calmly cast a glamour on it that made it appear as a fine silver chain with attached charm, and Ursula shut her mouth. The white silk gloves that matched the dress fit snugly under her ward bracelet. Her hair had been done up in enchanting cascades of waving curls, with sparkling pins and clips keeping each hair in place. Their sparkle matched the diamond earrings and necklace Ursula provided. To Lily's relief, the maid had gone light on the makeup, using more neutral tones with lots of shimmer in an attempt to make Lily appear younger than she was.

Once the ordeal was over, Ursula hurried off to see to a few last details with strict instructions for Lily to "not move an inch" lest she muss up her outfit. Sighing, Lily sat down on the bed, folding her hands in her lap. As much as she wanted to, it was too late to back out. She'd thought she could just show her face, smile at a few people, and then go hide. But Ursula had gone over the whole evening in detail, explaining how she would join her grandmother in a receiving line to greet every guest, then mingle with cocktails, dine, and lastly dance for as long as the guests remained.

"You *can* dance, can't you, dear?" Ursula had asked when she got to that part, a brief look of panic crossing her patrician features.

"Um, a little," Lily hedged. "I learned a few steps for our college social balls." What she didn't mention was that she usually bruised her partner's toes black and blue at the first such ball and had avoided the practice ever since.

"Well, that will have to do," her grandmother said, glancing upward resignedly as if searching for deliverance.

There was no way, of course, that Lily would last through all that. She planned to slip away as soon as she'd danced with enough partners to convince them of her deadly toe-bruising abilities. Ursula would have to find her to force her back, and she'd been contemplating hiding places throughout the trial of being dressed. Possibly that was why she didn't remember any of the names Ursula had thrown at her. Ah, well. Spilt milk and all that.

Lily felt a thrill of dread when she finally heard Ursula calling her name from the bottom of the grand staircase. Yet, this was not something that could be avoided. She was an adult, and she intended to act like it, if not in quite the way her grandmother was expecting.

Ever so careful not to tread on her dress, Lily descended the staircase with a grace that surprised even her. She supposed wearing heels all the time at work had given her a good sense of balance, as long as she wasn't trying to remember dance moves. At the bottom, Ursula took hold of her arm, dragging her over to the new arrivals. The ordeal had begun.

There were, indeed, only about thirty guests, which was far fewer than the house could accommodate. Yet, to Lily, the stream of people seemed endless. It was a fair mix of couples and singles ranging from early twenties to sixties. Many seemed present only for the status they added to the occasion, based on Ursula's constant whispers in her ear about each guest. Lily tried to smile even as she cringed inside. Her polite mask was a skill she'd picked up from all the work functions and staff meetings she'd had to attend at the library. Yet she'd never been in the crosshairs of so many single men and hawk-eyed mothers before. It made staying composed extremely difficult.

She shook hands, nodded, and spoke polite nothings to guest after guest, until Ursula finally towed her off for the pre-dinner mingle. Lily soon realized that her grandmother was, without knowing it, making her evening moderately bearable. If she kept her mouth shut, smiled and nodded, Ursula did all the talking, directing, and initiating for her. The LeFay family matriarch seemed content to tell everyone about her granddaughter rather than let her granddaughter speak for herself. Lily was content to let her, though the creative liberties she was taking with Lily's past rankled her.

Everything was going well until Ursula was pulled away by an elderly couple. She reminded Lily to find the setting with her name on it when the dinner bell rang, then disappeared into the crowd. It was so unexpected that Lily almost panicked, eyes searching desperately for the nearest corner to hide in.

"You look stunning tonight, Miss LeFay," said a voice behind her. She spun, a bit too vigorously as it happened, and wobbled precariously in an attempt to keep her balance. A strong hand took hold of her elbow and steadied her. Mortified, she forced herself to look along the hand to the arm, up the arm to the shoulder, and finally into the face of the stranger who had approached her.

His eyes were a stunningly beautiful green and were the best thing that could be said about him. The rest of his face was too angular and covered in a finely trimmed but rather weak beard. He was tall, skinny as a beanpole, and looked to be in his mid-thirties. Lily wracked her brain for his name and came up blank. Fortunately, he seemed to expect this.

"Daren Vance. A pleasure, ma'am," he offered, bowing over her gloved hand to brush her knuckles with his lips. Lily blushed and looked away, entranced despite herself. Without Ursula's chatter to hide behind, she had no defense. Her polite mask was no help when someone appealed to her romantic side—an unwanted disposition she'd long attempted to quash with practicality. She reminded herself she didn't know a single person here and that each one was only present to gawp at her, gossip, and, as had become apparent over the course of the evening, matchmake.

Lily managed a passable curtsy, keeping her eyes lowered as she murmured, "A pleasure, sir."

"I'm eternally in your debt for throwing this little party, as you've given me the pleasure of seeing the most beautiful thing I've laid eyes on all year," he said to her forehead, since she refused to look at him. The remark, though sappy and calculated, earned him a bit of a smile. "I have to wonder, where have you been hiding all this time?"

She was searching for a reply when more figures entered her vision, and she had to look up. Better to know your enemy than to flail about in ignorance.

"Good god, Daren. Do shut up. Your drivel could stun a door into blithering insanity. Run along, now, like a good lad." The speaker was the taller of the two men who'd joined their group, arrow-straight and perfect in every detail. If it weren't for the arrogant look of disgust on his face, he would have made an excellent Ken doll model. The man behind him was a shorter, less perfect version of the speaker.

Daren shot the proud man a look of thinly veiled hatred, even as he shrunk in on himself. Yet he wasn't quite finished. "I think Miss LeFay may socialize with whom she chooses. I would be happy to depart, should she wish." He turned hopeful eyes on her.

This blatant display of bullying did what no amount of urging on her grandmother's part could. Whenever Lily was conscious of herself, she was shy—cripplingly so in the face of eligible men. Yet as soon as she focused on something external, her inhibitions vanished. She wasn't going to donate an organ to this Daren Vance or anything, but she wouldn't stand for bullying either.

"I find Mr. Vance's company quite refreshing, sir. Were he to leave, I would no longer have any reason to stay." She held her head high and looked right into the proud man's eyes, remembering him suddenly from the receiving line: Mr. Charles DuPont himself, eldest son of the DuPonts and still quite single.

Charles's eyes flashed in anger, but it was quickly brushed aside in favor of a sardonic smile as if he recognized, and accepted, the challenge. "As you wish, m'lady," he said as he lifted her gloved hand to his lips. But instead of holding her gaze, as was proper, he lowered his eyes to her neckline. Annoyed—she was sure he was staring at her cleavage—she kept her expression even, remaining aloof from his display.

Sensing his position slipping, Charles released her hand and made a gesture in the air. She saw his lips move in silent command and suddenly there was a red rose in his hand, full and fragrant. He presented it to her, and she accepted the gift, blushing self-consciously and mentally cursing herself for not being quick enough to think of a fitting refusal. With little effort she could tell Charles and his companion were both wizards. It was obvious by Daren's look of hatred, no longer veiled, that he was not.

She was saved from further embarrassment by the dinner bell and fairly fled from the group after a hurried murmur of excusal. To her dismay, however, she found her grandmother had arranged the seating to place her squarely between Charles DuPont and William Johnston. Resigned, she sat, keeping her eyes on the table as everyone took their seats. A peek from under her eyelids showed Daren seated at the far end of a completely different table. Ursula, on the other hand, sat close by. Though she appeared engrossed in conversation, her beady eyes were locked onto Lily, making sure her granddaughter was where she was supposed to be: at the mercy of eligible young wizards.

Dinner was torture. Lily endured increasingly dull attempts to engage her in conversation—Charles and William would have had much more luck if they'd talked about anything but themselves—interspersed with cutting remarks about every other single male in the room. Mostly, Charles talked and William echoed him. They were ever so delighted that she was finally joining high society after her studies. Of course they would help her get acquainted with everyone worth knowing. All she had to do was stick close to them and she would be fine. She barely touched her food. Dessert couldn't come soon enough.

To her eternal shame, Ursula rose and made a speech, toasting her as everyone ate their dessert. She sorely wished she could vanish as easily as Sir Kipling did, or at least melt into her chair. Everyone stared, leaning in and whispering to each other as Ursula listed off academic awards Lily hadn't even heard of and dropped hints about her love life. She felt like a prize horse being auctioned off with her grandmother as the auctioneer, extolling her attributes so as to fetch the highest price. It was humiliating, and it was the last straw. Lily plotted her escape.

As chairs scraped back, marking the end of dinner, and the live orchestra traded quiet background music for a familiar waltz tune, Lily made her move. Dodging Charles's attempt to take her arm, she excused herself to the restroom and fled, sneaking off to the library instead. After finding a suitable book, she retreated to the most inconspicuous sitting room she could find and hid in a corner. She got through the first few chapters before she heard her grandmother's hunting cries.

"Lily? Lily, dear?" and then more quietly, as if to some-one else, "I'm so sorry, Mr. DuPont. I'm sure she just popped upstairs to freshen up. Perhaps a wardrobe malfunction. I'll fetch her down right away."

It took Ursula a few minutes, but she was obviously being thorough and so came fully into the room, spotting Lily in her corner. She looked furious.

"What is the meaning of this?" she hissed, eyes flashing and nostrils flaring.

"My feet hurt," Lily offered, trying to say no without saying no and therefore precipitate an explosion.

Stalking over and looming threateningly, Ursula spoke in a tense whisper. "You are embarrassing your whole fam-ily. I don't care if your feet fall off, you will march yourself downstairs, young lady, and entertain our guests, or so help me you will regret it."

Lily hesitated, considering her options. On the one hand, she was quickly growing to loathe her grandmother and everything she was trying to accomplish. On the other, she desperately wanted more afternoons like the one she'd spent with her father today. To get the latter, she had to please the former. Was it worth one night of discomfort? She had no intention of becoming like Henry LeFay, silent and submissive. Would giving in this time make it harder to say no in the future? She decided to take that chance.

Defeated, she followed Ursula back downstairs and danced the night away, stepping on as many toes as she could manage and speaking as little as possible. She showed no interest in any of the men, not even poor Daren. Some of them were nice enough, but most were snobbish and all of them dull. She tried to be as unpleasant as possible and was fairly sure she'd offended two-thirds of them by the time everyone left.

When the door finally closed on the last guest, Lily turned to trudge wearily up the stairs, counting the seconds until she could take the constricting dress off. But a cold voice stopped her.

"Where do you think you're going, young lady? Come here," Ursula said from the bottom of the stairs.

Lily considered ignoring her, but decided it was better to get it over with.

Ursula's face was full of cold fury, and Lily kept her eyes on the ground as the storm broke. "How *dare* you act so impolitely toward our guests! After I went to all this trouble and expense to help you, to make you accepted among our friends, you humiliate me by your behavior. Do you have any idea what kind of impression you've given to every wizard family in the area? How am I ever going to find you a suitable husband when you act so shamefully? You'll be lucky to find an initiate who wants you, at this rate."

Throughout this speech, Lily felt an unexpected build of temper. She'd intended to let it all wash away like water off a duck. Ursula would get over it. Lily could go back to being a nobody and studying magic. Everyone would leave her alone. But she had a bit of a temper from her mother. That woman could out-argue, out-bluster, and out-yell the biggest redneck in Alabama when she needed to. Lily's temper rarely showed itself, since she avoided letting people get close enough to offend her. Apparently she cared more than she realized, because words started slipping out of her mouth without her permission and her voice rose in agitation.

"What do you mean all *you've* done? You've done nothing but treat me like an object since you met me. You don't know me or care what I want. You didn't do any of this for me. If you had, you'd have asked me first and I would have said *hell, no!* And how dare you presume to 'find me a suitable husband'? How do you know I even want to get married? Or don't already have a partner? My private life is none of your dadgum business, and no one has the right to dictate who I should or shouldn't love, much less marry." Lily knew her stepfather's choice words were slipping into her speech, and somewhere inside she was mortified at her behavior. But mostly she was just angry. Really angry.

"If this is how you treated my mother, no wonder she ran off and took me with her. She spared me a lifetime of *you*." She punctuated her last word with a stabbing finger to Ursula's breastbone. The older woman stumbled back, her face a mask of horror, indignation, and shock. Some part of Lily's brain wondered if anyone had ever stood up to Ursula like this before.

"I'm finished with all this," Lily said, voice flat as she spread her hands wide to indicate the house and finery around her. "I'm going home where I'll live my normal, unfashionable life, work a respectable job, and spend time with my *real* friends until you learn how to treat people like human beings. And don't you ever speak about my love life to anyone again. That's my business, and I'll marry whoever I darn well please. Mundane or wizard, rich or poor, it doesn't matter." Finished, Lily stood there, breathing hard, finally processing what she'd just let pour unfiltered out of her mouth and trying to decide what to do about it.

"Well—I—I never—" Ursula spluttered, face turning red.

"Now, now, dear. Let's not lose sight of what's important," said Henry, making Lily start as he materialized at his wife's side, taking her arm in a calming hand. It was the first time she'd heard him speak. His voice was soft, but firm. "Lily is an adult and deserves to be treated like one."

"That does not give her the right to so disrespect—" Ursula began angrily, only to be cut off by a loud crack behind her. They all looked to see John Faust standing, palms together as if he'd just clapped. He must have amplified the sound to get his mother's attention, Lily realized.

John Faust came toward them, emanating a commanding calm in waves that Lily could actually *feel*, though she had no idea how or why.

"Mother, compose yourself. There's no need to get upset. Our friends will delight in a new opportunity to gossip about us, as they always have, and Lily is too beautiful a woman not to get whatever man she sets her sights on." Lily blushed furiously, feeling acutely embarrassed at such praise coming from her father. And not in a warm, fond way, but coldly calculating, as if he were simply stating a fact he had no emotional involvement in. "The family honor was damaged beyond repair decades ago. There are much more important things to worry about now, and you should let me worry about them. I am Lily's father, and I will take care of this. Go to bed, you'll be fine in the morning." As he reached her, he placed both hands on her shoulders and spoke a soft phrase. Then he kissed her forehead and stepped back. Lily was startled to see her grandmother's whole demeanor had relaxed and her eyes had gone glassy. Henry gently took his wife's arm and led her upstairs, looking back a few times in what seemed to be concern, though Lily wasn't sure.

Watching them go, every fiber in Lily's body had gone on full alert. What John Faust had done was simple enough, yet terrifying in its implications. He'd compelled his mother to be calm, forced it upon her. Yes, she'd needed it, but what right did he have to control someone else? It made her extremely wary. Compulsion magic was easily abused. It was paramount to assault to use it on another person without their express permission. Perhaps Ursula had given him permission in the past to calm her should she become upset? No, Lily thought, that woman didn't seem the type to want anyone else controlling her.

When John Faust's eyes turned to her, they were calm and welcoming. But now that she was paying close attention to every detail of his body language, she could sense how carefully he controlled himself. What she saw was what he wanted her to see.

"Lily. I apologize on my mother's behalf. She's had a hard time dealing with all this. I hope you'll forgive her. There's no need for you to go back to Atlanta. This is your home now, and we will do whatever necessary to make you comfortable. I thought a debutante ball would be a good way for you to get to know us, but I didn't realize how far Ursula would take it, or how uncomfortable it would make you feel. I apologize. Let me walk you to your room. I have lessons planned for the whole week that I'm sure you'll be eager to start on. There's so much I want to teach you. I'm greatly looking forward to it."

Nodding, Lily allowed herself to be helped up the stairs to her room, fixing a false smile on her face as she bade John Faust goodnight and closed her door. Inside, she was filled with fear. As she undressed—she'd sent the female construct away—Lily considered the situation. Tonight she'd realized her father was whatever he wanted her to think he was. He was a chameleon, changing his colors to suit his environment. This whole time he'd shown her only what she'd wanted to see.

This is your home now.

He'd said it so casually, as if conveying a statement of fact, not an option to be questioned. What if his words and use of magic on Ursula were all a subtle display of power, meant to assert his authority over her? But if all she'd seen was what he'd wanted her to see, then everything about him could be a lie just as easily as the truth. There was no way to know. She might be perfectly safe, an honored guest. Or she might be a prisoner. She decided not to wait around to find out.

Quietly, she packed her essentials, leaving behind her suitcase and all the new things Ursula had bought her, even the diamond necklace. Then she put on the jeans and tennis shoes she'd brought, just in case. Crawling into bed, she pretended to sleep while really watching the clock slowly count down the hours. Around one, she thought she heard the moans again but couldn't be sure. A wind had come up and it looked like it would rain. At two, she slid out of bed and cast a spell to silence her movements, then made her way stealthily down a back staircase. Her plan was to creep out the back door, find her car, and speed away before someone could stop her. She tried not to think about the magical protections John Faust had mentioned. Hopefully she could detect them early enough to avoid or bypass them. With that in mind, she focused on the terrain before her with both mundane and magical sense.

Thus she was taken completely by surprise when, in the process of fumbling with the back door lock, the hall was suddenly flooded with light. Lily spun around, almost dropping her shoulder bag as she faced down a fully dressed and very much awake John Faust LeFay.

"Going somewhere?" he asked, eyes glittering with something Lily could not name, but that sent chills down her spine.

She was caught.

Chapter 4

SINS OF THE FATHER

"**I** WOULDN'T ADVISE OPENING THAT DOOR. THE ALARM IS TRULY earsplitting." John Faust said conversationally as he eyed her defensive stance with her back to the door.

Lily straightened, lifting her chin high and gathering what courage she had. "I'm going home," she said.

He spread his arms wide. "But you're already home."

"I mean *my* home. Where I live. Where my possessions reside."

"I can have them retrieved in the morning. The northeast bedroom will do nicely, don't you think? It's closest to the library. You'd like that, wouldn't you?" He smiled.

Lily stared at him, openmouthed. "You don't get it, do you? I appreciate everything you've done, your hospitality, the food, the information. But I'm not going to uproot myself and move in with someone I've known a mere three days. I have my own life. It's mine and I like it. I'm sure we'll have plenty of time to get to know one another later. Right now I need to go home."

Folding his hands in front of him, John Faust nodded sympathetically. "I understand. Ursula can be rather... pushy," he said, taking small, casual steps toward her. "But as I told you before, all you need is to learn to say no. There's no need to run. Cowards run; weaklings can't face their problems. But LeFays...we know how to get what we want. You are a LeFay and you simply need to realize that this is where you belong." He was in front of her now, staring her down with his intense gaze.

Unconsciously, Lily tried to step back, anything to put more distance between herself and her father. But her back met the hard wood of the door and she flattened herself against it, looking away. John Faust was radiating power like a small sun. The effect was overwhelming, making her short of breath. Her heart pounded and adrenaline rushed through her body, singing its sweet song of fight or flight. The effect sent her thoughts tumbling as she searched them for a defensive spell that might help. But before she could gather her wits he leaned forward, putting both hands flat on the door, boxing her in on either side.

She tried to speak, voice coming out barely above a whisper. "I—I'm leaving, Father. Please, just let me go. You're frightening me."

"You are right to be frightened, daughter." His low voice was smooth as silk. "But if you obey me, then I am the only thing in the world you ever need fear. I can make you more powerful than any other wizard. Together we will shape the world into a better place for all our kind."

Against her better judgment, she raised her head, gazing into his eyes a mere foot from her own. His words stirred something deep inside her that she couldn't explain. A nameless fear, or was it a thrill of desire? For knowledge, for power, for belonging. Those eyes were so deep, bottomless pits of knowing. She felt a part of herself fading, falling. Who was Lily Singer?

Too late, she realized what he was doing and tried to come back to herself, to struggle. But by then his hands were already on her temples and he was murmuring powerful words that sent her into soft oblivion. The last thing she heard was his voice. "Sleep, Lilith, my child. I let your mother slip through my fingers. I won't make the same mistake with you."

She was floating, unattached. For a long while she did nothing, having no thought or desire beyond simple existence. Slowly, she became aware of things happening outside her warm bubble. Yet when she tried to move, her body was unresponsive, as if she were simply an observer on the sidelines. Part of her wanted to fight, but every time she tried, an overwhelming desire to sleep distracted her, and she lost track of time.

Finally, she stopped struggling and simply watched. Grey walls filled her vision, broken only by a bare wooden floor and a padlocked door at the far end of the room. Beneath her, she felt a narrow bed. Every so often John Faust would enter and gently lift her head, feeding her soup or helping her drink water. Once when he was leaving, Fletcher, the butler, met him at the doorway to take the dishes he held. She watched as they stood, conversing in low tones. Unable to raise her head to hear better, she caught only snippets of their conversation.

"...not decent—"

"...do as you're told...head of this house..."

"...her mother...never wanted..."

"No harm...not concern yourself..."

Soon the butler left, though not without casting a pitying glance her way.

Eventually, the room grew dark and John Faust no longer came. Time passed—she had no idea how much. She drifted from sleep to wakefulness and back again, dreams blurring the lines between the two. At one point she heard, quite distinctly, a low moaning. It sounded as if it came from the door, or beyond it, perhaps from a room across from her. But was she dreaming? Or was this wakefulness?

Another time, she heard scratching at the door, as if an animal were clawing the wood. When the scratching stopped, there was a faint sound, so low she could barely hear it. It could have been a meow, but she'd thought she'd heard words, too. It didn't make sense. Thoughts, perceptions, and dreams continued to intermingle until she finally slipped deep into true sleep.

A dull pain throbbing in her wrists, ankles, and around her neck woke her. Trying to shake off the drunken feeling of heavy slumber, she found she could move once again and sat up on her bed. When she swung her legs to the floor, they felt strangely heavy. Noting the door to her room—cell, more like—was shut and locked, she looked down to see thick iron bands encircling her wrists. They were on her ankles, too, and when she raised her hand to her throat she touched iron there as well. At the touch, her fingers went numb, then started to throb as hot pins and needles prickled across her sensitive pads. Everywhere the iron touched felt as if it had been submerged in ice-cold water, grown numb, then had hot water poured over it. The combination of numb throbbing and fiery ache was painfully distracting, though not so bad she couldn't stand. Wobbling uncertainly, she stumbled to the door and pounded on it, yelling for someone, anyone, to come. Though she had no clock, it felt like morning, late enough that light filtered in through the small, high windows over her bed, but early enough that nobody seemed to be up.

After yelling long enough to go hoarse, she gave up and slumped down against the wall by the door. There was no way to know for sure, but she suspected she was in one of the rooms by her father's workshop. This room gave her the same sense of unease and foreboding. Strangely, though, she had a hard time discerning the wards that should have been surrounding her. It felt as if she were trying to read Braille through a heavy wool blanket. Her magical sense was dulled and indistinct.

Well, if she were still at the LeFay estate, then there were constructs here. Perhaps they would help. She opened her mouth to speak the summoning spell but stopped, puzzled. She couldn't access the Source. Whereas it usually leapt at her slightest command, bubbling forth eagerly, now she could barely feel it at all. Something was suppressing her senses, getting in between her and her power. Concentrating, she bore down, trying by sheer willpower to break through. She finally felt a tiny trickle, but it was too feeble to fuel even the simplest of spells.

Panting from the effort, she leaned her head back against the wall and tried to collect her thoughts, refusing to give in to panic. Being in Pitts had been bad enough. There, she'd been able to access her magic but was afraid to use it lest it backfire in the unstable time loop. Here, she was flat-out cut off. Crippled. Hobbled like a horse who wanted to run. Never since she'd first learned she was a wizard had she been cut off from that glow of energy that lived inside, warming her soul. Gritting teeth against the growing pain in her extremities, she wrapped her arms around herself, shivering from the cold that slowly crept into her bones.

That was where John Faust found her when he finally came. He opened the door cautiously at first, then more quickly when he saw her on the floor. Concern flitted across his proud features as he bent toward her. "Lilith, whatever are you doing on the fl—"

"Get away from me!" she cried, half in pain and half in anger as she scrambled backward out of reach.

"Now, Lilith—"

"That's not my name!" she yelled, louder. All the anger and fear suppressed by his controlling spell came to the fore in a rush. She pushed to her feet, wincing in pain, and put the bed at her back. Raising her fists in a menacing stance, she glared at her father. Despite the bravado, she had no idea what to do should he approach. She'd never hit anyone in her life beyond a few warning swats at her stepsiblings when they were being particularly annoying. She was a scholar, for goodness' sake, not a fighter. But the temper she'd inherited from her mother was making another appearance. Backed into a corner, with no other recourse, she wouldn't go down without a fight.

John Faust must have found her defiance amusing, because a fond smile touched his lips, briefly smoothing his creased brow as he slowly approached. "You look so like your mother when you get stubborn. I loved her fire, and the challenge of controlling it. I always brought her around, in the end. Nothing can withstand logic, dearest, and I implore you to see reason."

He'd finally come within arms length, and Lily took an inexpert swipe at him, slowed by the heavy band around her wrist. John Faust easily sidestepped her blow, catching her wrist and pulling her toward him, his grip as strong and inexorable as the iron slowly burning into her skin. Though she tried to pull away, he got hold of her other wrist and gently drew her even closer, wrapping his arms around her in a tight embrace that pinned her wrists behind her back.

She struggled, but he was unmovable: a mountain of solid stone. Inhaling to yell for help—why, she didn't know; who was there to hear? —she caught the scent of sandalwood and smoke on her father's clothes. It brought back half-formed memories, so dim and ethereal she couldn't even be sure what they were, except the vague feeling of warmth and safety.

The fight went out of her as quickly as it had come. Exhausted and in pain, she surrendered to the embrace, turning her face to nestle against the crook of his neck. A flood of emotions overwhelmed her and, mortified, she began to weep. Tears ran down her cheeks to stain his expensive shirt. She felt like a little girl again. All she wanted was a father who loved her and took care of her. Was that too much to ask? Why couldn't he just hug her and make everything better? Why couldn't things be like she'd dreamed in her childhood, her family happy and together?

"Hush, child. There's no need to cry." He released her wrists and wrapped his arms fully around her, holding her tight. Despite having her hands free, she didn't resist. What could she do? She was weak and without magic.

"Why are you doing this?" she sobbed softly into his shirt, wanting desperately to understand, wanting her father to be kind instead of dangerous, understanding instead of controlling.

"It's for your own good, darling, I promise," he said into her hair. She felt his lips press briefly against her forehead, and her insides twisted in agony at the bittersweet counter-point between his tenderness and brutality. "This is where you belong. These unpleasant measures are an unfortunate necessity until you come to accept that. We have much to do, and I can't let you go, not even for a moment. Twenty-three years have been wasted already. I can't waste any more."

"But it hurts," she said, barely suppressing a gasp of pain as he pulled back to look at her, his movement shifting the iron shackles that abraded her skin.

His brow wrinkled once more, face filling with concern and confusion. "What hurts? The iron simply suppresses magic, it should cause no pain."

"My skin is on fire. Look." She pulled back further and he let go, taking the wrist she offered and examining the skin beneath the band. It was raw and inflamed, as if the iron bands had been chafing her wrists for weeks, not a few hours.

"Interesting," he murmured, moving to examine her neck and ankles as well.

"What?" Lily asked, trying not to sound as angry as she felt. There was no point in physical resistance, not unless she had a clear path of escape. Her brain was her best weapon now, and John Faust would drop his guard only if he thought she were properly cowed and obedient.

"Hmm, reaction to the wrought iron is consistent with historical accounts. Very interesting, though not completely unexpected, not with our lineage."

"What are you talking about?" she asked again, shifting restlessly. He seemed to have forgotten she was there, more concerned with his observations than her wellbeing.

"It is good news," he finally replied, taking her elbow to steer her toward the bed. She resisted briefly, but only out of pure instinct. "Please, sit," he encouraged, "we have much to discuss."

Once she'd sat down, he abruptly turned and disappeared out the door, locking it behind him—much to Lily's disappointment. He reappeared barely a minute later, carrying a small vial filled with dark purple liquid. "Drink this, it should dull the pain. I regret I cannot remove the iron until I am certain you've come around. I'm sure you understand."

She wanted to scream that, no, she didn't. But instead, she drained the vial, swallowing the bitter liquid and trying not to grimace as it burned a fiery trail down her throat. Almost instantly, however, the throbbing pain dulled to a whisper, and she relaxed in relief.

"There, that's better." John Faust smiled, pocketing the now-empty vial. "Hopefully, we won't have to bother with those restraints for long. You'll heal quickly as soon as they're off."

Lily refused to look at him, staring at the floor in silence.

Her father sighed. "Give it time, Lilith. You'll come around. Now, we have plenty of work to do, but first I need to know. What happened at the Clay museum? The police reports are rubbish, of course, and my agent seems to have disappeared. Since you were there, valiantly defending the tablet, I'm eager to know how it happened. What magic did you use? Did you defeat my agent? How was the Blackwell boy involved?"

A cold dread washed through Lily but she kept her gaze on the floor, hoping to hide the dismay marching across her features. Sebastian had been right. Of course he'd been right. Hot shame quickly replaced the dread as she realized her friends had been correct to warn her, but she'd been too blinded by curiosity to care. She'd alienated and hurt them when their only crime had been concern. Had she even learned any truth for all her trouble? Beyond knowing deep in her bones that John Faust was indeed her father, nothing else he'd said could be trusted. Had her mother really become afraid of magic? Or had she run away to protect herself and her daughter from a controlling megalomaniac? Had her mother sat in this very cell, years ago, plotting her escape?

John Faust remained silent, probably assuming Lily was considering her reply when in reality her mind was miles away. But when she still didn't speak, he put an encouraging hand on her shoulder. "It's all right, daughter. You needn't worry. That job was only a test. I wanted to see how you would react to such a situation, whether you would run and hide or stand and fight. You made me very proud. I only wish to know the details."

"A woman died, Father! Died!" Lily burst out, jerking away from his touch and glaring up into his face. "We *all* almost died because your cursed agent summoned a greater demon. How could you gamble with people's lives like that? You're insane. You don't care about anyone or anything but your stupid plans, and I'll have no part of them."

Angry, she stood, moving to the far side of the cell and turning her back on him. She'd meant to play it cool, to go along and seem complacent, then slip away at the first opportunity. But she was too furious. At herself for her stubborn blindness, at her father for being a conniving, deceitful bastard. His betrayal hurt far more than it should, having known him for only a handful of days. Perhaps it was because she'd had such high hopes. Perhaps she'd projected too much of her own need on him, only to have it brutally slashed to pieces by his matter-of-fact unconcern.

She heard a sigh behind her, and the rustle of cloth. Her back grew warm as he came to stand behind her, his presence palpable. A hand rested gently on her shoulder, but she shrugged it off angrily.

"Don't do this, daughter. Don't turn away from me like your mother did. You are precious to me, my beloved child. Won't you give me a chance? A chance to show you how much I love you?"

Desperate, yet dreading what might come next, Lily turned, looking up into a face filled with concern, even love. But she knew it could turn cold and hard in a moment's notice. "I'll give you a chance," she told him quietly. "Let me go home. Give me space and respect, let me be *me*. Then I'll know you actually care, and I'll do my best to see your point of view. We can learn together...be a family..." she trailed off, begging him silently in her head to say yes.

But something in her words must have been wrong, because his face darkened, making her heart sink. "That's what your mother said, right before she ran away, taking herself and our daughter out of my life forever. She had no right to do that, and neither do you." His face grew even darker, anger and hurt showing plainly in a moment of vulnerability. "What she never seemed to have grasped, and neither have you, is that you are part of this family. A LeFay. As such you are bound to obey. There is no choice, there is only my will. And you *will* obey me."

He stepped closer, looming over her as his body radiated power, battering her senses.

Lily stood on a precipice. She could almost feel the ground plunging away before and behind. Whatever she did in this moment, it would change her life forever. Her father was correct, she was a LeFay, and there was so much they could do together. Was he right to demand obedience? But what about her? What about Lily Singer and all she had become? Was it right to forsake herself and the principles she'd been raised to hold dear—respect, honor, truth, compassion? Were those principles worth losing her father's love forever?

In that moment of indecision, something her stepfather had said long ago came back to her. "Well, honey, if you don't stand fer something, you'll like as not fall fer anything."

If she submitted now, what would John Faust ask of her in the coming days? Months? Years? Where would she draw the line? Her mother and stepfather had loved her unconditionally, whether she obeyed them, agreed with them, or even liked them.

The balance tipped and she made her decision, even as the knowledge of its consequences tormented her.

"No," she whispered through numb lips, barely able to meet her father's gaze. At her words, something inside him broke, she could see it in his eyes. The door he'd opened slammed shut and his face became an emotionless mask. Something else shattered, then, but this time it was her heart.

Stepping back, he regarded her, eyes coldly calculating. "You leave me no choice. The fate of wizardkind is more important than either of us, or our feelings." His voice caught briefly, but then he continued, words as hard as steel. "If you will not help me willingly, then you will help me unwillingly. I tried to spare you this, but you've brought it on yourself." With that he whirled, opening the door with a wrench and closing it with such force that the walls seemed to shake. She heard the rattle of bolts and felt a dim touch of magic closing in, securing her prison.

A sob caught in her throat as the awful reality spread through her quivering body: she'd just lost the family she'd spent her whole life searching for. Stumbling back against the cell's wall, she slid down to curl in a huddle on the floor, sobbing over the fragments of her broken heart.

She didn't know how long she lay there, but, judging by the dimming light, evening was coming. She'd pushed herself up to lean, listless, against the grey wall. Whatever painkiller John Faust had given her was wearing off, and her extremities throbbed again with a fiery ache. She was considering pounding on the door to call for help when she heard a soft tapping and a quiet voice.

"Miss? Miss, are you all right?" It sounded like Fletcher.

Scrambling on all fours, she crawled to the door, putting her ear to the keyhole. "I'm here. No, I'm not all right. Please, let me out, I beg you."

There was a long pause. "I'm sorry, Miss, but I couldn't even if...there are powerful enchantments. I'm sorry," he repeated, really sounding it. "It was much more simple all those years ago when I helped your mother."

"Wha—what do you mean?" Lily asked, voice quavering. "If you helped her escape, why didn't you warn me when I first came? If you knew what kind of man my father is...why?"

Fletcher sighed loudly enough for Lily to hear it even with a solid door between them. "We'd hoped he'd changed."

"We?" Lily asked, confused.

"I am in the service of Master Henry LeFay, Miss, not his son."

"So you *all* knew? You *all* just let him do this to my mother? To me?" Lily felt the indignation and betrayal only faintly, as if she no longer had the ability to feel.

There was more silence and an even deeper sigh. "I cannot speak for Madam LeFay. I suspect she would ignore a genocide in her own bedroom if it threatened to upset her social status. Mr. Henry LeFay is a quiet man, concerned with maintaining the family honor. John is powerful, more powerful than both his parents put together. He acquiesces to his father in matters of business and keeps his...endeavors quiet. In return, my Master does not inquire into the nature of his son's work. But family matters, what with us all under the same roof, well...when things grew to be too much with your mother, he...encouraged me to help her. But there is nothing I can do for you now, Miss. I am no wizard."

"Yes. Yes, there is something," Lily breathed through the keyhole, suddenly remembering the scratching sound she'd heard the night before. "I have a familiar, a cat named Sir Kipling. He can take word to my friends. They'll help me."

"A...cat?" Fletcher asked, dubious.

"Yes, he's special. He'll understand everything you tell him."

"Very well," he agreed slowly. "Where would I find this...cat?"

"I heard him last night scratching at the door. I'm sure he's hanging around the grounds. If you just call his name softly and tell him I sent you, he should show himself. Tell him I'm a prisoner, and to go get Sebastian and Madam Barrington. He'll know what to do."

"I'll do my best, Miss Singer." And with that, he was gone.

Lily sat in the chair she'd glimpsed on the landing the first time she'd visited her father's workroom. Her arms, legs, and forehead were strapped to it, immobilizing her. Not that the straps were necessary. She was already weak as a kitten. It had been two days since she'd sent Fletcher to find Sir Kipling, and in that time John Faust had been busy. True to his word, he used her for his experiments whether she liked it or not. The iron bands on her wrists, ankles, and neck had drained her of strength, making her barely able to walk, though regular doses of the purple liquid kept the pain in check. John Faust recorded her reactions carefully in his notes, having an eduba of his own that followed him around, floating as if on an invisible pedestal. He seemed to find the weakening effect fascinating but wouldn't tell her why the bands affected her so. Of course, the copious amounts of blood he was extracting for his tests didn't help, either. She could do nothing but sit and watch. At least he answered her other questions, saying that just because she'd decided to be stubborn didn't mean he couldn't still educate her.

Eyes closed, she was half dozing in the chair as John Faust examined another blood sample. Though Oculus—the raven construct—was silent as a whisper, she knew it was perched above her on the odd-looking frame that arched over the chair. The frame was solid metal, curving up in two vertical rings set at right angles to one another, forming a sort of globe around the chair that was suspended in the middle. Each circle was intricately etched with dimmu runes, half of which Lily didn't even recognize. She'd given up trying to puzzle out their meaning or purpose. As of yet John Faust had declined to explain.

"Yes! At last..." John Faust's triumphant cry roused her and she opened one eye, ignoring Oculus's beady stare.

"What is it?" she asked, voice toneless and expression wooden. Ever since her father had rejected her, she'd felt as empty and barren as a desert. It seemed every drop of anger and hurt she possessed had already been cried out on the floor of her cell. Now she simply felt detached.

"I found the match needed to confirm my theory," he said, voice clinically professional. Whereas Lily felt dead inside, John Faust appeared to have become a machine. He stood from the strange device he'd been peering into, walking to an adjacent table to notate his findings in several notebooks. Then he grasped his eduba—a larger volume than Lily's own and bound in black leather with little adornment—taking it from its hovering place beside him and propping it on one arm as he wrote in it. He wandered over to her chair, scribbling absently, before looking up to examine her. There was no emotion in his eyes. They were as flat and calculating as if he gazed at a set of mathematical calculations, not his own daughter.

"As I've explained," he began, talking at her instead of to her, "I've long sought to find the gene that makes us wizards. Since the gift is hereditary, it must exist. Once found, it could be studied to learn what exactly gives us our powers, and possibly be replicated through cloning. If we were to develop a way to introduce this gene into a mundane embryo, it might be the key to saving us from extinction. The technology to do such a thing might take years, even decades, to develop. But I believe we will find it. Today, your blood has enabled me to isolate such a gene. This is the first step toward a greater good that outweighs any cost we might pay to achieve it. It is unfortunate you lacked the vision to participate willingly in such a historic venture." He turned away, back to his worktable.

"But would we want to make mundanes into wizards? Without the proper upbringing or training, giving such dangerous gifts to the general population could be disastrous to all of us. Do you truly believe humanity is ready for such power?"

"Of course not," he replied, not turning to her. "Candidates would be carefully selected from current wizard families and other, reputable households within high society. Mundane society is not capable of bearing such a burden. The average mundane is barely worthy of life, much less being responsible for such a gift."

"So your plan is to simply maintain our existence, not to change the status quo?"

"Hardly, daughter." He did turn toward her then, a tiny spark of amusement in his eyes. "Multiplying in number is only the first step, merely a process of preservation to stave off extinction. We were meant for so much more than simply existing." He came forward, going behind the chair and fiddling with something on the frame. "Have you ever read translations of the Uruk tablets? Of course not," he continued without letting her answer, "you wouldn't have access. In any case, they speak of the gods giving Gilgamesh magic so that he and his descendants could rule mankind. Wizards were meant to guide humanity in a glorious history of enlightenment, scientific advancement, and learning. Instead, they dwindled in power and allowed mundanes to rule, eventually succumbing to the fearful superstitions of the people they attempted to help. They were ostracized, hunted, and slaughtered."

He came back around to the front of the chair, facing her squarely. "I do not intend to make the same mistake. Once wizards are strong again in both number and power, we can reveal ourselves to the world and fulfill our duty to guide society into a more enlightened age. If we are not powerful enough, they will strike out in fear or try to enslave us. Wizards cannot and will not bow to the whims of mundanes, nor serve as their mercenaries. They must fear, respect, and love us."

Lily blinked slowly, considering her father's words. They were compelling, in a way, and his goal of enlightenment a worthy one. Yet who would decide right from wrong in this new age? The world existed in a balance: hot and cold, day and night, life and death. Governments had internal balances, countries balanced each other. What would balance wizards' power if not their small numbers and need for secrecy? Her mentor's words just weeks ago came back to her: *The saying that absolute power corrupts absolutely is no empty aphorism. Where magic is concerned, it is a deadly reality.* Lily didn't want wizards to die out any more than her father wanted them to, but his methods were reprehensible, and his ultimate goal could destroy humanity just as easily as save it. He had to be stopped. There was nothing she could do physically to oppose him, but if she knew his plans, perhaps she could get the information to someone who could.

"So, you've found the gene. Congratulations," she said without emotion. "But we are far from being powerful enough to control humanity."

"A correct observation," John Faust acknowledged, turning to one of his worktables to collect a handful of something Lily couldn't see. When he turned back, she saw they were small disks of engraved metal the size of quarters, with one side covered in a white film. He began to stick the disks onto her—the white must have been some sort of adhesive. They went on her temples, at her neck, over her heart, and on her wrists. "That is where you come in."

"Me?" she asked, feeling a twinge of unease. It was the first emotion to stir in her for several days.

"Yes. As your DNA was the key to finding the gene, so it is key to finding the source of the power we need, possibly even the key to immortality. Just think of all the good we could do if we no longer had to worry about growing feeble, our minds failing with the passage of time?"

Lily's blood ran cold. "What are you talking about?"

"Why, Morgan le Fay, of course," he said matter-of-factly. "Surely you realized we are her direct descendants? You're named after her mother, after all, Igraine. I wanted to name you Morgan, but Freda wouldn't hear of it."

"Wh—what?" Lily spluttered, shocked. "You mean Morgan le Fay as in King Arthur? But she's just a legend."

"Really, Lilith. I'm disappointed in you. Morgan was as historical as Merlin and Arthur, though, of course, mundane accounts have romanticized history and gotten the facts wildly wrong. One thing they did realize, however, was that Morgan's powers were not entirely human. Have you never wondered why they named her le Fay, from the French *la fée*, meaning fairy? Somehow she acquired fae magic, most probably given. But there simply isn't enough documentation on the fae to know for sure. That's something I wish to discuss with your friend, the Blackwell boy."

"Sebastian?" Lily asked, now alarmed. What did he want with Sebastian?

"Oh, yes. He knows quite a bit more than he lets on," John Faust said. Her mind immediately went to Grimmold and the other odd things he'd let drop. John Faust misinterpreted her realization for surprise and chuckled. "He never told you, did he? Not surprising. If I knew of the fae I would also be reluctant to discuss it. Perhaps once he is my guest here we can ask him together."

"But what's all this have to do with Morgan le Fay and making wizards more powerful?" Lily asked, trying to distract him while pushing the thought of a captive Sebastian out of her mind.

"I'm trying to find her, of course. She is still alive, some-where. There's a reason her body has never been found, nor that of Arthur or Merlin. They're all hidden somewhere, per-haps at Avalon, if it exists. Even if I'm wrong and she is dead, there will surely be clues, documents, perhaps artifacts with her that we can gain immense knowledge from. Wizards as a whole are rather reluctant to share their secrets. That is why we have lost so many of the powerful spells that made our ancestors great. Dead or alive, Morgan will give us the power we need."

This is ludicrous, Lily thought, struggling to even con-sider the possibility. Yet, she herself was a wizard. How much more ludicrous could it be that Morgan le Fay was a real person? Her ancestor, no less. "But how am I supposed to help you find her? I know nothing about her."

"Fortunately, you don't need to," he explained, stepping back to examine his handiwork. "You have the strongest manifestation of her fae blood that I have found in any of our line. Using several advanced spells of my own invention, this device can use your unique blend of magic to search for other such instances. We are all connected, don't you see? Every living thing is connected to the Source. It is what gives us life. Only the three races of magical creatures—wizards, fae, and angels—can use it, of course. But it touches even mundanes. I initially tried to use Vera—"

"Who is Vera?" Lily asked.

John Faust turned back to his worktables, still speak-ing. "Vera Haas, Ursula's mother. The Haases are only dis-tantly related to the LeFays through their maternal line, but I thought it would be enough. It wasn't, unfortunately, and I'm afraid the magic drove her mad. You may have heard her at night, she rather enjoys raising a fuss when others are abed."

Horror-struck, Lily shrank away from John Faust as he returned to the chair. "You monster," she whispered, unable to take her eyes from him. "How could you?"

"Easily. She was quite eager to help make our family great again. She felt that, at her age, she had little else to contribute, especially after her husband was murdered by the Blackwells."

"What!" Lily exclaimed.

"Never fear, I've improved the spells since then. It is unlikely you will suffer any harm."

Lily began to struggle weakly, each new revelation sending a shock of life and fire to her limbs, returning her will to fight. "What do you mean, 'unlikely'? I could go mad; how can you do this?"

"Well," he said tightly, a flash of anger flickering across his face, "if you hadn't destroyed that lugal-nam, I wouldn't need to take such drastic measures. I had intended to use it to find Morgan. But you blundered in, ignorant of the facts, and destroyed one of the most priceless treasures ever entrusted to wizardkind. Then you had the temerity to interfere in my acquisition of the Tablet of Eridu, the power of which could have—"

"But you said that was a test," she protested.

"Of course it was. That doesn't mean I expected it to fail. You turned out to be more powerful than I expected, which is why I could delay our meeting no longer. I still want to know how you did it, but that can wait until later."

"There might not be a later," she said desperately, still struggling as he tightened the straps holding her down. "You said yourself, this might drive me mad."

"That is highly unlikely, but I'm willing to take the risk."

"Why? Don't you I—love me?" She stumbled over the word, trying to keep the quaver out of her voice, but unable to hide her pleading.

He stopped and stared at her, face a blank mask once more. "How I feel is irrelevant. Nothing must stand in the way of the greater good. That is a fact your mother could never accept. That is why she ran away with you, to sabotage my research."

Lily had thought she couldn't feel any worse, but her father's words sent a shock of hurt and betrayal through her that jarred her to the core. The shock did something to her head, and she felt the blackness of her childhood crack. It leaked memories long hidden, or perhaps simply suppressed. She remembered needles, and pain. Crying for her mother. Her father's stern voice.

"What did you do to me?" she whispered in disbelief.

John Faust didn't reply, simply continued his preparations. Once he'd tightened her straps, he began removing the iron bands, to "prevent them from interfering with the spell" as he explained tonelessly, once more speaking at her, not to her.

She felt immense relief, a freeing and lightening sensation as each one was removed. Yet, she was still very weak. Would she be strong enough to cast in her state? Even now, the stress and shock of just the last five minutes had drained her. She closed her eyes, resting for a moment as he removed the band from her right wrist.

"Hmm, we shall have to remove this," he said.

Lily's eyes flew open in panic as she felt him tugging at her ward bracelet. Of course, how could she have forgotten it? It would prevent active spells from influencing her in any way she didn't allow. The compulsion magic John Faust had used was passive and only worked if the subject allowed it a first grip, which she foolishly had. But the ward bracelet would surely protect her from his experiment.

The bracelet didn't budge, much to John Faust's annoyance. He left momentarily and returned with a pair of scissors. They could not cut the cords, surprising both of them. "Where the devil did you get this?" he asked, throwing the scissors aside in frustration.

When Lily did not reply, he sighed and placed his hands on the bracelet, speaking words of power obviously meant to break or neutralize the ward. In a flash of white light, John Faust cried out in pain and jumped back. He stared at his hands in disbelief, and Lily saw red welts on them in the shape of her bracelet's beads. She couldn't help the smile that crept across her face.

"Defeated by a little ward, Father? I'm disappointed in you," she taunted weakly, feeling reckless despite her helplessness.

He stared at her coldly, smoothing his face to hide any trace of emotion. "We shall see." Turning back to his worktable, he stopped short as Oculus suddenly spread its wings and croaked loudly. The construct beat the air, his croaking turning into caws of alarm.

"What in the world—" John Faust cursed and hurried to descend the landing stairs, headed for the workroom's entrance.

Lily could just barely see the door from where she sat. As John Faust approached it, the whole thing began to vibrate. There was a loud cry outside the room and the door exploded inward, knocking John Faust off his feet.

Lily could have cried in relief and actually felt a tear or two in the corners of her eyes at the sight that greeted her. There in the doorway stood Madam Barrington, Sebastian, and—

"Mother!" Lily cried. Tears now streamed freely down her cheeks as she began to half sob, half laugh, overwhelmed by relief.

Freda Singer didn't look up at her daughter, keeping her eyes fixed on her ex-husband as he scrambled to his feet. But her voice was full of all the love and concern Lily had desperately wanted from her father. "It's all right honey. Don't cry. You're going to be just fine."

There was a sudden bang and a yowl, and Lily struggled to see through her tears. It looked as if Sir Kipling had tried to sneak around John Faust and had been hit with some sort of spell that flung him into the air. Her familiar landed safely on his feet, unhurt thanks to his ward collar, even if the tip of his tail was a bit singed. Now he crouched by Madam Barrington's feet, hissing and spitting at her father. To Lily, who could understand him, it sounded like a string of curses so colorful she was momentarily shocked, wondering where in the world her cat had learned such foul language.

"How dare you touch my student, LeFay. You are a disgrace to our kind." Madam Barrington was too conservative to curse but looked as if she wanted to. Hairs that had come loose from her strict bun now stood up in all directions as her whole body crackled with power. Her eyes were alight with rage, frightening in its intensity. Lily had never seen her teacher so angry.

"She is my daughter," he replied coolly, eyes flicking between his opponents, gauging them. "I believe that gives me more right to her than you."

"No one has any right to her, you pig-headed bastard," Freda shot out, looking just as angry as Madam Barrington. Lily almost felt sorry for her father. Very few things could make her mother lose her temper. But when she did, all bets were off. "She belongs to herself, and if you lay one more slimy finger on her, I'll curse you myself."

"Is that any kind of welcome, *darling*?" John Faust taunted, polite mask cracking under the strain. "It's been more than twenty years, after all. But I knew you would return to me someday."

"Drop dead," her mother spat.

His face twisted into an angry snarl. "So sorry to disappoint, but by the time I'm done, I will be immortal."

"Heaven help us," Freda retorted.

"Enough," Madam Barrington said, her sharp voice cracking like a whip. Freda's mouth formed into a thin line, lips turning white with the pressure of being pressed together. Madam Barrington eyed her opponent's ready stance and outstretched arms. She began speaking, but her voice faded in Lily's ears as she focused on Sebastian. He stood behind both women, looking up at her helplessly. She could tell he wanted to rush to the rescue but wisely held back, understanding what he was up against. If only she could create a distraction, get John Faust's attention to waver for a moment. That would give her friends the opening they needed.

The straps holding her to the chair were as tight as ever, keeping her immobile. But of the iron bands, only the one on her left wrist remained. She felt stronger than she had since this ordeal began, but was it enough to cast a spell? She closed her eyes and reached inside, fighting past the now much thinner veil between her and the Source. Her lips formed words of power, whispering them in a desperate plea. All she needed was a little bit of magic, just enough to...

A large, glass beaker at the edge of one of the worktables by the stairs wobbled, then fell. It plunged two stories to smash on the workroom's bottom floor in an explosion of glass and liquid.

John Faust reacted instinctively, head whipping toward the source of disturbance. Even as he realized his mistake and turned back, Madam Barrington and Freda sprang forward on the attack, and all hell broke loose.

The women's voices combined, calling out powerful words that shot bolts of energy at a retreating John Faust. They rebounded off his defenses, shooting wildly around the room in a wave of destruction as he responded in kind. Lily could only stare, shocked at the sight of her mother casting spells as well as at the whirlwind of magic that was three wizards locked in battle. Her attention was soon pulled away, however, as she spotted Sir Kipling making a beeline for the landing stairs, followed closely by Sebastian.

Unfortunately, she wasn't the only one who had spotted them. Oculus launched itself from its perch atop the circular frame, cawing the alarm as he dive-bombed Sir Kipling, sharp beak seeking out tender flesh. The feline jumped aside and swiped at it, sharp claws scoring across the construct's metal body.

Alerted by the raven's cries, John Faust was somehow able to peel away enough attention from his battle to shoot bolts in Sebastian's direction. Before the cry of warning even left Lily's lips, Sebastian had whirled, black staff crowned with shining green light appearing in his hands in time to catch the blast of energy aimed at his chest.

He started forward as if to enter the fray but was stopped by Sir Kipling's frantic meow. Somehow Oculus had dug its claws into her cat's back, its strong wings beating furiously to pin him there as it pecked at his eyes. Sebastian turned and swung his staff like a batter hitting a low ball. It connected solidly with the construct's metal body, and the raven went tumbling off into a corner, shrieking raucously. It scrambled to its feet, then crouched to take wing once again when something tiny and squeaking dive-bombed it, whirling around the bird's head and distracting it from its plans.

Now free, Sir Kipling raced up the stairs to the landing. Sebastian followed more slowly as he backed up the steps, staff between him and John Faust. For the moment, however, Madam Barrington and Freda were keeping her father distracted, their spells sending books, chairs, even shelves flying. Windows shattered and light globes fell from the ceiling, crashing to the floor and adding shards of glass to the destruction around the combatants.

Jumping up into her lap, Sir Kipling meowed worriedly and nosed her bound wrists. He tried to bite the leather straps but was gently pushed aside by Sebastian. His staff had disappeared to wherever it stayed—she had to remember to ask him when things quieted down—and he deftly undid the straps holding her captive. As soon as her hands were free, she threw her arms around his neck, trying not to start crying again. The movement took all her strength to do, so she couldn't even jerk back when Sebastian swore in pain. He grabbed her arms and pried them off, staring in shock at the iron band on her left wrist. She could just see an angry red burn on his neck where it had touched him.

"Wrought iron. That bastard," he muttered to himself. "Calm down, Lily, it's all right. I've got you," he said to her, shifting her to the side and ignoring her protests. One arm behind her back, the other under her legs, he lifted her in his strong arms. Huddled against his warmth, she finally let go, head falling weakly to rest on his shoulder, her strength completely spent.

She was barely aware as he carried her down the stairs, taking a circuitous route behind fallen bookshelves and columns to stay away from the battling wizards as he fled the room. Exiting the door, he called over his shoulder, "Fall back! I've got her!"

He took off down the hall, Lily bouncing in his arms. There was a bellow of rage and a massive explosion behind them, making Sebastian falter momentarily as he stumbled and regained his footing, trying not to drop her.

As they passed through the grand entryway and she struggled to keep her eyes open, she caught sight of Ursula through the drawing room door, bound to a chair and gagged. Beside the door stood Henry, hands in his pockets, watching them go with a sad expression. Her strength fading fast, Lily wondered if what she saw was real or if she were dreaming again.

She was jarred back into partial wakefulness as Sebastian barreled her into the back of a beat-up car. He dived in after her, yelling, "Drive! Drive!"

"Okay, okay. I'm going!" a familiar voice yelled back. Was that Tina? Lily couldn't think any more, exhaustion from her ordeal overtaking her as the rumble and sway of the car pushed her over the precipice into sweet oblivion.

Epilogue

"**D**O YOU THINK SHE'LL EVEN WANT TO TALK TO ME?"

"Of course she will, dear. Do not be silly."

"I'm not sure, maybe it would be better if I go. If she wants to see me, I'll come back later."

"I will hear no more of this nonsense, Freda. You remain exactly where you are until she wakes. You are a guest in my house for as long as you need. It is high time she apologized to you, and you have quite a bit of explaining to do yourself, as I recall."

"But in her current state—"

"Not another word. I shall go make tea and bring it up."

A sigh. "As usual, Ethel, you know best."

"Indeed."

A door opened and closed, and the sound of footsteps faded. Lily struggled to open her eyes, feeling as if she were swimming up from a great depth to reach the source of the voices. Her eyes slowly opened and she recognized her surroundings as a guest bedroom in Madam Barrington's house. What caught her attention, however, was the figure sitting on her bed. Though the person's face was turned toward the door and partially covered by bandages, it was familiar nonetheless.

"Mother?" she croaked, throat dry as sandpaper.

Freda Singer turned toward her, face full of relief as well as apprehension. "Oh, Lily, you're all right." She raised a hand to caress her daughter's cheek, a smile on her lips even as tears glistened in the corners of her eyes.

Lily stared at her mother, drinking in the sight. That curly brown hair, soft grey eyes, and stubborn mouth that nonetheless was quick to smile and laugh. Quarrels forgotten, she weakly held up her arms for an embrace, wanting only the warmth and love she'd missed for so long. Freda bent, wrapping Lily in a gentle embrace, kissing away the tears on her cheek even as her own fell and intermingled with them.

They stayed that way for a long time. As far as Lily was concerned, she never wanted the moment to pass. But eventually Freda pulled back, handing her daughter a glass of water from the bedside table and searching her daughter's eyes as she drank.

"Can you ever forgive me, Lily?" Freda asked, words barely above a whisper. Her request brought back memories and images, and Lily's brow creased as she recalled what had happened.

"Why, mother? Why didn't you tell me?" She didn't need to specify. Freda seemed to understand the all-encompassing nature of the question.

"I thought I was protecting you, dearest. You know I never meant it to come to this. I thought if I kept you away...if I hid everything that connected us to him, even magic, he could never touch you. Never hurt you again."

Lily looked away, trying not to remember the cold touch of iron and the emptiness of a broken heart. She searched for something to say, to break the tension. "Are you alright?" she asked, glancing at her mother's bandages.

"Oh, it's just a scratch." Freda waved her hand in dismissal. "A bit of flying glass."

"And...John Faust?" Lily asked quietly.

"We didn't manage to kill him, if that's what you're asking. Though he *will* need to build a new workshop," she said with grim satisfaction.

Lily's eyes darkened, remembering a cold, hard chair and the blankness in her father's eyes as he dispassionately discussed using her as research material.

Freda saw the look, and her shoulders slumped. "I'm so sorry, sweetheart," she said, voice full of guilt and pleading. "I never thought this would happen. I only wanted to protect you."

Lily averted her gaze, wanting to bite back. She wanted her mother to feel some of the hurt she'd suffered, the frustration of years spent wondering about her past, not knowing the truth. But then she remembered something her father had said. *I loved her fire, and the challenge of controlling it. I always brought her around, in the end.* What had her mother endured, all those years ago? Did she deserve to be punished for protecting her daughter as best she knew how? Did their family really need any more animosity than it already had?

It was then that she noticed the purring vibrations at her feet. Craning her neck, she saw Sir Kipling curled up on the covers, warm yellow eyes fixed on her. He made no noise, simply blinked contentedly. This subtle display of feline forgiveness—his complete lack of resentment or withdrawal despite her actions—warmed her heart and she felt it soften.

Pushing back the hurt and anger, Lily looked at her mother and attempted a smile. She echoed Annabelle Witherspoon's words as she said, "I know...and I forgive you. Also, I'm sorry for yelling at you and staying away all this time. It wasn't right."

Her mother's face broke into a smile so big it brought her face to life. Her eyes danced with joy as she hugged her daughter tightly. "I forgive you, sweetheart. Always."

"Please, Mother, gently," Lily gasped, feeling the tender skin on her neck protest the violence of the embrace.

"Oops! Sorry, sweetie," Freda apologized. "I'm just so happy to have you back." Tears still glistened in her eyes, but they were tears of joy. "You'll come home to visit, won't you? Everyone is dying to see you, especially your brother Jamie. He...well, I think I should let him tell you himself, when you see him."

"Of course I'll come," Lily promised, smiling. "After all, I have a thousand questions, and I'm far too tired to listen to all your answers right now."

"I'll tell you everything, I promise."

"You'd better," Lily said, giving her mother a look of mock severity.

There was a soft knock on the door, and Madam Barrington bustled in with a tray of tea. Sir Kipling, nose no doubt alerting him to the presence of milk, raised his head and eyed the tray with considerable interest.

"Ah, you are awake, Miss Singer. I am glad to see it," said Madam Barrington.

Lily exchanged a knowing glance with her mother, and Freda nodded. She rose and headed for the door.

"Wherever are you going, Freda?" Madam Barrington asked in surprise.

"Lily and I have come to an...understanding. I'll be back. Right now I think it's time for *you* to do some explaining." She winked and slipped out of the room.

Lips pursed, Madam Barrington set her tray down and poured Lily a steaming cup of tea, adding just the right amount of milk and sugar. She helped Lily prop herself up with pillows against the headboard and handed her the teacup. Lily winced as she shifted, noting the bandages wrapped around her wrists and more on her ankles, by the feel of it.

They sat in silence as she sipped, staring at one another. She couldn't read Madam Barrington's expression, and she felt awkward, wondering what to say.

"I must...apologize for my dereliction of duty," her teacher began, saving her the need to speak. Madam Barrington's words were halting, as if she forced them out with difficulty. "Through my inadequate and selective teaching, I left you vulnerable to attack from another wizard. It could have cost you your life, and I would never have forgiven myself had you come to lasting harm."

"Let me guess," Lily asked bitterly, "Mother made you promise to keep me in the dark?"

Madam Barrington nodded and sighed. "I have known both sides of your family for some time. When your mother left, it was quite the scandal in the wizard community. Nobody quite knew what had happened, though I had always distrusted that LeFay boy. So when I received a call from Freda, a decade and a half after she disappeared, I was just as surprised as anybody. She said I was the only one she could trust and, since you had plans to attend my school, implored me to...mentor you. Apparently your words before you left made an impression. She felt guilty but was afraid to tell you anything. I felt it was unwise to hold anything back, to operate on half-truths, but I gave my word. Now I see it was a mistake, and for that I apologize."

Again, Lily felt the resentment rise in her, but she pushed it back. She'd forgiven her mother and could do no less for her teacher who had done so much for her the past seven years. "It's done and past. Think no more of it."

"Ah, but I do, Miss Singer...Lily." She said the name softly, tentatively. Her eyes held a tenderness Lily had never seen before. "You are the daughter I never had, you see. Long ago I...I loved a man. We wed against my family's wishes, but he was killed barely months later on the German front. World War I was brutal, and my Arthur was hardly the only casualty. I never recovered from the loss, and I emigrated to America soon after because I could not stand to be reminded of him." Her voice faded and her eyes grew distant. Lily stared in wonder, fascinated by this new openness she'd never even glimpsed before.

Madam Barrington's eyes returned to the present, and she smiled sadly. "I should have treated you as you deserved to be treated, with honor and truth. You are a strong woman, Lily, and very powerful. I knew you could handle the knowledge I wanted to impart—your parents raised you well. But I listened to others instead of my own instinct. I want to make that up to you. There is so much more you have to learn, if you will allow me to teach you."

Lily's throat constricted with emotion and she reached for her mentor's hand, giving the cold, bony member a reassuring squeeze. Madam Barrington's admission of guilt and offer of assistance meant more to her she could have anticipated. It eased the pain of loss in her father's rejection, knowing that her future, her heritage as a wizard, was not closed off simply because she refused to acquiesce to her father's corrupted morals. There were other great wizards besides her father, and they would help her.

"Of course, Ms. B. I would like that."

"Call me Ethel, dear," she insisted, smiling softly.

A plaintive meow cut off Lily's reply. "If you two are done being all mushy, I have a serious question."

Madam Barrington's eyebrows rose quizzically, but Lily just smiled and eyed her cat. "And what would that be, O noblest of felines?"

"Are you done with the milk?"

Lily laughed heartily, but before she could explain her mirth to Madam Barrington, a knock on the door distracted her and Sebastian poked his head in. "Mrs. Singer said you were awake. Could I, um, come in?" he asked, looking awkwardly at the floor and not at his great-aunt.

"Well, Lily, you have quite the parade of visitors today." Madam Barrington rose. "I shall leave you both to it." She headed for the door, pausing as Sebastian slipped inside and cleared the doorway. Gazing at him with pursed lips, she finally spoke. "Do not tire her out, nephew. After all the trouble you went to to save her, you might as well finish the job and let her recover properly." She swept out of the room, but not before Lily thought she glimpsed a twinkle in her teacher's eye.

"I told you," Lily said, grinning at Sebastian.

"What?" he asked, sitting on the bed. Sir Kipling, seeing an unprotected lap, got up, stretched, and moved in to remedy the situation.

"She doesn't hate you. I think she's even starting to like you," Lily replied.

"Hmph," he grunted, still not looking at her.

They fell silent, the awkwardness in the room almost palpable.

"I'm sorry for not trusting you," Lily blurted out, desperate to say it before she lost her nerve. "And for being horrid about Tina."

He finally looked at her, relief shining in his eyes. There was something else there, too, something she couldn't name.

"I'm sorry, too, for being jealous and all. I guess I was kind of a jerk, even if I meant well."

"Yeah, you were. But it's all right." Lily grinned, then sobered. "I haven't exactly been the sort of friend you deserve, either. You've always been there when it mattered. I shouldn't have doubted you."

He took her hand gently and gave it a squeeze. "I'll always be there for you, Lil. I promise," he said, face as earnest and open as she'd ever seen it.

She looked away, unable to keep the words from slipping out. "What about Tina?"

His eyes clouded, but he didn't look away. "She's...complicated. We're just having fun together, you know? Teaching each other some witchy tricks. She's...kind of wild, and not a very nice person. Not like you." He smiled warmly at her. "You actually care about people. She only cares what she can get out of you."

"Oh," Lily said in a small voice, not sure what to think.

"I'm your friend, and always will be. Even if," he paused, rearranging his face into what was obviously supposed to be a smile, but looked more like a grimace, "even if you do go out with Agent Doofusface."

Lily rolled her eyes, trying to act casual even as her heartbeat quickened and she felt warm inside. Then she remembered something. "You...you were right about everything, of course." In for a penny, in for a pound, she thought. "About my father. He was behind the museum job. I should have stayed away."

Sebastian shrugged. "Hey, look on the bright side. At least now you know what part of town has all the butt-heads in it. Avoiding them will be easy."

Lily laughed. She'd missed his irreverent humor and mischievous ways, even if they did annoy her. But her thoughts returned to her current situation, and she grew serious again. "The problem is, I can't avoid them."

That got her a raised eyebrow. "Don't tell me you didn't learn your lesson the first time," he said. "If you start acting all shifty again, I'll tie you to your bed myself. I'm sure Sir Kipling will volunteer to sit on your chest until we talk some sense into you."

"It will be a sacrifice, but I am prepared." Sir Kipling didn't even bother opening his eyes, simply remained splayed out on Sebastian's lap, luxuriating in the tummy scratches he was receiving.

Ignoring her feline's sarcasm, Lily shook her head. "No, it's not that. John Faust...my father..." she sighed, suddenly tired beyond imagining. "He...has plans. Wizards ruling the world and all that. Knowing what I know, I can't just ignore it, even though I'd like to forget the entire thing ever happened."

"Hmm," Sebastian said, noticing her drooping posture and heavy eyelids. "Maybe we should wait to have this conversation until after you've recovered. And your mom and ye old bat should probably be in on it."

"Sebastian!" Lily exclaimed, eyes opening wide for a moment. "Don't call her that. She'll never like you if you keep being so impertinent."

"Fine, fine," he said, hands raised in surrender. "The point is, you need rest. Mr. Fancy Pants won't take over the world in the next few days, I promise." He stood, much to Sir Kipling's displeasure, and gently took the teacup from her hands, helping her shift back down into a prone position. She winced as the sheets brushed against the raw skin around her neck. It had been an awkward angle to bandage. The pain reminded her of all the questions she'd been meaning to ask him. He'd never lied to her, that she knew, but he certainly wasn't open about his past.

"Why did the iron hurt me? And you, look what it did to you." She reached up, pointing to the fresh burn mark on his neck.

"Weeelll," he answered slowly. "Iron is poisonous to fae. So if you had any connection to fae magic, it might affect you."

She remembered her father's revelation that they were descended from Morgan le Fay, and that the woman had somehow acquired and passed on fae magic to her descendants. "That explains why it hurt me. But it hurt you even worse. Are you related to the LeFays?" She felt suddenly and inexplicably afraid. What if they were kin?

"Of course not," he scoffed, and she relaxed, trying to hide an unconscious blush. "I just...well, you know I've had dealings with the fae. They kind of...rub off on you."

Lily examined him, knowing a non-answer when she heard one. Her piercing stare was interrupted by a massive yawn. "There's more to that story than you're telling me, but I'm too tired to pry it out of you," she said, finally letting her eyes shut. "But don't think you can wiggle out of an explanation. You owe it to me."

"Hmm, we'll see, sleepyhead," he replied. She heard a rattle of dishes, indicating he'd picked up the tea tray still full of scones, crackers, cheese, and a selection of fruit. "Now, since you won't be needing this, I'd be glad to, uh, dispose of it for you," he said lightly.

Lily smiled into her pillow, cracking an eye to look at him but not having the strength to scold him properly. She did notice Sir Kipling glaring at him in displeasure, probably because the impertinent human was stealing his milk. Sebastian turned to go, then hesitated. Bending over, he planted a soft kiss on her forehead and whispered, "Sleep well, Lily," before slipping out the door.

Two days later, Lily was just packing the clothes and other personal items her mother had brought from her house when Madam Barrington entered the guest room. The woman nodded to Sir Kipling, who sat primly on the bed-spread, supervising all activity.

Turning to Lily, she eyed her student's slow and careful movements, meant to avoid disturbing the bandages on her ankles and wrists. "Are you sure I cannot persuade you to stay a few more days? You are not yet fully recovered," her mentor said.

"I'm well enough to want my own bed." Lily smiled at her mentor. "Besides, I have to be back at work tomorrow and I'd rather drive myself. But thank you...for everything."

Madam Barrington sighed, but nodded. "Very well. Inform me when you feel up to continuing our conversation of yesterday. I don't approve of anyone rushing off with mad notions of heroic grandeur, but I certainly agree LeFay must be stopped."

"How much harm can he do, though? You don't think Morgan le Fay really exists, do you?" Lily asked, shoving the last of her clothes into a backpack and straightening slowly.

"Quite a bit of harm, actually. And yes, Morgan le Fay existed. There is an unfortunately distinct possibility she is still alive, as well. However," she continued, raising a hand to forestall Lily's protests, "why I believe so is a conversation for another time, as are the details of what we must do to prevent his finding her. The first step is for you to recover. Then, I believe you are planning a much overdue visit home?"

Lily nodded.

"After you return, I have much to teach you and very little time to do it. While we work on bringing you up to your full potential, there are some people you should meet on both your mother's *and* your father's side who may be able to help you. No, do not look at me like that. Not all LeFays are as delusional and controlling as your father and grandmother. Also, I shall need to instruct you in the proper use of this." She held out Lily's eduba, its red cover embossed in gold gleaming with its usual magical sheen.

"Where did you find it?" Lily exclaimed, eagerly taking the volume. She'd thought it had been left at the LeFay estate along with her other things. She'd never expected to see it again.

"An extremely competent butler by the name of Byron Fletcher brought it to me, along with your shoulder bag. The bag is downstairs."

"Thank you," Lily said, holding the book tight to her chest.

"No thanks needed, my dear. Being the daughter of John Faust LeFay, I suspect you have a very difficult, though exciting, future in store. I only hope I can teach you what you need to know to survive." Her expression was serious, and she nodded briskly before turning and exiting the room.

Eyes distant and thoughtful, Lily sat on the bed, one hand absently petting Sir Kipling while the other rested on the eduba in her lap. A difficult and interesting life, indeed, she thought. She could not deny her relation to John Faust, no matter how much she wished the memory of him away. Nor could she forget his crimes against both her and her mother. Was knowing truth worth the cost, after all? She wasn't sure. If this was freedom, it certainly didn't feel like it. She had more to worry about now, not less, and a whole new set of scars inside.

Of one thing, however, she was certain: she was Lily Singer, not Lilith LeFay. And now that she knew the truth, pleasant or no, she had to do something about it.

She rubbed her face with both hands and sighed. "We have a lot to do," she lamented. "And somehow I feel things are only just starting to get interesting."

Taking advantage of her distraction, Sir Kipling eased onto her lap, settling into a comfortable catloaf on top of her eduba. "You should stop worrying and pet me," he advised.

Recognizing a sound piece of cat wisdom when she heard it, she did as she was told.

Glossary

Agnes Scott College - a private liberal arts college in downtown Decatur, Georgia, located within metro Atlanta. Founded in 1889, the name was changed in 1890 to Agnes Scott Institute to honor the mother of the college's primary benefactor, Col. George Washington Scott. Though originally offering classes to elementary age and up, by 1906 the name was changed again to Agnes Scott College and remains today a women's-only college.

aluminum - a metal favored by wizards for its usefulness in absorbing large amounts of magic because of its high energy density potential. Safer and more stable than lithium, it is widely used in crafting spell anchors (see dimmu runes) either as a raw material or an inlay. While spells can be cast onto any substance but wrought iron, aluminum better absorbs the magic fueling the spell, thus making the spell more potent and long-lasting (as long as it is cast in conjunction with the proper dimmu runes and sealing spells).

angel - one of the three species of magic users (human, fae, and angel/demon). Spoken of in myth and lore, their origin, powers, and purpose are largely unknown to modern wizards. It is said that they are the stewards of heaven and the most powerful of the three species.

Basement, the - the magical archive beneath the McCain Library containing a private collection of occult books on magic, wizardry, and arcane science, as well as an assortment of artifacts and enchanted items. Created in 1936 during the library's original construction, it is accessed through a secret portal in the broom closet of the library's own basement archive. At any point in time, the Basement has a gatekeeper, the wizard tasked with its maintenance and protection and upon whom rests the control of its magic. This collection of knowledge was bequeathed as a public resource to wizardkind, but, because of the decline of wizards in modern society, has been very little used by anyone but its gatekeeper. Lily Singer is the current gatekeeper, with Madam Barrington as her predecessor.

battle magic - a dangerous form of quick casting requiring an intuitive mastery of Enkinim along with an adroit enough mind to shape magic on the go. To battle-cast, one must react largely on instinct. Without as much time to carefully control and constrain the magic used, there is much higher risk of accidents or backfires.

circle of power - a method of joint casting where two or more wizards join hands, forming a physical circle to aid in pooling magic. This allows for the casting of more powerful spells as well as spells that need to be controlled by more than one wizard, such as a household ward. While any wizard strong enough can break or circumvent another wizard's spell, only the original caster/s can alter it.

construct - a crafted being, usually built in the likeness of a man or animal, enchanted with abilities. Though complex to make, they can be crafted out of almost any material. While they can be built to act and respond in a very lifelike fashion based on the parameters of their controlling spells, they are not alive in the biological sense and can't be killed. Their magic must be broken or altered for them to stop working. Used for everything from manual labor to mobile wards, messengers, guardians, and spies, they can be created to respond only to certain people, commands, or circumstances.

crafting - the art of creating and enchanting objects. Such objects, once made, can exist and operate separately from their creator or even magic in general, as the controlling spells are anchored to dimmu runes carved, inlaid, or otherwise affixed to them. To craft properly, you must not only know the properties of your materials, but also the dimmu runes needed to attain the desired result.

debutante ball - a formal "debut" or "coming-out" presentation for young ladies, usually from upper-class families, who have reached the age of maturity and are to be introduced to society. Originally, it meant the young woman was eligible to marry, and part of the purpose was to display her to eligible bachelors and their families with a view to marriage within a select upper-class circle. Historically, because of their small numbers, it was the most effective way for young wizards to find a match among other wizards or initiates. It was also one of the only places considered safe for wizards to gather in large numbers.

demon, greater - a fallen angel. They are those who rebelled and were cast down from heaven, their magic corrupted. Each has their own unique name by which they can be commanded, if one is brave enough to speak it and powerful enough to master its owner. They are creatures of great power, hate, and thirst for destruction.

demon, lesser - corrupted fae. Demons cannot create, only destroy. Therefore, to acquire underlings, greater demons can perform a ritual to force a part of themselves into a minor fae, something small and weak like a water sprite, to take over its immortal body and turn it into a corrupted, ugly, twisted mockery of its former self. This corruption cannot be undone. The lesser demon becomes a slave to its master and cannot disobey. This is why the fae hate demons so much, and why fae magic is particularly useful in opposing demons.

dimmu - [dim + mu = {dim = to make, fashion, create, build (du = to build, make + im = clay, mud)} + {mu = word, name, line on a tablet}] the Enkinim word for runes of power, the script used to write Enkinim, the language of power. In and of itself, this script is not magical, and a mundane could write it all day without achieving anything. Dimmu runes are used by wizards to anchor their spells. Infused with magic from the Source, these runes enable and guide the carrying out of the desired enchantment and can preserve the enchantment's effect long after the spell is cast.

ebony staff - a fae staff made of twisting ebony wood belonging to Sebastian Blackwell, a gift from the fae. At the top the branches, as of the roots of a tree, flare out to twist around a glowing green gem embedded in the wood of the crown. With the abilities he was given, Sebastian can summon it from the fae realm at will, but as soon as he releases it, it disappears back from whence it came.

eduba - [e + dub + a = {e = house, temple, plot of land} + {dub = clay (tablet), document} + {a = genitive marker}] the Enkinim word for library, used by ancient Sumerians to indicate the houses where their clay writing tablets were kept. To a wizard, however, it describes a book containing their personal archive of knowledge. Similar to the mundane notion of grimoires, edubas are full of much more than simply spells. They accumulate centuries of history, research, and personal notes as they are passed down, usually from parent to child or teacher to student within powerful wizard families. The knowledge in them is magically archived, such that you must summon the desired text to the physical pages before it can be read. This allows for vast stores of information to be carried around in one physical book.

elwa - fae word of greeting. It carries deeper meaning, however, than a simple hello. It is a request to commune with or share the presence of the named fae. The request may be denied or ignored, in which case the supplicant must withdraw. It is considered extremely rude to ask a second time.

Enkinim - [Enki + inim = {Enki = Sumerian god of creation and friend of mankind} + {inim = word; statement; command, order, decree}) words of power, the language of magic by which wizards control and direct the Source. Named after the Sumerian god Enki, who, it was said, taught mankind language, reading, and writing.

fae - one of the three species of magic users (human, fae, and angel/demon). Myth says they were created to help steward the earth, and that long ago they worked side by side with man to nurture it. But they have long since faded from sight and memory, and very little reliable record remains about them (though theories abound).

fae glamour - a type of fae magic by which fae disguise their true shape. They also use it to create illusions or temporarily change the appearance of inanimate objects. While wizards can cast their own type of glamour to achieve a similar effect, their scrying spells cannot see through fae glamour. It can be defeated using a seeing stone, something only fae can make. A fae can see through another fae's glamour.

familiar - a companion creature, being, or entity of some sort. Used in different contexts for witches and wizards. A witch familiar is usually some kind of spirit or creature with which they've made a bargain and formed a partnership. Some such beings can take the form of animals to avoid detection, thus the stereotype of witches having black cats. These dealings can be dangerous, however, and often lead to the practitioner changing, knowingly or not, by simple association. "Something given, something gained" is the witch's way. Most wizard familiars, on the other hand, are nothing more than loyal pets wearing enchanted collars. In rare cases, however, a skilled wizard could create their own familiar by crafting a mechanical body and enchanting it with abilities. These construct familiars were used for everything from manual labor to acting as mobile wards, messengers, protectors, spies, and more.

Gilgamesh - figure from ancient Sumerian lore. Opinions differ on whether or not he was historical. Possibly also mentioned in Biblical text by the name of Nimrod. In wizard legend it is said he was the original recipient of magic from the gods, and all wizards are his blood descendants. Considered the most powerful wizard in all of history—almost a god—he searched for, but never found, the source of immortality.

Grimoli'un - a mold fae befriended by Sebastian Blackwell, who calls him Grimmold. The *'un* of the name denotes masculine character. Grimmold has a sense of smell so good he can track things across dimensions. He has a weakness for specially aged pizza (Sebastian's usual bribe in exchange for Grimmold's services) and is very allergic to soap or cleaning fluids of any kind.

human - one of the three species of magic users (human, fae, and angel/demon), and the only one of the three with a direct connection to the Source. Whereas fae and angels/demons were created with a set amount of magical power proportional to their status, humans have no innate limit. They are limited only by their own will, discipline, and skill, as well as the frailty of their mortal bodies. Also, not all humans can use magic. While all fae and angels/demons are innately magical, only certain humans descended from the wizard lines manifest the ability to access the Source and manipulate magic. It is thought the difference is genetic and inherited, but no one yet knows how or why.

initiate - a term traditionally used to indicate a member of a wizard family who is not a wizard. Because not all children born to wizards or wizard-mundane couples could use magic—yet were still raised within the magical community with knowledge of its secrets—there arose the need for a distinguishing word for someone not magical, yet not ignorant like a mundane. Because these mundane children of wizards often became the butlers, valets, housekeepers, etc., of wizards, the term initiate has come to mean someone who works for a wizard family, caring for them and keeping their secrets. It is an old-fashioned term, generally used by the very traditional. Most modern wizards simply call all non-magic humans mundanes, whether they know about magic or not. With the decline of wizard families and magic use in general, along with society's general acceptance of, rather than fear of, magic, the existence of initiates in the traditional sense has all but disappeared.

Jastiri'un - an elemental fae befriended by Sebastian Black-well, who calls him Jas. The *'un* of the name denotes masculine character. Jas can control light and sound (mechanical and electromagnetic waves). Like most pixies, he has a weakness for alcohol, which Sebastian often trades him for various services.

Lake Lanier - a large man-made reservoir built in 1956 to provide hydroelectricity, navigation, flood control, and water supply for Atlanta. It is located about forty miles northeast of Atlanta.

lugal-nam - [lugal + nam = {lugal = king; master (lu = man + gal = big)} + {nam = planning ability; destiny}] literally translated *master of destiny*, it is the name given to a device created long ago by powerful wizards that can loop time by creating alternate timelines that repeat until the magic ends, at which point they rejoin "real" time. Made of clay and about six inches long by an inch and a half wide, it looks like a cylinder made up of rotating dials.

McCain Library - the library of Agnes Scott College, a private liberal arts women's college near downtown Atlanta. Built in 1936 to replace the smaller Andrew Carnegie Library constructed in 1910, it was originally still called the Carnegie Library, then later renamed the McCain Library after the college's second president in 1951. Complete with four main floors, a grand reading room, and three attached floors dedicated to the stacks, this building is Lily Singer's workplace and domain. She is the college's archives manager, and her office is located on the library's main floor. The basement floor contains the library's archives as well as the portal to the secret magical archive of which Lily is the gatekeeper.

mundane - a term used by wizards to denote non-magical humans. Generally, mundanes are ignorant of the existence of magic, the notable exception being witches. Other enlightened mundanes include members of wizard families who were born without the ability to use magic. These non-magical members of the wizard community were traditionally known as initiates. Historically, the term mundane was derogatory and insulting. Accusing a wizard or initiate of being "mundane" was paramount to calling them ignorant fools. The wizard community looked down on mundanes and considered them little more than animals. The fact that mundanes regularly executed anyone they suspected of using magic helped to solidify wizards' negative attitude toward them. That attitude has largely disappeared with the advance of society, though there still exists a lingering feeling of superiority among wizards.

Oculus - Meaning *eye* or *sight* in Latin, this is the name of John Faust LeFay's construct familiar crafted in the form of a raven.

Pilanti'ara - a plant fae befriended by Sebastian Blackwell, who calls her Pip. The *'ara* of the name denotes feminine character. As a plant fae, Pip has a certain area she is responsible for. Within that area she cares for all growing things. Like most pixies, she has a weakness for alcohol, which Sebastian often trades her for various services.

Pitts - a tiny town in south central Georgia. It is the location of Lily Singer and Sebastian Blackwell's fated adventure with the lugal-nam, a time-looping device that trapped them in Pitts until they could find it and save everyone from the time loop.

pixie - any fae that are small, quick, and flighty. This is purely a human term and has no relation to actual fae taxonomy (naming and classification). However, it is true that most pixies are energetic, fun-loving, and have a weakness for alcohol, which they can metabolize in vast amounts compared to their body mass without getting drunk. Of all the fae, they are the ones most familiar to, and seen by, humans because of their curiosity and lack of fear.

power anchor - a crafted object—usually something small and wearable like an amulet, necklace, or ring—that wizards use to focus and amplify their magic so as to cast more precise and powerful spells. For particularly powerful spells, wizards can create a one-time-use, secondary power anchor which they might draw or carve on the floor to further channel their magic.

runes of power - also known as dimmu runes, these are the symbols used to write Enkinim, the language of power that shapes magic. They are similar in appearance to the cuneiform script used in Mesopotamia during ancient times.

seeing stone - traditionally a triangular stone with a hole through it, though the stone can be any shape and still work. In ancient times these stones were made by the fae and given to certain humans so they could look through the hole and see past fae glamour. Few were preserved and passed down and so are rare today, for the fae have long since withdrawn from regular contact with humankind and give no more such gifts as they did in times past.

seeming - a kind of second skin or magical glamour wizards use to conceal things from mundanes. This kind of concealing spell is incredibly complex and detailed, even feeling real to the mundane touch. Therefore it must be crafted into a permanent object, such as the limbs of a construct servant to make them appear human instead of machine. It is also possible to weave it into clothes, such that when a wizard puts the clothes on, it changes their appearance or causes them to disappear. This type of glamour is easily spotted by other wizards, and so is only used to fool mundanes.

Source, the - the place from which all magic comes. While many creatures and parts of nature are innately magical, filled with the Source's power, wizards are the only beings in the universe born with an innate connection to it and the ability to draw on it at will. The Source is not sentient, only raw power. Magic drawn from the Source has to be shaped and directed by the caster's will using words of power (Enkinim). Incorrect use of Enkinim or poor control over a spell can cause backfires or spell mutations, resulting in a different outcome than intended and sometimes causing the injury or death of the caster. Though many known, reliable spells exist, the power of the Source is, in theory, limited only by the willpower and knowledge of the caster. Though safe to use within limits and with the proper training, many wizards over the years have died from overestimating their own strength or attempting dangerous spells which they did not properly understand. Thus, use of magic by modern wizards is in decline. With the rise of mundane technology, many wizards feel magic use is not worth the trouble or cost.

spell circle - a simple line or mark on the ground providing a visual aid and anchor to the casting of any sort of circle, such as a shield circle or circle of containment. Spell circles can be permanently engraved or carved into a surface accompanied by dimmu runes that add to the stability and effectiveness of whatever casting is being done.

spell of: compulsion - used to control another human being. Only works with the initial willingness of the subject, usually gained through subtle suggestion or trickery. Once the subject has been compelled for the first time, however, they are particularly susceptible to it again even if they try to resist. Traditionally a type of magic only openly used on mundanes, as it is not "polite" or "decent" to compel another wizard.

spell of: containment - a kind of spell circle used to contain magic. It is usually cast as a safety measure when doing spell work.

spell of: conveyance - a type of spell that can transmit sensory input, whether audio, visual, or tactile, from one item to another, even over great distances. Variations of this spell class can be used for many things, even a wizard version of the mundane cell phone.

spell of: shielding - a kind of spell used to shield the caster from magic. One type—a barrier through which magic cannot enter—is often cast as a spell circle. Another type—a selective spell that blocks only incoming active or targeted magic—is commonly used in personal wards.

summoning circle - a series of demonic runes and symbols used exclusively to summon, control, or commune with demons. Anyone, mundane or wizard, who knows the correct runes and words can summon a demon. A summoning can not be completed without knowing the name of the demon being summoned, because it is the demon's name that gives the summoning circle its power. If incorrectly drawn, a summoning circle may simply become ineffective. Or, if a more serious mistake is made, it may successfully summon, but not control the demon. Once active, a summoning circle cannot be dispelled by simply removing the marks. Only magic can break it. Though fae magic is especially effective in destroying all things demonic, certain wizard spells can remove a summoning circle as well.

Tablet of Eridu - an ancient clay tablet inscribed with cuneiform, relating incomplete accounts of the origins of the world, the gods, and mankind. Underneath the cuneiform are hidden invisible dimmu runes which outline some of the most primitive, yet potent and dangerous spells known to wizardkind. The tablet was broken many centuries ago and some of the pieces rediscovered during the 19th century by wizard archaeologists. It is currently on loan to the Clay Museum at Emory University in Atlanta, GA, from the Hermann Hilprecht Museum of the University of Pennsylvania.

Thiriel - the fae who gave Sebastian Blackwell his ebony staff.

truth coin - a silver coin given to Sebastian Blackwell by his father. It is inscribed with dimmu runes and enchanted to grow warm in the presence of lies. The degree of warmth is directly proportional to the degree of the lie.

ward - magical protection of some kind, usually cast into an anchor such as a bracelet (personal ward) or into runes set in/around a location (stationary ward). Ward spells can be customized to do a variety of things. Personal wards usually contain a combination of a shield spell along with various minor spells that help protect the bearer from weariness, sickness, or other physical harm. Stationary wards put up around a house or created to protect a certain location or object, can be set to protect against specific things (just wizards, or alternately, just mundanes, for example). They can also be customized to prevent the passage of physical objects, sound, light, etc.

witch - a mundane who, through trades, favors, and alliances with other beings, gains magical power or the service of said beings. "Something given, something gained," is the way of a witch. While uncommon, the other two magical species (fae and angels/demons) have been known to form alliances with humans, mundane and wizard alike. Besides directly gaining other beings' magic, witches also often trade for the services of various supernatural beings. Many witches favor demonic pacts, as demons are the most eager for contact with humans. Such pacts, however, usually end badly for the witch, or else the witch is irrevocably changed, sometimes tricked or forced into subjugation to whatever demon they were trying to control. Spirits in their various forms are one of the other more common partners of witches. But since they are incorporeal and have no need for physical things, they can be hard to bargain with and, by nature, are unstable. Fae, while shy of humans and largely unknown to them, do occasionally form pacts. Historically, witches who allied with the fae were known as druids, but the term has largely fallen out of use because they are now so rare.

wizard - a human with the ability to access the Source and manipulate its power. The ability is thought to be genetic, as it seems to be passed from parent to child. Legend says magic was given to Gilgamesh and so only his descendants inherited it. Like most inherited genes, it can be diluted by mixing with normal human genes. So a wizard marrying a mundane is less likely to produce wizard children than a wizard-wizard union, though even those are not guaranteed to have all wizard children. A wizard's abilities are not instinctive, they are a skill that must be taught and mastered to use effectively.

words of power - the language (Enkinim) used by wizards to control their magical power. Passed down over the centuries, these words help shape and direct a wizard's spells, both activating and limiting their effects. Though many set spells exist, new ones can be discovered and old ones customized. The stronger a wizard's will, the more adroit their mind, and the better their understanding of Enkinim, the more they can do with magic. Magical experimentation can, however, be extremely dangerous.

wrought iron - a metal which repels magic. Spells cannot be anchored to it, affect it, or pass through it, and it dulls the effectiveness of any magic in its vicinity. Because fae and angels/demons are beings of pure magic, it is poisonous to them. It will burn them on contact, its presence weakens them, and it will kill them if ingested in large quantities. A wizard wearing iron or standing near iron will be hampered or completely prevented from casting, depending on their strength and skill. Iron does not, however, hurt humans in any way beyond a slight weakening effect that is a result of blocking their access to the Source. Only wrought iron has these characteristics. Other mixtures of iron alloy such as steel have little or no effect.

Turn the page
for a preview of Lydia Sherrer's
third Lily Singer Adventures book

LOVE, LIES, AND HOCUS POCUS: ALLIES

Now in paperback, ebook, and audiobook

Chapter 1

THICKER THAN BLOOD

What kind of music do cats like? Under normal circumstances, this would be a difficult question to answer—one which scientists and cat experts have, no doubt, puzzled over for decades. Lily Singer, on the other hand, didn't have to puzzle. In fact, she didn't even have to ask. She was informed, loudly and unequivocally, that cats prefer jazz, specifically ragtime. This was the obvious answer, she was told, because country was too whiny, rock too angry, pop too undignified, and classical too boring—though it was an acceptable substitute. The expert in question? Sir Edgar Allan Kipling, magical talking cat extraordinaire. What, exactly, made Sir Kipling an expert on cats' taste in music Lily had no idea, but she'd learned it was best not to argue with one's cat. At least, not if you disliked losing.

So it was that she spent the first half hour of their drive shuffling through radio stations until she found one that met Sir Kipling's exacting tastes. How he even knew about jazz, or ragtime for that matter, was a mystery to her. Up until several weeks ago, he'd been a normal cat. At least, as normal as a wizard's cat could be. For Lily Singer was not just the archives manager of Agnes Scott—a private women's college in Atlanta, Georgia—she was also a wizard. And being a wizard meant odd things often happened. In Sir Kipling's case, a mysterious entity had gifted him with human intelligence and the ability to be understood by, but only by, his mistress. That same entity had helped Lily, her mentor Madam Barrington, and her witch friend Sebastian Blackwell stop the theft of a powerful magical artifact, with the side benefit of defeating a greater demon intent on eating them.

Yet Sir Kipling hadn't been the only one to come away changed. The entity's otherworldly touch had made her ward bracelet—the wizard equivalent of body armor—more powerful than any magical artifact she'd ever seen. She'd been told the bracelet would protect her, and protect her it had. Not just against demons, but against her estranged father, John Faust LeFay.

She'd spent years searching for him, allowing a rift to form between herself and her mother and stepfamily in the process. Yet in the end it was he who found her. She discovered, too late, why her mother had left him in the first place. A powerful wizard in his own right, her father showed his true face when he attempted to use her in a magical experiment that could have driven her insane—if it had worked. Rescued at the last minute by her friends, Lily was left devastated, wishing she could erase the knowledge of who her father really was: an egomaniacal sociopath. The truth may have freed her, but with that freedom came a burden of responsibility. It was, in fact, the reason for her current road trip with her musically opinionated cat.

They were on their way to Bertha, Alabama, to see her family for the first time in seven years. This reconciliation or "strengthening of the ranks," as her mentor called it, was the first step in preparing Lily and her allies to stop John Faust's insane plan to repopulate the world with wizards so they could "benevolently" rule mundane society. Completely aside from her father's questionable ethics—the ends justify the means, all is permissible for the greater good—she was quite sure any wizard interference in mundane affairs, or vice versa, would end in disaster and bloodshed. Even if John Faust's desire to preserve the dwindling wizard race was a worthy cause, his methods and ultimate goal were untenable.

Of course, stopping John Faust was easier said than done. Besides being exceptionally intelligent, highly skilled, and downright rich, he was also a respected member of the wizard community—well, respected by some, feared by others. Any attempt to recruit allies against him would be met with scoffing or outright hostility.

Lily hadn't known any of this herself, unfortunately. Her mother, Freda, had spent the past seven years colluding with Madam Barrington to keep Lily as far away from other wizards as possible, all in an attempt to keep her hidden from her father. Their attempt had backfired rather spectacularly, of course, but as angry as it had made Lily, she couldn't blame them for trying to protect her. The dynamics of current wizard society were something her mentor had only recently explained, now that the cat was out of the bag, so to speak. It made their prospects look pretty bleak, though when Lily made a comment to that effect, Madam Barrington had cryptically implied they weren't as friendless as it might seem. But before they did anything else, she first insisted Lily go visit her family.

It wasn't that Lily didn't love her stepfather and stepsiblings. She was just so…different. She didn't fit into their country way of life. They were perfectly content to drive tractors, raise crops, and enjoy the simple but rigorous life of Alabama farmers. Lily, on the other hand, disliked working outside. Knowledge was her milk and honey, and all she'd ever wanted was to read, study, and be left alone. Growing up on a small peanut and cotton farm with four younger siblings to take care of didn't afford much alone time. She'd been happy to leave and was apprehensive about returning.

Even so, she missed her family more deeply than she cared to admit and was worried how they would react to her visit. What if they wouldn't forgive her long absence? How was she going to explain about wizards and magic? Should she even try? What if they thought she was abnormal? What if they rejected who she'd become? These doubts, and more, were why she'd never come home. It was easier to keep her distance and bury her loneliness than to deal with the possibility of rejection.

"You know," came a silky meow to her right, "you really should stop worrying. It only makes you cranky." Sir Kipling twitched his whiskers, not lifting his head from where he lay curled up in the passenger seat. He was quite the picture, his large, fluffy gray body taking up a good part of the seat while his white-tipped tail hung over the side, slowly flicking back and forth.

"How in the world would you know if I'm worrying?" Lily asked, annoyed.

"You smell different."

"I smell—" Lily stopped herself, and sighed. She should know by now not to try to fathom her cat's maddening ability to know far more than he ought. He claimed it was all part of being a cat, which was hogwash, in her opinion. She was sure the entity who had given him human-like intelligence had given him far more than that, but so far Sir Kipling was playing dumb. So Lily simply grumbled about his "cat magic" and left it at that.

Silence returned to the car. Lily had turned off the radio to give herself room to think—all right, worry—and she stared blankly at the road. The passing scenery, a mix of coniferous woodland and verdant peanut and cotton fields, offered no comfort. It was only a three-and-a-half-hour drive from Atlanta to Bertha, and they were approaching the end of the journey. As familiar landmarks became more frequent, her apprehension grew, exacerbated by Sir Kipling's exaggerated sniffs and whisker twitches. Of course, such behavior didn't make him appear quite as disapproving as he probably thought it did, owing to the white circle of fur around his right eye and the splashes of white on his nose. They made him look like a crotchety old gentleman with a monocle, twitching his mustache, an amusing picture if Lily could have looked at it instead of at the road ahead.

In no time they were passing Eufaula. The sight of it recalled vivid memories of her and Sebastian's "virtuous" break-in of the Shorter Mansion museum during their attempt to undo the Jackson family curse. And, of course, of Sebastian's theatrical "escape" kiss. It had been suspiciously enthusiastic for being only a ploy to throw off the security guard. At the time she'd put it down to his generally over-the-top nature, but ever since he'd helped save her from her father's clutches, she'd wondered. Of course, it wasn't the kiss itself that made her blush now as they drove past the quiet Alabama city. It was the memory of how it had made her feel. Feelings she had promptly, and appropriately, quashed.

"You should have asked him to come with us." Sir Kipling commented, once again out of the blue.

Lily pushed her glasses further up on the bridge of her nose and kept her eyes fixed on the road. Sometimes she wondered if her cat could read minds. "I have no idea what you're talking about."

"Oh please. Don't insult me," Sir Kipling meowed. "Your body temperature just shot through the roof and you're blushing. You're thinking about Sebastian." It was not a question.

"That's ridiculous," Lily protested, attempting a casual tone. "I could be thinking about any manner of embarrassing things." Self-conscious but trying to hide it, she reached up to tuck a wayward strand of her chestnut hair behind an ear. Most of it was caught up in the usual bun at the back of her head, but there were some strands that just refused to stay put.

"I suppose you could be," Sir Kipling admitted. "But you're not, because you also smell—"

"Alright, fine!" Lily interrupted, having no desire to know what she smelled like when she was thinking about Sebastian. "So I was thinking about him. But only because I'm relieved he's not here. He would just make things worse. Imagine trying to keep him out of trouble and deal with my family at the same time. What a disaster."

"Mmm," Sir Kipling murmured, obviously unconvinced. "Of course, his absence also conveniently lets you avoid confronting your feelings."

Lily looked away from the road long enough to glare at her cat. "Who elected you matchmaker? I'm dating Richard, for your information—"

"You mean that lawman who suspects you're lying about

everything? At least Sebastian already knows you're a wizard."

Sir Kipling's comment earned him another glare as Lily's insides squirmed. "Sebastian is an uncouth reprobate with entirely too many secrets of his own. In any case, he's taken up with that witch, Tina. If you ask me, they deserve each other." Lily knew her words were harsh, but Sir Kipling's barb had stirred an uncharacteristic defensiveness in her.

"I see. So, since when does one coffee translate into 'dating'?" He asked, eyes still closed.

"Well, there would have been more," she pointed out, "but things got in the way." Things like being kidnapped by her father, to be precise. She'd only just recovered from that fiasco when Agent Grant got back in touch, hoping to schedule another date. They'd settled on next Friday evening. Or at least she thought they had. She'd written it down on a slip of paper by the phone but hadn't been able to find it the last time she'd looked. She would look again when they got home. That is, if she survived the weekend with her family.

"If you say so," her cat said, dropping the matter, much to Lily's relief. Faced with the dubious task of navigating familial relationships, this was no time to face the complicated tangle of emotions that were her feelings for her troublemaking friend.

Thanks so much for reading Lily, Sebastian, and Sir Kipling's latest adventure! Don't miss future books in the Love, Lies, and Hocus Pocus universe by signing up to my mailing list at www.lydiasherrer.com/subscribe for new release alerts, behind-the-scene sneak peeks, book giveaways, and chances to help me out in the story-making process.

Reader reviews are essential to a book's success by helping other readers discover stories they might enjoy. Plus they are a great way to show support for your favorite author! Please consider taking a moment to leave a review for Love, Lies, and Hocus Pocus Revelations on Amazon.

If you want to explore more of the Love, Lies, and Hocus Pocus universe, then come join my motley crew on Patreon www.patreon.com/lydiasherrer. You'll get awesome rewards like exclusive monthly short stories (found nowhere else), snarky swag, and series backstory.

I'd love to connect with you online! You can find me at:
www.lydiasherrer.com
www.facebook.com/lydiasherrerauthor
www.instagram.com/lydiasherrer
www.twitter.com/lydiasherrer
www.youtube.com/c/lydiasherrer

ABOUT THE AUTHOR

Award-winning and USA Today-bestselling author of snark-filled fantasy, Lydia Sherrer thrives on creating characters and worlds you love to love, and hate to leave. She subsists on liberal amounts of dark chocolate and tea, and hates sleep because it keeps her from writing. Due to the tireless efforts of her fire-spinning gamer husband and her two overlords, er cats, she remains sane and even occasionally remembers to leave the house. Though she graduated with a dual BA in Chinese and Arabic, after traveling the world she came home to Louisville, KY and decided to stay there.